THE PRISONER OF ACRE

Also by Murray Bailey

Ash Carter Singapore series:
Singapore 52
Singapore Girl
Singapore Boxer
Singapore Ghost
Singapore Killer
Singapore Fire
*Singapore Rain

Ash Carter Near-East series:
Cyprus Kiss
The Killing Crew
Troodos Secret
**Wolfe's Gambit

BlackJack series:
Once A Killer
Second To Sin
A Third Is Darkness

Egyptian series:
Map of the Dead
Sign of the Dead*
***The Lost Pharaoh

Black Creek White Lies

* A novella
** A Bill Wolfe short thriller
*** A Yan-Khety mystery

The Prisoner Of Acre

Murray Bailey

First published in Great Britain by Heritage Books.
This format first published in 2024

123423477

copyright © Murray Bailey 2024

The moral right of Murray Bailey to be identified as the author of this work has been asserted in accordance with the copyright, Designs and Patents Act of 1988.

All rights reserved. No part of this publication may be reproduced, stored in a retrieval system, or transmitted in any form or by any means, electronic, mechanical, photocopying, recording, or otherwise, without the prior permission of the copyright owner.

All the characters in this book are fictitious and any resemblance to actual persons, living or dead, is purely coincidental.

Three Daggers
An imprint of
Heritage Books, Cornwall

For my wife, Kerry.
We are light travelling through space.

ONE

A haze of cigar smoke swirled around the dark wood-panelled walls like a living thing. The two men often met here, the elite members' club an intimate cocoon from the outside world. Illumination came from the dim glow of antique lamps on each linen-draped table. Heavy drapes of dark green velvet blocked the tall windows, keeping out the bright Jerusalem sunlight. They also muffled the indistinct murmur of conversation.

The man contributing most to the smoke leaned back in his leather chair, puffing contentedly on a fine Cuban cigar. He was tall and broad-shouldered although the last few years of fine living had layered his frame with a generous padding of fat. He moved with a deceptive grace, a lightness that belied his sheer mass. People said he gave the impression of a bear dancing on its hind legs. Although he didn't like that analogy.

Across from him sat a thin unassuming figure though his piercing slate-gray eyes betrayed a formidable intellect. The smoker knew there was power coiled beneath the man's expensive black suit and bland façade.

The thin man was the genius behind the organization. He could have passed for a teacher or an accountant. An average man in his forties with a receding hairline. Only his lined face spoke of a hard early life. In his youth, he'd survived through brute force and ruthlessness. Now he possessed the easy confidence of a man accustomed to comfort and wealth. The unassuming man had reinvented both himself and the organization he'd created.

Within these shrouded walls, the true power brokers of Jerusalem and Tel Aviv rubbed shoulders, subtly shaping affairs through whispers in trusted ears. The cigar smoker drew luxuriant smoke into his mouth, savouring his proximity to the hidden levers moving the world outside. And their ignorance.

The thin man swirled the brandy in his glass. "Now the other matter." He spoke softly, without obvious affectation. Yet when he unleashed the force of his personality, he could make his voice hit men like a crashing wave.

The smoker said, "You've been teasing me."

The thin man smiled.

"You have a date?"

The other man glanced around although no one could hear, let alone understand.

"A week on Saturday," the thin man said. His fingers on one hand splayed out. Five days. Then he repeated it, followed by two. In twelve days. After such a long wait, it was finally happening.

"We'll be ready." Cigar-man said, his rumbling voice muffled by the plush furnishings. "Everything is in place for the next phase."

"What about our friend?" His slate eyes glinted as he swirled the brandy again.

The smoker huffed a quiet laugh. "Ever the doubter. Don't worry, he'll play his part. We have ample leverage." Cigars and rich food were the smoker's obvious vices. He collected secrets and weaknesses, exploiting them meticulously to support the organization.

"And the man in Tel Aviv?" the thin man said through the curling blue smoke.

The cigar smoker nodded. "He's prepared. A true zealot. Fanatically and financially loyal. He's got a big future with us, I think."

The thin man nodded, seemingly satisfied. He swirled the brandy some more, contemplating it. "The Armistice is imminent. A new dawn is breaking across this land. The time has come for our order to emerge from the shadows."

"You sound like a politician!" The cigar smoker chuckled deep in his chest. "So, the war is over?"

"The war will never be over, my friend."

It was undoubtedly the truth and they could profit from it. War and the greed of men. Thousands of years of history. Things had never and would never change.

The smoker flicked ash into the crystal tray and raised his glass.

The thin man stopped swirling his brandy. "To new beginnings."

"Let the games commence," the smoker answered as their glasses rang together. "Let the games commence."

TWO

It was unclear which type of AWOL Sergeant Alfred Duffy was, and I'd never known a case like it.

Most AWOL soldiers disappear for a few extra days without permission. Dealing with a personal matter, they need more time than permitted. Occasionally, that personal issue leads to problems such as drunkenness. Their priorities change and they need to be reminded by the army of their duty.

That's the first type.

The second type is the deserter. Officially, the term only applies in time of war, or when warned to go on operations. Otherwise, it's recorded as *Long-term AWOL*. But it's effectively the same thing. The individual no longer wants to serve and deliberately walks away.

Duffy had been a Buff—the nickname for men in the Royal East Kent Regiment. He'd been temporarily assigned to Provost Company 225 based in Cyprus. Armed with a two-day pass, he walked out of Dhekelia Garrison without a word of where he was going.

He'd been gone for a week and not been traced. Opinion was that he was hiding out somewhere in Cyprus. But he wasn't. A phone call to the provost marshal's office told us otherwise. Duffy had made his way to Israel and then walked into Acre Prison where he'd handed himself in.

Which was why I was involved. Ordinarily, an SIB officer wouldn't be engaged in a straightforward arrest. But this was far from straightforward.

The British mandate for Palestine ended on the fifteenth of May 1948. We'd left the newly formed state of Israel surrounded by invading Arab nations. On the whole, the Jews hated us, and the Arabs despised their once allies. We'd walked away and left the country at war. Thousands had died. Hundreds of thousands of Arabs had been displaced.

Since then, I'd been back to Israel on a sanctioned mission. It didn't mean they liked me, but I had status and approval.

And that was why I was involved. A simple job: travel to Acre and return with Duffy.

Three of us arrived in Haifa on Sunday the third of April 1949 and were met by the police. We were plain-clothed and allegedly unarmed. As usual, I carried a Beretta hidden in an ankle holster.

Because of the tensions, we would only identify ourselves as military if absolutely necessary. Which suited me. Turning up in a British Military Police Land Rover would have made us a target without a doubt.

We were given an old Austin 6 and told to go directly to Acre. We were not to deviate. Our boat home was in the evening, and we were told to be on it. Come hell or high water.

My colleagues were Roscoe and King. They were young but had also served in Mandatory Palestine so knew what to expect. And they both knew Duffy.

We walked to the car-pound and found the Austin sitting in the sun. Black leather seats were tacky with the heat. It smelled of horses, which I figured came from the hair in the seat padding. We wound the windows down to let out the hot thick air.

King drove. Roscoe sat behind me in the back.

The car rode hard, like it had no suspension. And probably didn't.

"The buggers have fixed it," King said, referring to the car's handling.

"Better than walking," I said.

"And the alignment's off."

"Just drive carefully."

We went through the first checkpoint on the edge of the town and my colleagues tensed. But it was fine. One glance at our official papers and we were on our way again. The IDF soldiers didn't even search the car.

"Things are getting better," I said because last time I'd been here, I'd been stopped and searched frequently. "We'll be fine."

We went north, the road shimmering in the late morning sun. The air blew fresh off the coast and the car's interior cooled. My skin stopped sticking to the leather.

We thumped over potholes, and metal ground against metal. King grunted as he fought the steering, but there was otherwise no talking once we were motoring. We'd done all the talking on the boat.

I'd asked them about Duffy. Neither knew him well.

"Keeps himself to himself," Roscoe said.

King shrugged. "He's all right. Never a problem."

"Anything personal?" I probed.

"I found out he's a Fulham supporter," Roscoe said. "Not a heavy drinker. Rubbish at cards and darts."

They provided some other useless information before I asked the burning question.

"Why did he go AWOL?"

They had no idea.

"Did he tell anyone he was going to Israel?"

"No," King said. It's the answer I expected because the investigation to date had assumed he hadn't left the island.

Roscoe said, "Do you think he meant to join an Arab militia?"

There had been over eighty deserters in the final months of British rule. Most were pro-Arab and had joined the Arab Legion, the Transjordanian Army, or the Arab Liberation Army. A few foolhardy men had joined smaller, more radical militia such as the Army of the Holy War.

No one had left to join any of these groups for almost a year.

"Perhaps none of them wanted him," chuckled King. "Too boring for them."

"That would explain why he handed himself in," Roscoe added.

I guessed it would. The ALA were in the north. If Duffy had hoped to join them but had been rejected, then it would make sense. He'd have had nowhere to go, so he'd handed himself in. Ordinarily he might have just returned to base, but he'd been in an enemy country. Finding his way back to Cyprus would have been problematic. The Israeli Army were patrolling ports and any stranger without papers would be treated with suspicion. Maybe even shot.

Handing himself into authorities was probably his safest option.

I said, "After Palestine, was he assigned or did he volunteer for the provost?"

King swivelled and stared at me. "Damn. It's relevant isn't it?"

I nodded.

Roscoe said, "Did he volunteer?"

King said, "No one volunteers in the army."

"He volunteered," I said. "He wanted to be in Cyprus. Which means, he probably wanted to be close to Israel."

"Maybe he planned this way back then," said King.

Roscoe whistled. "Someone should have asked."

"I did," I said.

"Does it matter?"

"Not now," I said. "Now he's in custody. It'll be interesting to find out why he did it."

"And what went wrong," King added.

The six miles along the coast followed the railroad for most of the way, and I found myself wondering if thumping along the rail tracks would have been any less uncomfortable.

There wasn't much traffic, maybe more than last time I'd been here. There were fewer armoured vehicles and only occasional private cars. Taxis and buses on the other hand, were doing a good trade and trucks were coming out of Haifa laden with food and goods. Despite the war, Israel was thriving, it seemed.

Finally, we crossed the rail tracks and followed the curve of the land to the ancient city of Acre.

The old city of Jerusalem is majestic and astonishing. However, my first reaction to Acre, through the haze of hot air, was one of awe. A giant walled city dating back to the Ottoman Empire, holding a violent sea at bay. White foam waves crashed up the sides of worn stone walls. They'd withstood the battering for thousands of years. And within those embattlements I could see towers and more fortified structures.

King stared with his mouth open.

His attitude changed as quickly as a lightning bolt. There was a checkpoint at the city gate and these soldiers looked anxious.

Guns pointed at our heads, and we were told to get out. I'd warned the men to stay calm, and they tried to look passive as we were frisked.

"Don't look them in the eye," I'd said. "And let me do any talking."

I showed our papers and waited as the junior IDF men debated their veracity. They made us wait. A queue of trucks formed behind us, and a horn blared.

One of the soldiers stormed off to deal with the offending driver while another soldier told us to hurry up and get back in the car.

"Jesus!" Roscoe said, panting from the excitement.

"They're just nervous," I said.

Acre was only ten miles from the official border with Lebanon. Since the war, the front had moved much closer and had totally subsumed the Jewish settlement of Hahariya which was just a few miles north of us. The Arabs had been pushed back but Acre was still within ALA bombing range and had seen heavy fighting during the war. The soldiers had every right to be nervous.

King fired up the engine once more and we rolled away and toward one of the city gates.

From far off, we'd seen a castle within the castle—a citadel. It had been the home of the Crusaders for a hundred years as their bridgehead to recapture Jerusalem. Despite its Ottoman heritage and Jewish control, I could imagine Richard the Lionheart on the ramparts, watching us approach. He'd undoubtedly disapprove of the way we'd scuttled away from the country in '48.

We didn't go into the citadel itself but followed a sign to an adjacent entrance.

King drove up to the gates where a police officer flagged us to a halt. I got my first glimpse of Acre Prison, box-like with newer walls than the fortress behind it.

The cursory check of our papers told me he'd been briefed about our impending arrival, but there was something else in his eyes. He wasn't uneasy like the IDF checkpoint guards. This policeman looked embarrassed, I thought.

The gates were opened, and we drove under an arch into a broad courtyard. I saw men hurrying. We got out, and I walked into a room marked *Head Officer*. Roscoe and King shuffled their feet, and I asked them to wait outside.

Behind a desk, a small man with round spectacles and an awkward smile, looked up. Above his head on the wall was the Israeli flag and a photograph of David Ben-Gurion. The name on the desk read: *Captain A Gruner.*

"Ah. Captain Carter," he said, offering me a bony hand to shake.

"Here to collect Sergeant Duffy," I said unnecessarily.

"Please sit," said Gruner, and I took the chair opposite his desk.

"Were you here before?" he asked, referring to the British rule.

"In Mandatory Palestine for a while."

"And here, at Acre?" The British Army had run the prison back then.

"No," I said, "Never in Acre. Not even as a tourist."

He gave me his awkward smile again. Maybe it was sympathy. "It's not the army here anymore. The police run the prison now," he said. I could see that. My guess was that the army were too busy fighting the Arabs. There was no prison service in Israel yet per se. Before the new state, the Jewish Agency had a military force, the Haganah. But they had no need for prison guards since the prisons were run by the British. On the other hand, Jewish policemen worked within the British forces which included assisting with the prisons. So it made sense that the police were running Acre Prison.

I suspected the best of the police were being deployed elsewhere in the key cities of Jerusalem, Haifa, and Tel Aviv. Gruner and his team were probably the underperformers, the men who would have been let go if there hadn't been a shortage of expertise.

Gruner said, "Numbers of prisoners here halved once you left. Of course, the British had incarcerated our patriots along with the criminals."

He chuckled.

Outside, the shuffling sounds grew louder. I turned expecting to berate my men. However, a junior Israeli policeman was standing in the office doorway, breathless and worried.

Gruner glared then after a pause said, "Any news?"

I saw the young man make hand gestures that I couldn't interpret.

"One minute, please Captain," Gruner said, irritated. He got up and left the room. I could hear whispers before Gruner barked in Hebrew.

He returned with a red face. Moisture prickled on his upper lip.

"What is it?" I asked, standing.

Gruner breathed and cleared his throat. "We just went to get him—your man. And well, you see—"

"Spit it out!" I said, starting to lose patience.

"He's gone. Your Sergeant Duffy is missing."

THREE

Gruner took me to the cell where Duffy had been held. Roscoe was with me. King stayed in the courtyard with the car.

The catcalls and clamour of inmates was an angry buzz. Duffy's cell door lay open. Two guards looked uncertain, trying to appear busy but doing nothing to find my man.

On the way, Gruner said, "We knew you were coming... I assumed... When I sent for him, I assumed..." He swallowed hard and shook his head. "It appears your man was allowed some exceptional exercise. We're looking for the officer who took him. I'm sure everything is fine. I'm sure he is fine."

"He better be," I said.

"We just can't find them at the moment. They're not in either of the exercise yards... or obvious places."

Gruner paced. Hate-filled faces pressed up against bars watching us, jeering. I caught Roscoe's eye and saw he had the same concern as me.

The scenario that was forefront in my mind was that a guard or inmate had exacted revenge on Duffy. He'd have been the only Brit in the prison and a target for anyone with a grudge.

The cell had two cots, both beds unmade. There were the usual scratch marks on the stone walls, a tally of days, writing, and seemingly random lines.

"Where's the other prisoner?"

"They'll be together."

"Also missing?" I said, and he nodded.

So we had two prisoners and a guard unaccounted for.

"What's his name, this other prisoner?"

"Abu Hajjar," Gruner said. "A gangster. Been here a few years. Never any trouble, even—"

I sucked in the warm sour air as he spoke, then interrupted. "A gangster? Is he in for murder?"

"Most of the inmates have—"

I shook my head in disgust. "You put a British soldier in with a known killer."

"I…"

Shouts outside the cell stopped his apology—assuming that's what he'd have given. Feet pounded down the corridor.

"Maybe they've found him," Gruner said with relief. "It'll just have been a misunderstanding."

But it wasn't and they hadn't. The man Gruner had sent away had returned with another guard—a sergeant. The sergeant had blood on his forehead and a fearful look on his face.

"Is he the missing guard?" I asked.

"One minute," said Gruner before intercepting his men. They spoke, their voices lost in the background racket.

"This way," Gruner said to me once they'd finished their urgent discussion.

"Were you Duffy's guard?" I asked the sergeant.

"Yes."

"He's escaped?"

"Yes."

The five of us jogged along the corridor, the noise from the inmates rising to fever pitch. Down a flight of stone steps took us to another corridor. This led to a door in the citadel wall. It opened into a courtyard.

The sergeant went through and said something I didn't hear.

"What?" I said to Gruner beside me.

He was panting. "The idiot... he showed him the fortress. Was trying to be nice, I understand."

We went into the main part of the ancient castle. Romanesque and Gothic. Towers and pillars. The Crusaders had used it as headquarters and a hospital. The Order of Saint John—the Hospitallers. The British had used it as barracks. Now it was empty except for bright sunlight and stray cats.

Gruner and his men had stopped. Not in awe of the citadel but uncertainty. My initial assessment of the senior officer had been correct. Totally incompetent, he hadn't a clue how to deal with this situation. It wasn't in the manual, so he needed instructions.

"All right," I said. "Explain what happened."

"Duffy overpowered my sergeant after he opened the door back there."

"Then start searching the castle!"

"Right!"

Gruner sent his first guard scurrying back to fetch more men. As the man disappeared through the door, I turned my attention to the sergeant.

"Duffy hit you after you opened the door?"

"Yes, sir."

"What did he hit you with?"

"With that." The man glanced down and pointed to a smooth, round rock the size of a fist. A rock like that could do severe damage, possibly kill. The blood on the guard's forehead was a trickle about an inch long. Admittedly, there was dirt and grime, but I saw no sign of blunt force trauma.

I spun the sergeant around, put his arm in a half-nelson lock.

Gruner glared at me. "Captain!"

I ignored him and growled into the guard's ear. "Where've they gone?"

"The tunnels." The man's response was an embarrassed mumble.

I looked at Gruner, whose eyes had bulged. Was it with disbelief or something else? He cleared his throat, then shook his head. It was a message for the sergeant, not me.

"Tunnels?" I asked.

The sergeant's jaw tensed. He said nothing, his focus still on Gruner.

The door opened and the first guard reappeared with others behind. Gruner stopped them with a raised hand.

"Go back and check the cell," Gruner said.

The guard's face contorted as he tried to process the change in orders. First told to fetch others and search the fortress, now told to search the empty cell. Then the guard noticed that I had hold of the sergeant.

"Sir, I—"

"Now, man! And shut the door behind you."

The guard backed away, then forced the others through the door and shut it.

That left me, Roscoe, Captain Gruner and the sergeant, alone again.

"Whatever this is, you'd better tell me." I paused. "And no more bullshit! What's going on?"

Gruner swallowed. "There are tunnels under the citadel. Built by the Crusaders."

"Where do they lead?"

"To the port."

I let go of the sergeant's arm. "That's where they went? You're sure?"

"Yes."

"How long ago?"

"Fifteen, maybe twenty minutes ago."

I thrust the sergeant toward Roscoe.

"Go with him. Take King. Go to the port and wait where the tunnels come out."

Gruner nodded at the sergeant, and the guard followed Roscoe out of the courtyard.

"All right," I said to Gruner. "Take me to the tunnels."

FOUR

I had a theory. The sergeant had been coerced by the other prisoner. Maybe Duffy had been deliberately incarcerated with Hajjar. After all, Captain Gruner had told me there wasn't overcrowding. There were half the number of inmates there used to be. Duffy hadn't needed to share a cell.

So, Hajjar wanted the British soldier. Perhaps they had history. Perhaps it was personal. Or Hajjar wanted a prisoner of his own.

After the British had departed Mandatory Palestine, thousands of our Arab employees had been left behind. They'd been our friends and colleagues, but few had rights to British citizenship. Perhaps Hajjar thought he could use Duffy as ransom for a passport.

Gruner hurried me to the great hall. Coats of arms, tapestries, and flags adorned the walls. Three long, dark wooden benches ran the length of the room and I guessed this had been used by the British Army as a mess hall of sorts.

"This way," Gruner said, giving me no time to marvel at all the history. We pressed on, through smaller rooms and then to an alcove. It seemed to be a dead end, but it wasn't. A sharp turn showed an opening hidden to one side. We squeezed down on narrow spiral steps, hands against the walls for safety. I could hear his heavy breathing above our footfall.

I had questions spinning in my head. Why hadn't Gruner wanted the sergeant to mention the tunnels? What was the secret? Why didn't he want others to know? However now wasn't the time to ask such questions. We'd wasted enough time, and the fugitives were getting away.

Cooler air came up from the darkness. At the bottom, Gruner switched on a flashlight. We were in a vaulted room held up by Romanesque pillars.

He started moving off, but I stopped him and gripped his shoulder.

"Listen."

I held my breath and hoped I'd hear running feet, hoped I'd have confirmation that Duffy was down here. But I heard nothing except dripping water.

"OK," I said. "Let's go."

Below ground, was like a city beneath a city. Without a guide, I'd have been lost in minutes. Gruner knew where he was going, darting through the darkness, his torch flashing against pillars and uneven flooring, room after room. And then we came to a tunnel.

It was long and straight, about six feet by eight feet wide and with an arched roof. As Gruner's light swept around, I saw neat stone blocks. Quality workmanship, far better than a typical castle's sally port.

My feet splashed in water.

"From here it's wet," Gruner said. "Not much deeper though."

After a hundred paces, we were rising out of the water. It was getting lighter and another fifty brought us to an open gate.

Roscoe and King were standing in the bright sunshine looking in. The sergeant was behind them.

Emerging from the tunnel, I saw we were east of the city, by the old port. A gaggle of citizens formed a semi-circle a few paces off.

"Heard you coming a while back," King said. "Knew it was you, sir."

I nodded, understanding. "Because you know where Duffy is?"

Roscoe said, "About twenty minutes ago, two men were seen coming out of here. One white with red hair. Must be Duffy." He nodded. "The other one was an Arab. And bugger me if Duffy didn't get into a Bedford Fifteen Hundred." That was a typical British Army truck.

We were already moving toward our little Austin, parting the crowd and forgetting Gruner and his incompetent crew.

"Anyone else?" I asked, my mind whirring. "A driver?"

"Duffy got in the driver's seat," King said.

Roscoe added: "An Arab-looking man also got in. No mention of anyone else."

King started manoeuvring through the narrow streets, following the line of least resistance, heading north out of town.

"Any witnesses mention prison clothes?"

"No," Roscoe said.

Now I had a new theory. Duffy had brought the Bedford truck to the old port and left it in Acre. He'd then walked into the prison and waited. Twenty minutes before we arrived, he'd been let out by the sergeant. He'd escaped from the very place he'd surrendered to. With a get-away vehicle waiting in the right place. Probably had a change of clothes too. All waiting.

Which could only mean one thing.

It was planned. He'd arranged for the truck and he'd bribed the sergeant and he knew about the tunnels.

However, I still had no idea why he'd done it.

FIVE

Outside the city, we came to the checkpoint again and queued behind a bus. On the far side there were two trucks and a taxi. The IDF checkpoint men did the same as before but they were more focused on the arriving vehicles than those at the head of our queue. Of course. Any threat to the city wouldn't come from people leaving.

The soldiers alternated the traffic through their barbed wire blockade. A truck laden with crates of fruit came through. The bus moved forward and was waved through the gap.

King rolled toward the soldiers. I held out our papers.

A young man peered in, looked at each of us before stepping back.

A taxi came through and passed us, going into the city.

Our soldier waved us forward.

King rolled toward him.

"Has a Bedford truck come through in the past twenty minutes?" I called.

The young man scrutinised me and held his hand out for the papers that he had barely glanced at before.

"English?"

"Here with permission," I said calmly. "A Bedford truck—have you seen one?"

Another truck, overflowing with badly tied sacks, came through the checkpoint. The vehicle behind us sounded its horn. We'd missed our slot.

Another soldier came over, looking flustered. He waved frantically. *Go through now!*

I got out.

Two rifles immediately aimed at my head.

I raised my hands. "All I need to know is whether a Bedford truck has been through recently."

"Yes," the second man said. "I think it was. Old army."

"Two men inside?"

The car behind blared its horn again. Another soldier came over and a truck on the far side joined in the angry honking.

"Yes."

The third man said, "A problem with their papers?"

They conferred, all eyes and guns still aimed at me.

"Everything seems to be in order," I heard the second man say.

The third soldier lowered his gun. "Right. Get back in your vehicle. Now move!"

I dropped my hands and climbed into the car. King trundled forward as I pointed to the gap in the barricade. Then I told him to stop.

"Which way did it go? North or south?" I shouted to the second soldier, the one who'd seen the Bedford.

Most of the traffic was going to and from Haifa. Out of Acre and south.

"The green truck went left," the third man said. "North."

I waved a thank-you although it probably wasn't noticed or appreciated.

"What do you think?" asked Roscoe after we'd passed the checkpoint.

"That Duffy didn't have a problem getting out."

"And he's heading for the frontline," said Roscoe.

"Maybe."

King said, "He's joining the ALA after all."

We passed vacated hamlets with small craters and walls peppered with bullet holes. When we came to the town of Nahariyya we saw the damage done by the heavy bombardment. But we also saw building work. Bulldozers cleared rubble and workers laid bricks.

I admired their tenacity. The frontline was mere miles away. The fighting could swamp this town again in a heartbeat. And yet the Jews rebuilt, and they hoped. It's what they'd been doing for fifty years or so, although now the land was officially theirs and no longer British.

"There's someone behind us," King said. "Flashing his lights."

I turned and looked at the vehicle in our dusty wake. It was travelling faster than us, its headlights dancing and blinking on and off.

"Stop," I said. It looked like a jeep, and when our dust cleared, I could see it was gray and probably military.

We sat and waited for whatever was coming.

The sun bounced off our metalwork and now that the air no longer rushed through the car, I felt the heat again.

The jeep overtook, then stopped and reversed. It came right up close so that we couldn't just pull away if we decided to leave in a hurry.

It was a real Jeep as my American friends would say, as opposed to a topless Land Rover. It had IDF stencilled on the side and there was one occupant.

A woman got out, one hand hovering over a holstered gun. She wore a khaki blazer and a long skirt. On her head was the cap of an officer.

Her stride was confident as she approached my side of the car.

"Who are you?" she demanded.

I held out our papers.

She took them, and her half-second's glance told me she had checked they were on official paper rather than reading the detail.

I said, "Captain Carter, Royal Military Police. We're here to escort a prisoner."

The woman looked at Roscoe in the back, maybe wondering briefly if he was the prisoner, then realizing a prisoner wouldn't be in the back on their own.

"Where is he, this prisoner of yours?" she asked.

"He escaped from Acre Prison. We're looking for him."

She nodded. I noted her warm brown eyes were wide set. Their lack of reaction to my response told me this wasn't news. Which begged a question. Before I could speak, she said, "You think he's heading for the frontline?"

"He came in this direction. So, the frontline seems likely."

She said nothing for a moment. I felt the seat warming up even more. And we were wasting time. Duffy was ahead of us and getting away. The sad truth was that he'd probably reached the border before we'd got through the checkpoint.

Then the IDF officer surprised me.

"What's Sergeant Duffy's connection with Abu Hajjar?"

I looked at her hard. She knew precisely who we were and what we were doing. That's why she hadn't been surprised earlier.

"Well, Captain?"

"I don't know."

She took a long, deep breath that strained the done-up button on her blazer.

"Right," she said as though drawing a conclusion. "Get out of the vehicle."

We all started to move, but she shook her head. "Just you, Captain."

I climbed out but left the door open.

"Are you armed?"

"No," I lied.

She looked at the shape of my jacket. "Lift it and turn around."

I complied, showing that I didn't have a Sam Browne belt or gun in my waistband. All I was armed with was a pair of handcuffs intended for Duffy.

"Thank you," she said. "Now, your authority stopped at Acre. You do not have permission to drive around the country. And you know why?"

I waited for her to continue.

"Because we are at war, Captain. You could be up to no good. Your job was to come in, pick up Sergeant Duffy and leave. Nothing more. Was it?"

I didn't respond. A taxi went past, going south. It was only the second non-army vehicle we'd seen on the northern road since leaving Acre. She glanced at it then switched her full attention to me, thinking, possibly calculating.

She had neat, high eyebrows above the wide brown eyes. Her mouth seemed small with close teeth and yet she was attractive. And she intrigued me.

She did the jacket-straining deep breath again. I wanted to tell her to undo a button but resisted the urge.

"Right. Here's what we'll do. You're coming with me." She ducked her head to look at King. "And you two will drive back to Haifa and get on the next boat out."

"Sir?" Roscoe said.

I looked back down the road. There was white dust in the wind from demolition work. A volley of gunfire suddenly crackled through the air but it was far off to the north.

"It's an order," she said. "Of course, the alternative is that I arrest you all—suspected enemy sympathizers."

We were wasting time. She could try and arrest me and would fail. If my hands didn't stop her, I was sure my Beretta could. However, that would take more time.

Duffy was getting away. The clock was ticking.

Maybe it was already too late to catch up with him.

Maybe I stood a better chance with this lady's help.

I made a decision.

"All right," I said and shut the Austin's door. To the men inside, I said, "Get yourselves home and write it up—let the provost marshal know that I'll report in as soon as I have something."

I climbed into the passenger seat of her Jeep. King started the engine but didn't move. I guessed he and Roscoe were discussing things. Maybe they were questioning whether they should follow my instruction or make sure everything was kosher.

I swivelled and waved them away.

King nodded. He reversed and then swung the little car around.

My driver undid her jacket belt and buttons. I almost breathed with relief for her. She thumped the Jeep into gear and started going in the opposite direction.

"OK," I said, "tell me what's really going on."

"Lieutenant Eva Weiss. Eighty-second battalion."

"OK." I noted that her uniform showed she was a second lieutenant, so the most junior of officers. "And what else?" I asked.

"I'm not concerned about your Sergeant. I'm tasked with finding the escaped convict, Abu Hajjar."

More gunfire could be heard ahead and right.

"We can work together," she said. "What do you think your man is doing?"

"He's broken out with an Arab, so my best guess is that he's joining your enemy."

She nodded.

"But we're too late."

Eva glanced at me then back to the rutted road. As we'd travelled north, the once smooth lanes were bomb damaged and trammelled by tanks and heavy vehicles. Doing less than twenty miles an hour, she steered to avoid the worst of it.

I could see the hills and knew the frontline was getting close. I knew the Israeli Army was spread thinly around the borders but based on the tanks and tents in the haze ahead, it appeared the whole lot were camped on the Lebanese front.

No way had Duffy driven his truck through that.

Eva stopped and expressed the same thought.

"Where then?" I asked.

"Can't be west," she said.

"Unless he had a boat waiting. And that seems unlikely."

"East," she said and turned the wheel.

At first, we bumped over rough terrain but then picked up a route going east. The road climbed with hills ahead as well as to our left.

I said, "You think he was looking for a place to cross?"

"There are mountain goat passes. Maybe in a Jeep or Land Rover they could make it, but in an old truck? I don't think so. Not unless he's crazy."

"I doubt he's crazy," I said. "Maybe he doesn't know."

She kept her eyes on the road. There was no other traffic out here. "You think he didn't realize it would be impossible to just drive to Lebanon? Of course, there is the other option. Perhaps he's heading for Syria."

"Maybe," I said, unconvinced. So far, Duffy's planning had been incredible. At least it seemed that way. He may have escaped with an Arab to help him. Because of everything else, I'm sure he had a plan for afterwards. Surely, he wasn't just driving blindly into the mountains in an unsuitable vehicle.

"Stop," I said. "We've got this wrong."

She applied the brakes, slowly rolling to a halt.

"What?"

The dust settled as I squinted toward the hills ahead.

"What?" she prompted. "Now you're thinking we should have gone to the coast?"

I swivelled my attention to her. "Duffy expected me to come after him. Maybe he expected you or someone like you as well."

"Right," she said dubiously.

"He had a plan. He wanted us to come this way. He wanted us to get lost in the mountains."

"Right," she said again, still unconvinced.

"Back up to the track we passed a short while ago."

Reluctantly, it seemed, Eva turned the jeep around and we went west. The sun was past its zenith and bright in our eyes.

"Here!" I yelled.

She stopped, and I got out.

"There are tracks—tyre marks."

"They could be old, could be—"

"I think they're fresh." I returned to the Jeep, my heart pounding. He'd turned here, I felt certain.

With my hand on the windscreen frame, I stood and scanned the land ahead. Eva drove steadily.

She shook her head. "I don't get it."

"He's doubled back."

"This road is no good for—"

She stopped mid-sentence. Off to the right, in a gully, was a green vehicle with its backside in the air. Within seconds, we'd closed the gap enough to recognize a truck. A Bedford Fifteen Hundred.

SIX

As the crow flies, 75 miles approximately due south, a man in Tel Aviv office received a message. A clerk had taken a telephone call and the note read: Your uncle has asked for help, please call urgently.

"Something about plumbing," the clerk told him. "I couldn't quite get it. He sounded anxious and uncertain. I suppose that's why he ended the call before I could put him through."

The man in the office shook his head. "The old fool. There's always something." He thanked the clerk and added that he'd call back later.

He waited ten minutes and casually left the building. After a short stroll, he arrived at a hotel where he asked to use the telephone. He'd paid the staff in advance for its use, just in case.

Money wasn't an issue. Secrecy was.

In a private room, he asked the operator to connect him to a number in Acre. They knew each other's names. When he'd called and left a message, the other man had used his. It couldn't be helped, but no one would put two and two together. No one would figure his involvement.

And even if someone did, they wouldn't get very far.

Although he was part of the organization and knew the plans, the man in Tel Aviv only had one contact above him: Cuban Cigar-man. Maybe he was the boss, but it was unlikely. Second from the top, the man from Tel Aviv told himself. Of course, Cigar-man might have been far from the top, but the man in the Tel Aviv hotel didn't think so. The chain could be long but that would involve too many people. Long enough to protect identities. Too long and there would be the risk of failure.

The man who had called from Acre about the plumbing was a different man. A nobody. Someone who Cigar-man had provided information on. Someone who would do what he was told.

The man from Tel Aviv didn't know Cigar-man's real name. He didn't need to. Not even a code name. The man from Tel Aviv had coined the name Cigar-man after they'd met. Before that, he thought of him as the man from Jerusalem with a deep voice. Much later when they met for the second time, the man from Tel Aviv thought he'd got the nickname wrong. When he stood, the man was as big as a bear. Tall with wide shoulders and a heavy frame.

Whenever the man from Tel Aviv rang the Jerusalem phone number he'd been given, the other man always answered. So Cigar-man was rich and important. He could afford a private telephone and was available whenever it rang.

Which surely made Cigar-man one of the elite. Which would mean his boss would be too. How many layers in the upper echelons could there possibly be? Second from the top, was Tel Aviv-man's conclusion.

Years ago, the man from Tel Aviv had been making money from a less than legal source. It hadn't been much, just cash on the side. Low profile, sleight of hand deals. The British authorities weren't looking closely. The police and army had bigger issues with insurrection and terrorism rather than worry about petty crime. But the criminals knew what he was up to. It was impossible to hide it from the people he did the deals with. And when he was contacted about a big opportunity, he was proud that he'd been selected. The organization must have had a large pool to fish in but had chosen him. They figured they could trust him to keep their secret. And they were right. He'd been asked to do as instructed by any message using the right code word. He'd received three such notes and done as they'd asked. Each time he'd been paid handsomely—an envelope of cash pushed under his door. He never met any of the messengers until a youth he'd never seen before, or since, took him to a meeting place in Jaffa's old town.

He remembered the evening like it was yesterday.

The sky was gray with the onset of night but Arabs on the street could have seen him. But no one looked closely despite a Jew being in their midst. It was before the tensions had reached boiling point. Arabs and Jews still worked together although this was the Arab town and the Tel Aviv man carried a gun, just in case.

Before disappearing, the youth told him to go inside the old building, walk through to the back and then go up the flight of steps.

Cigar-man had been in the darkness with a wide brimmed hat pulled low. The man from Tel Aviv didn't see him straight away and was surprised by the whispered voice.

"Put the gun away." The voice was deep and alluded to Polish heritage. "Good. Now sit."

The man from Tel Aviv complied.

"You've done well," the man in the dark said. Sitting closer, the Tel Aviv-man could smell tobacco. Not the cheap, stale smell he was used to, but aroma of expensive Cuban cigars.

"The jobs—you've been testing me," the man from Tel Aviv said. The last task had of course been illegal but it also took a certain attitude. Money above all else. Even patriotism. Anyway, he told himself afterwards, selling a few old guns to the enemy wouldn't make a jot of difference to the outcome of the full-scale war which would come. And he'd guessed it was a test of his loyalty and nerve.

"On a number of levels," the shadowy man said and appeared to nod. "Would you have killed if I'd asked?"

The Tel Aviv man had thought about that already. He'd known the answer immediately. "Yes," he said.

"That's what we thought," the man said.

We. Others. A chain of command probably. That's how these things worked in his experience.

"We trust you and you'll be well rewarded." The man from Jerusalem lit a cigar and the flame from the match briefly illuminated the room.

Another test, the Tel Aviv man thought. All this subterfuge. Cigar-man wouldn't let his face be seen. So, the man from Tel Aviv looked away and was rewarded.

"Well done, again."

A bundle was slid across the shadowy table between them. An envelope full of money. More than a year's salary. And then Cigar-man told him of their audacious plans. He was told he had an important role. He had one contact in Acre and needed to convince another in Haifa to do a simple job when the time was right. The organization planned an initial shipment. The first would be small. Once proven, they would go into a full-time operation. Like a business, he said. In plain sight but invisible.

Cigar-man provided a second envelope, smaller than the first, and said it had instructions for the recruitment of the man in Haifa. The Tel Aviv man would have to wait until he was back home to read it and be shocked by the contents of the envelope.

At the end of their meeting, Cigar-man had provided his telephone number in Jerusalem. He said he expected any problems to be dealt with. That was his job. "But if you can't deal with something, you call me. A last resort."

"When do we start?" the Tel Aviv man asked.

"Anytime. It could be next week. It could be a year from now."

It hadn't been either. It had been almost thirty months. He suspected it was linked to the Armistice. It made everything easier for the organization. He had no name for them and didn't need one. He just needed to do his simple job and make sure nothing went wrong with his part of the operation.

He just needed to wait for the signal.

The first of which had come three weeks ago. Now everything was well advanced.

"You called about the plumbing," the Tel Aviv man said when the phone in Acre was picked up.

He heard the man on the other end swallow before speaking. "Yes. It's…"

"Do we have a problem?"

"I don't know. I thought I'd better call."

The man in the Tel Aviv hotel closed his eyes and took a calming breath. The contact in Acre was an old imbecile. Unfortunately, the organization had little choice. Perhaps they could have replaced him but then that might have raised eyebrows and questions.

"Just tell me," the man in Tel Aviv said.

"There's been an escape… from the prison."

"And that's a problem?"

"They escaped through the tunnels."

Static crackled on the line while the Tel Aviv man thought. Then he said, "How many men escaped?"

"Two."

"Do they know?"

"About the shipment next Wednesday?"

The Tel Aviv man suppressed irritation. The other man had already mentioned tunnels. Now he unnecessarily said shipment next Wednesday. *Idiot!*

"Do the prisoners know anything?" His voice was clipped.

"I don't know."

"Did they disturb anything in there?"

"No. They used the left tunnel." Two tunnels built by the Crusaders, one real, one a decoy. The decoy one was what would be used by the organization for storage.

"Could it have been a coincidence?"

"Yes. Likely just a coincidence. It's just the timing. Just over a week before it arrives. I wasn't sure. I didn't call you straight away but then I thought…"

The Tel Aviv man took another calming breath. No point in upsetting the fool in Acre.

"All right," he said. "Thank you for letting me know. It's probably nothing but you did the right thing to call."

The Acre man started to speak but he cut him off. "Call me again if anything changes."

SEVEN

"He crashed," stated Eva as we looked at the upturned Bedford. "I knew these roads were too bad for a truck."

I jumped down before the Jeep's wheels stopped turning.

The truck did indeed appear to have crashed. I touched the exhaust pipe and felt heat. This was Duffy's escape vehicle. No question.

"Bodies?" Eva called as she got out of the Jeep.

"No."

"They must be on foot," she said hurrying over. Her gun was out.

I checked the cab for signs of blood and found none. Then I scanned the scrub. I figured they were now at least thirty minutes ahead of us. We'd lost time at the checkpoint and in the exchange with Eva. Thirty minutes on foot, hurrying—they'd be at least a couple of miles away. We weren't in the mountains, but the land undulated with big rocks and gullies. They could be out there. Anywhere. Any direction.

"They'd go west," said Eva.

"Why?"

"Water. Any other direction and they'd run the risk of dehydration. They need civilization. Out here they'd find abandoned Arab villages. And they're no good for water.

The Arabs poisoned the wells before they left—rotten dead animals dropped in."

I was looking westward, thinking.

"If they're smart, they'll go for water." She started walking down the slope. "We should at least check around to make sure they aren't hiding... or sheltering from the sun."

I followed through dry grass, our shoes kicking up dust.

Eva was ten paces ahead when she jumped and screamed. I saw the flash of something whip close by her legs.

Crack! Crack!

Her sudden gunfire caused ground-birds to scatter into the air.

Then she screamed again, although this time it was more anger than fear.

I caught up with her and looked down. At her feet was a snake at least four feet long. It was headless. Blown clean off.

"I hate snakes," Eva said, her voice trembling. "Scared the life out of me. Did you see the way it sprang up?"

She was fiddling with her gun.

"A problem?"

"Jammed," she said, her voice returning to normal. "Good job I got it with the second shot."

She continued to play with the mechanism, and I guessed it was a delaying tactic. How many more snakes were out there?

I turned my attention to the countryside, half-looking for where Duffy may have hidden. I couldn't see any disturbance.

Back the way we'd come, our passage had left an obvious trail. Would it disappear in twenty minutes? Half an hour? Probably not.

"You're in luck," I said. "They didn't come this way."

I walked back to her Jeep. She followed.

"Why?"

"No tracks. The ground doesn't look disturbed."

At the road, I took twenty paces and found where the truck had come off. The surface was uneven, holes and stones as big as oranges. But were they big enough to cause the truck to swerve and leave the road?

What had Eva said before shooting the snake?

If they're smart.

So far, Duffy had proven just how smart he was. He'd pulled off an escape, unimaginably hard—especially in the current climate.

I continued walking. And then I saw it on the other side of the road. Off to the left was a scuff mark. A casual glance would have missed it: a smooth patch of dusty ground, a few inches wide and a foot long.

A tyre-spin.

I got on my haunches and looked at the nearby dirt. Maybe it was the light or the heat, but I could imagine the four wheels. A small passenger car had been parked at the side and then driven onto the main strip.

I closed my eyes and pictured it.

Eva was close. She said something but I held up a hand, not wanting her to disturb my mental image. I was back in the Austin 6 with King driving.

While we'd been stopped by Eva, a taxi had gone past. Only two non-army vehicles had gone toward Acre as we'd travelled north. A private car and the taxi.

I saw the first vehicle in my mind's eye. It was small and black although covered in dust. A driver and no passenger.

I shook my head. The image went and the taxi came back. It looked gray. Maybe it was the dust or maybe it was originally gray. One driver, one passenger. But the passenger had been in the front, not the rear.

A taxi. Practically invisible unless you need one. A Bedford Fifteen Hundred may as well have had a big sign on it. *Follow me! Look, here I am!* That wasn't a smart choice—unless you wanted to send your pursuers in the wrong direction.

Duffy was smart.

"Back to Acre," I said. "They're in a taxi and they're going the other way."

EIGHT

"You're good!" Eva said, her voice full of genuine admiration. She'd asked me to drive and was dismantling her pistol.

"Finding people—it's one of the things I do. But let's not count chickens. We've not found them yet. All I know is that they intended to shake us off, and they were last seen heading for Acre."

"Damn!" she said, fiddling with the gun.

I waited.

"The extractor claw is broken."

We re-joined the main north-south drag and passed the spot where she'd pulled us over.

"They're way ahead," she said, looking into the distance. "We won't catch them now. They're in the wind."

"Not necessarily."

"I like your optimism."

It wasn't optimism, it was perseverance. "Don't quit until you've lost."

"Sounds like a mantra."

"It was one of the things my boxing coach used to say. Get knocked down, you get back up. You fight until you can fight no more. If you go in with any other attitude, you've lost before the fight even starts."

I flashed back to an early boxing match. Coach Sammy was yelling words I couldn't make sense of. But I learned the lesson. I thought my opponent was strong and I was weak. I was on the ropes, losing, but I dug deep, and my sudden burst of energy surprised him. The psychology helped. He went from believing he'd won to facing defeat. And I beat him.

She nodded. "No quitting."

I said, "And the other thing he taught me was don't assume the other man believes he'll win. Everyone has self-doubts."

"True in war," she said.

"Undoubtedly."

"But it can also work the other way around," she said, and I shot a glance at her. She continued: "Overconfidence. If your opponent believes they can win they may underestimate you."

Smart, I thought, and realized we had a mutual respect going on.

She said nothing for a moment before throwing me with her next comment.

"Do you hate us, Captain? Do you hate Jews?"

It was a fair question. The last two years of the British Mandate had been particularly tough. Jewish terrorists, the Irgun and Stern Gang, were intent on driving us out. It was a state of fear, and many British soldiers did hate them. Separating the terrorists from innocent public was a mental challenge.

"No," I said, "I don't hate you. In fact, I have Jewish friends. One of my best friends is a police inspector."

Eva swivelled, looking at me. Her eyebrows climbed higher than I thought humanly possible. "What's his name?"

"David Rosen. Based in Tel Aviv."

She looked back at the road. "Not a name I've heard before."

"Other friends too," I said, thinking of my ex-landlady. Our intimacy had been short-lived, but I still thought fondly of Erika.

"If not hate, then what about distrust?" she said.

"Not at all."

"That's good to know."

I continued to race back the way we'd come, the Land Rover thumping hard over the uneven road. Finally, I could see the checkpoint outside of Acre. I'd been trying to visualize the taxi.

How did I know it wasn't a private car? There was writing on the side. I couldn't see the letters clearly. Maybe ending in *rcb*?

It was small to midsize. I might have guessed an Austin 8, but the grill was distinctive. Narrow with vertical lines as opposed to the Austin's horizontal. There were also four headlights compared to the Austin's two.

"Slow down," she said. "At this speed they'll be worried. I don't fancy getting shot by my own side."

I'd already started braking and dropped the speed to thirty miles an hour for the final hundred yards. Then I slowed even more until the Jeep trundled to a halt in front of a soldier with his hand up.

She said, "Let me do the talking."

"Ask about the taxi: possibly beige with a long narrow front grill and four headlights."

"OK." Eva climbed out.

The guards relaxed as she walked toward them, presumably recognizing her uniform. I heard her speak in Hebrew and guessed she'd asked for the officer-in-charge because the man she addressed pointed to a second soldier beyond the barrier.

Eva marched over and started talking to the second man. It began friendly enough, but after she showed him her gun, it got heated. I watched and heard a short, terse exchange between them. In a protective manner, he had a hand on the grip of his own pistol.

I saw Eva shake her head and stomp back to me with a face set like thunder.

"You wanted his gun," I said as she got in.

She said nothing and waved her arm. The boom-barrier raised to let us pass.

"What did he say about the taxi?"

"It came through less than half an hour ago. The Arab was driving, so they didn't think anything of it."

"Did he know the make?"

"No."

"What did he say?"

She looked across at me, and her eyes still burned. I thought she wasn't going to reply but after a beat she said, "He thought it was British and the colour isn't beige it's pale green and covered with dust."

The ancient, fortified town passed on our right and I scanned ahead. It was a barren region. To the left was scrub stretching to low hills. There were old Arab villages out there, abandoned since the war. The road ran almost parallel to the sea for a few miles, then deviated for a section where the sand and infirm ground stretched a mile from the coast.

Haifa was about ten miles ahead. The westerly wind pelted the Jeep with sand. I drove very fast. Despite Eva's conversation, we'd been quick through a roadblock and he wouldn't be driving too fast. Even subconsciously Duffy wouldn't want to draw attention to himself.

Maybe we'd reduced the gap between us.

"I outranked him," said Eva, still angry. I knew she was talking about her exchange with the soldier at the check point.

"You ordered him to hand over his weapon."

"I'm an officer. I outranked him," she said again. "He should have obeyed. He argued that he didn't have to obey because of his duties and my being in the female division. Like my rank meant nothing because he's a man!"

She fumed some more and then pressed herself hard against her seat and stared at the road.

At the Haifa roadblock, I jumped a queue of three trucks until a soldier flagged me to stop. Eva stayed in her seat; her eyes fixed on some far-off point.

I asked the soldier about a taxi, and he said three taxis had passed through in the last twenty minutes. They'd all driven straight on. Two had turned toward Haifa. One had continued south. However, none of them matched my description. Then he remembered a fourth taxi, before the others. He described it as olive rather than green and it was a Ford. It had also gone straight on.

So we hadn't closed the gap by much, if at all.

I wondered whether Duffy could have gone past and then doubled back. He could have taken the southern road into Haifa. However, at the next roadblock, they said they'd stopped the pale green taxi and confirmed the driver had been Arab. The passenger spoke a little Hebrew but could have been British. I asked if the white man had curly red hair but the soldier only recalled a cap. Which made sense. Duffy had covered up his obvious hair.

I kept the conversation short and we were soon on our way. Possibly faster than the fugitives. They had queued and been questioned. I reckoned we'd closed the gap a little.

They'd continued along the road to Tel Aviv which was a long straight stretch.

Driving fast once more, I thought about Eva's treatment by the male soldier.

"One day there will be equality," I said. "One day there won't be male and female divisions. Maybe there will just be the army. And you shouldn't forget that the Israelis are already way ahead of the rest of the world."

She made a grumbling sound.

I said, "The Woman's Royal Army Corps has only just been established in Britain—"

She interrupted: "You think we're ahead but we're not really. I was in the Palmach."

I was impressed. The Palmach was the elite strike force of the Haganah.

She continued: "A third of us were women. We carried guns and we fought, but frankly the Women's Corps is just like yours. Officially, we aren't allowed into combat. So, until that changes, you can call your divisions whatever you like but there won't be equal status until there's equal treatment."

"Ever heard of Dr James Barry?"

She looked at me, the first time she'd stopped staring ahead since her argument at the Acre checkpoint.

"He was a highly respected surgeon in the army back in the eighteen hundreds. Rose to the equivalent rank of Brigadier. And when he died, they discovered the subterfuge." I shot Eva a glance. "You see, James Barry was actually a woman."

"Your point?"

"That a hundred years ago, women couldn't be surgeons. Things change."

She didn't comment and I returned to thinking about the terrain. I knew this stretch of road, having driven it many times during my time serving in Mandatory Palestine. Forty miles, passing villages on either side and roads twisting east toward the mountains.

Eva returned to her own thoughts, although she seemed a little more relaxed after our conversation. I found myself thinking of my favourite book: *The Count of Monte Cristo.* In the story, a sailor, Edmond Dantes is wrongly accused of being a Bonapartist traitor. He is imprisoned on a fortress island for fourteen years with a mad monk as his only friend. When the monk dies, Dantes switches places with the body and escapes when it is cast into the sea.

The rest of the story was much more complex, with Dantes assuming identities and plotting his revenge against the men who caused his imprisonment.

It made me wonder about Duffy and a small part of me admired what he'd done. Breaking out of a high-security prison was no mean feat.

Dantes had seized an opportunity. Duffy had planned everything. He'd arranged for his arrest and then cleverly escaped.

But there was a significant difference between Duffy and Dantes. Duffy had wanted to be in the prison before he escaped. I went over it again and again. However, as we neared Tel Aviv, I was still no closer to understanding what his motive had been.

NINE

"We've lost them," Eva said after a long silence between us. We'd reached the final checkpoint before Tel Aviv and I'd asked the soldiers about the taxi, probably olive, possibly a Ford. They hadn't seen it. Or, to be precise, they'd seen plenty of taxis but couldn't remember noticing the one we were chasing.

"That's it," she said.

"Not necessarily." I backed up and pulled to the side of the road.

Eva raised her eyebrows at me. "So where now? Shall we keep going in the hopes that we bump into them? Maybe they'll run out of fuel."

I heard defeat and sarcasm in her tone.

"Don't quit until you've lost," I said.

She shook her head. "But you need to recognize when you *have* lost."

Which was true, but I hadn't reached that point yet.

"Do you have a map?"

She pulled one from under the dash. I got out and spread it on the Jeep's hot bonnet.

Eva joined me.

"What are you looking for?"

"Sometimes it's better to stop and think," I said, "rather than charge ahead."

"You still believe you can find them?"

"I've found people before."

"A hundred percent success rate?"

I shook my head. "No, however quitting gives you zero percent chance of finding them."

A taxi came through the checkpoint the other way and passed us. I pointed at it.

"Kesher," I said. "The taxi firm around here is Kesher. If the soldiers at this checkpoint had seen ours they might remember it wasn't a Kesher!"

"What company was it?" she interrupted.

"I don't know, but it wasn't a Kesher. They use Israeli Olds, exclusively."

I expected her to ask more questions. I thought I remembered *rcb* written on the side but now I doubted myself. It might be American or British. It could be a Ford and I knew many people, even Brits regarded some Fords as British.

Rather than ask a follow-up question about the car, she asked, "Where've they gone then?"

The truth was, they could be anywhere. Assuming the information from the checkpoints was correct, and they did head south from Haifa they could have taken any of the minor roads into the hills.

I'd driven over the mountains in the past. Some of the roads were fine but most were not. People had Jeeps or Land Rovers for a reason. Once off the main drags, you relied on a purpose-built vehicle or four legs.

There was another thing I'd learned about human behaviour—especially of people fleeing. They tended to turn in a natural direction.

A right-handed person entering a room without a specific target will typically turn left. Most people progressing on a circuit will go anticlockwise. But not everyone. However, someone favouring a choice such as a direction will repeat that pattern. Most likely as not.

I ran my finger north from Acre to where Duffy had turned right and gone east to the hidden taxi.

I then ran my finger south from Acre the same distance took me to Haifa. But the checkpoint guards on both sides had seen the taxi. My finger continued south. It passed the town of Alit. A few miles later, was an area called Nahsholim.

"Really?" she said. "A kibbutz? You think they're at a kibbutz?"

"No," I said. "That doesn't feel correct. However, they turned right before, which I think it could have been instinctive. The same with the distance." I tapped the map. "Do you know this place?"

"Vineyards."

I kept going south. Netanya felt too far, but the settlement at Hadera interested me. Exactly halfway between Haifa and Tel Aviv.

It was on the wrong side of the road but I liked the symmetry. Not the same distance as they'd gone north but halfway. And it had minor roads fanning out in other directions.

"A throw of the dice," I said, packing up the map. "Hadera."

Eva shrugged and sighed.

I said, "I'm not ready to quit."

"They most likely continued through the checkpoint. They just weren't remembered."

"My gut says Hadera."

She sighed again. "Fine."

I turned the Jeep around and went north. Now that it was no longer a race, I took it easy. Beside me in her seat, Eva still looked tense.

"Relax," I said. "It can't be your fault if we don't find them. Your superiors will understand."

"This is just prolonging the pain," she said after a thoughtful silence. "They aren't in Hadera."

"We'll see."

"Aren't we just as well stopping at every township along the way?" We were approaching Netanya. "Here, for example."

I thought not. "Too big. They're going to dump the taxi." When she looked at me, I shook my head. "A feeling. Duffy is smart, we're agreed on that. The taxi was good for slipping through checkpoints on major roads. Now he needs a vehicle for rougher terrain."

"Based on what?" she asked, incredulous.

"Experience."

"You could look pretty foolish."

I smiled. "Won't be the first time and it's not like anyone else will know."

"All right," she said because it was her car and her decision, "We'll just check at Hadera and then I'll drop you off in Haifa. You can catch the next boat home."

Eva went quiet again and didn't talk for the twenty-odd minutes it took to reach Hadera. From the road, as we passed through agricultural land, I had no idea how large the town was. I guessed perhaps ten thousand people lived here. I saw shops and a school, and I thought I'd made a mistake. It was bigger and in a series of blocks. Geometric. Ordered. Too big. No place to dump a taxi.

"I was wrong," I said.

Eva sighed. "Back to Haifa then?"

We were at the junction with the main north-south drag. We were on the east side and my gut now said that Duffy would have gone west.

I crossed the main road.

"Where are you going now?" Eva asked.

"Instinct," I said. "Another final throw of the dice."

The ground was all ochre rocks, stretching into lighter-coloured sand. A few shacks and cypress trees speckled the land. The road went straight to the coast and then, about a hundred and fifty yards ahead, it split at a T. On the left was a low brownstone building: a coastguard station.

I slowed to a stop.

"What?" she said.

"There's a car. Left-hand side of the building. Tucked out of sight."

"Is it the taxi?"

"Too far to tell," I said.

She drew her gun.

I drew mine from my ankle holster.

She stared at me. "You didn't…"

"A small lie," I said. "I apologize. At least we have one working weapon between us."

I rolled the Jeep forward toward the T-junction, stopped and got out. The coastguard station had a stubby lookout tower and radio masts. I couldn't see any sign of life except for gulls wheeling through the sky beyond.

"Split up or approach together?" I asked.

"Together," she said, waggling her useless gun. "I'll follow. If you don't mind?"

I didn't. I also didn't expect them to still be here. They'd swapped cars; taken an off-road vehicle and gone. A quick switch. Maybe an hour ago. No need to hang around.

They'd probably gone long before we reached the Tel Aviv checkpoint.

Unless they were waiting for a boat. I didn't think that made sense. All the complexity and changes of direction.

Whether there or not, we weren't taking any chances. I left the road with Eva one step behind and crept along the rocks toward the building. All the time, I kept an eye out for movement. If they were watching for us, someone would have been in the tower, but there wasn't. If they were here, then maybe they didn't expect to be followed. Not this far anyway. A needle in a haystack.

"It's the taxi," I said as we got nearer and recognized the shape of the grill. And beneath the sand and grime, I could see olive paintwork.

Eva picked up a stick—jetsam, I guess—and weighed it in her hand like a baseball player about to go out and play. Another weapon. More use than her damaged gun.

"Let's hope you don't—" I started to say, but a jolt to the back of my head stopped me.

Just before the blackness flooded in, I think I heard her say, "Sorry."

TEN

The man in Tel Aviv went to the hotel and used the telephone to call the office in Haifa. A secretary answered and said the boss was busy.

"He'll speak to me," Tel Aviv-man said calmly and gave her the code word.

The boss came on the line seconds later, out of breath. He was in his forties and overweight. Tel Aviv-man imagined the fat man's greasy hair and bloated face. No doubt he'd run to the telephone and was dripping with sweat.

They'd met only twice and this was the second phone call. The man in Haifa owned a transport business. Three years ago it had been small with only five lorries in his fleet, and one warehouse. Now he had twenty trucks and three buildings. His business was booming since the British had left, although black-market trade was driving it rather than anything legitimate. But that wasn't the leverage the organization had over the transport boss. They had the photographs.

After meeting Cigar-man in Jaffa, the Tel Aviv man had opened the second envelope and seen the pictures. He'd admit it to no one, but they made him sick to his stomach. Ordinarily he might have considered paying the fat man a visit at night. A couple of shots to the head, with blame directed at the Arabs. But the organization needed transportation and the fat man had accepted his role. No questions except for when he'd get the negatives.

"After the job," the Tel Aviv man had said. Although he didn't say there would be multiple jobs. Nor did he say that the negatives would come with a bullet. Because once the fat man had the originals, the organization no longer had their leverage.

With the man in Haifa on the line, the Tel Aviv man waited. He let the fat man sweat even more.

"Are you still there?"

Tel Aviv man said, "It's happening." He heard a swallow. "We need three."

"Yes."

"You remember how to set them up?"

"Yes. And no drivers."

"We'll provide the drivers. You just need to deliver them to the port in Acre and collect them from Sarafand."

"Sarafand? But—"

"It's deserted and secure," Tel Aviv-man said, relaying the information he'd received. The destination had changed since the British had deserted their bases. Sarafand was isolated and perfect for their purposes.

The fat man cleared his throat. "When?"

That was three weeks ago. Since then the man from Tel Aviv had sent a message requesting a fake delivery for Sunday. He'd followed up with a phone call and used the code word.

"You know the date?" he checked with the fat man.

"Don't worry," the horrible man in Haifa responded. "The trucks will be there, just as required."

Part of Tel Aviv-man wanted the fat man to let them down. Not because it would be a problem for the organization but because it made his skin crawl just thinking about the photographs he had hidden beneath his floorboards. On the day he destroyed them, he'd sleep better at night.

That evening, after his third beer, the man from Tel Aviv decided he wouldn't shoot the other man twice in the head. He'd shoot him twice in the knees and set fire to the man's house. With the fat man inside.

ELEVEN

Of course, Eva's Land Rover was gone. I had a golf ball of a lump on the back of my head but no broken skin.

The coastguard building wasn't locked. They'd been here. They'd been waiting.

For Eva.

Eva's Jeep had been their off-road vehicle. Rather than leave it for them, Eva's job had first been to make sure no one followed. Duffy had guessed we'd be sent to recover him.

If we'd delayed a day, probably sorting out paperwork, he'd have gotten clean away. But we came immediately because I had clearance. We'd been right behind him.

The switch of vehicles near the northern border might have been enough to lose us, but they wanted to be sure. Maybe if her gun hadn't jammed, she'd have gotten rid of me earlier, probably when I guessed where they were waiting.

That's why she'd been so quiet on the drive. She'd been wondering how to deal with me.

Despite the pain in my skull, I had to admire the planning. They'd considered almost everything. I figured their plan had been for Eva to drop me off at the port after a fruitless search. But I hadn't given up and I'd tracked them down to this remote spot.

Eva had made a blunder but I hadn't spotted it. It was only now that I realized and kicked myself for not challenging her. When we got to the mountains she'd said they'd make it in a jeep but not an old truck. But she'd never asked me what vehicle they'd been driving. She'd known about the Bedford Fifteen Hundred.

No point in beating myself up about it now, though. Always move forward. Don't dwell on the *if-onlys*.

So, what could I learn from this place?

There were two wooden chairs and a pile of cigarettes. I counted eleven in two rough piles. There was a length of rope on the floor. Which intrigued me because it was knotted in the middle and possibly cut at each end. Maybe it was relevant or maybe it had been there for a long time.

I figured the station hadn't been operative for over a year. The British used to watch out for immigrants trying to land illegally along this stretch of coast. It served no purpose anymore.

Dust covered everything. There was a map of the coast spread on the bench by a broad window that overlooked the sea. It was tatty and old and yet didn't appear to have the same dust as most other things.

Outside, I checked the taxi. It was a Ford Pilot. I'd never seen one before but was pleased with my visual memory. It was a four-seater but with a single door on each side. The company name on the door was *Barclo*. I'd failed to visualize that, but the brevity combined with speed and dust justified my failing.

I pulled away the steering column and attempted to hot-wire the car. Nothing happened: no spark at all. When I lifted the bonnet, I saw why. They'd removed the distributor cap. No way was it going anywhere without that.

There was, however, a working radio in the building. I transmitted, made connection, and asked for a message to be passed on to the police in Tel Aviv. Five minutes later, I was relaying my story to my friend, Sub Inspector Rosen and he was arranging for me to be collected.

Then I radioed Alexander Barracks in Cyprus and spoke to provost marshal, Jim Dexter.

"You're coming back," he said after I updated him.

"No, I'm not quitting yet."

"Oh?"

I asked him to pass on a message to SIB Command to let them know I was staying in Israel. "With their permission," I added graciously.

"Let's hope so."

They'd be fine, for a while at least. Unless, or until, I was needed for something else.

"Could you send me an unmarked Land Rover and Duffy's file?"

"Of course."

"I'll also need papers," I said, guessing that the hunt for an AWOL soldier wouldn't be enough of a reason to be allowed the freedom of the new state. Last time I was here, to find the Killing Crew, had been in Israel's interest. They might care about their escaped prisoner, but they wouldn't give two hoots about Sergeant Alfred Duffy. Not unless he became a terrorist, that is, and I had no evidence that he would.

To Dexter, I added: "Ask SIB Command to come up with authority for me to stay—a travel permit as a minimum."

"Where will you be, Ash?"

"I'm going back to Acre," I replied because when uncertain, the best approach is to start at the scene of the crime. It was good advice I'd been given in the early days of my training.

For Duffy, that was the escape from Acre. I ensconced myself in a cheap hotel on the outskirts of the town. I also checked in with the local police station and let the inspector there know what I was doing. I also gave him

Sub Inspector Rosen's details as a contact. He would vouch for me while I stayed in Acre.

My next visit was to the prison. Captain Gruner didn't need to help, but he was generous. He said he was happy for me to see Abu Hajjar's cell. He'd also accompany me through the tunnels. We'd follow the escape route once more, looking for anything of interest. I didn't know what a clue would be. He didn't either.

The only thing in the cell was scratches on the wall, marks counting the days and maybe some doodles. I spent time, carefully copying the marks. I used four sheets of paper, one for each wall.

"Any idea about this?" I asked.

Low down on the right-hand wall beside one of the cots was a star of sorts: three intersecting lines. To the left were five straight lines, followed by four horizontal lines and other marks, followed eight vertical lines. The vertical ones were the most like a tally, although the fives didn't have a bar through them.

"None," said Gruner. "All the cells have scratches on the walls. I'm afraid they probably don't mean anything."

I moved the bed and found another star. Gruner was wrong, I was sure of it.

Once I'd finished, we followed the route to the door to the citadel, went through the courtyard and into the castle.

Gruner led through the rooms and into the tunnel. They were full of history and secrets, but the damp walls told me none of them. Using a torch, I shone it around, hoping Duffy or Hajjar had dropped something, anything that could help. I found nothing.

There was an old Jew sitting on a stool outside when we emerged into sunlight.

Gruner spoke to him. The man grunted. Then I noticed what looked like another entrance.

"Two tunnels?" I asked the warden.

"A fake one," Gruner said. "I think the Crusaders used it as some kind of trap for anyone thinking they could get into the citadel this way. Old Moishe here, charges for people to look."

"You don't mind?"

Gruner shook his head and shrugged. "Doesn't do any harm. The right-hand one just dead ends now. I think there used to be a water trap. Plus Old Moishe stops anyone getting into the real tunnel."

I walked back the way we'd come, noticing how the stone went from rough-hewn to fine, chiselled blocks. However, I still saw nothing enlightening. As we walked through the final subterranean hall, I asked Gruner about the thing that had bothered me the day before.

"You didn't want to admit these tunnels existed," I said, remembering the non-verbal exchange between the Gruner and his sergeant.

"No, but—"

"But?"

"I figured your man Duffy knew and you might have known."

I waited for more.

After a few paces, he added: "You Brits discovered them but only a few remaining people know. And... well the new government"—his tone suggested that his opinion of them wasn't high—"well, the Minister of Education and Culture has instructed that the tunnels be sealed."

"Why?"

We climbed the spiral staircase and came out in the great hall before he answered. "It's to do with imperialism. Crusaders equal British rule, I think. If it weren't for the fact that the citadel was originally Ottoman, it would be razed to the ground. It makes no sense to me, but that's politics for you."

When I left, he gave me a firm handshake with his bony hand, and a copy of the Arab's prison file.

Hajjar was classed as a dangerous, violent criminal. It was alleged that he was a member of a gang known as the Orbit Men. The file included a photograph in which he was naked except for a loincloth.

The gang name meant nothing to me, so I asked for information. Which wasn't as straightforward as it sounds. I telephoned Sub Inspector Rosen who then asked the local police inspector to bring me newspaper clippings.

I got a handful of reports that were from the late 1930s and early 1940s. It transpired that Orbit was a corruption of Obit which was short for obituary. Bodies were marked with an 'M' as a message that the Orbit Men had been responsible. They appeared to be a typical criminal gang involved in crime, ranging from serious assault to armed robbery. The robberies intrigued me. This gang didn't target banks, it appeared. The two articles I read involved the theft of artefacts. One was from a museum and one from a synagogue. This second one referenced an audacious theft from the Dome of the Rock.

Hajjar had been arrested in 1945 after digging and looting the ancient site of Arad. He'd been the only survivor of a gang of eight. They'd tried to shoot their way out when surrounded by the police.

I found an article that implied Hajjar had been the leader of the gang.

After Hajjar's imprisonment, the Orbit Men's activity stopped. Or at least that's what it appeared since there were no further reports. There had been plenty of so-called criminal activity reported in the papers though. April 1945 had seen the surrender of German forces and the start of a massive influx of Jewish refugees into Mandatory Palestine. The Stern Gand and Irgun had been active for years, Zionists fighting for a Jewish state. When the second world war ended there were full-scale riots in Jerusalem and Tel Aviv, and bomb attacks on the railway system. Terrorists targeted the British like never before and the papers were probably more focused on that than the activities of petty criminals. It was just an opinion, but maybe the Orbit Men hadn't disbanded when Hajjar was arrested. Maybe they just became old news.

The news breaking that evening was about the Armistice. TransJordan had signed a ceasefire agreement after a month of hard negotiations. People celebrated long and hard into the night although I suspected the war wasn't truly over. The enemy weren't withdrawing and, most sensitively, they still controlled East Jerusalem and sacred Jewish sites.

On my second day in Acre, a courier arrived with Duffy's file and a message that the Land Rover had been delivered to Haifa port. However, before I could do anything, I needed to wait for the travel permit.

Duffy's file told me that he'd been based in Haifa for two of his three years in Mandatory Palestine followed by Acre. He'd been assigned to prison duties which was interesting. I wondered why and found that he'd been involved in an incident. He'd been acting as security for a group of oil workers. They'd been attacked by Arabs and of the four security detail men, one had been killed and two badly injured. The injured men had been repatriated and Duffy had been reassigned.

There was no suggestion of inappropriate behaviour on his part, and it genuinely looked like he'd been assigned to prison duty to protect him.

Even the Army could be sensitive at times. Or at least, a senior officer concerned for his men.

His record at Acre Prison had been exemplary with no suggestion of a relationship between Duffy and any prisoner. Hajjar, the Arab who escaped with him, was not mentioned.

Nor did I find a link between Duffy and the Orbit Men.

I'd asked for information about Second Lieutenant Eva Weiss. She'd told me she was in the eighty-second battalion. The Woman's Core of the IDF.

I got nothing.

I called Dave Rosen and asked again. He said he'd find out what the problem was. Later that day he called my hotel and told me the news, I'd half expected.

"No such person," he said.

"A fake name."

"Undoubtedly."

I said, "But I think she was genuine. Her name was made up, but I'd bet she was in the eighty-second. And I'd bet she was ex-Palmach. She was particularly pissed about how the women were now treated."

He said, "I'll find out if there's anyone AWOL."

"Thanks. They probably didn't go off-piste until four days ago—let's extend that to a week. A female officer missing, not just AWOL, within the last week. And find out everything you can, right down to where they lived, if you can."

I shopped for casual clothes to last me for a few days and kicked my heels while I waited.

On Wednesday night, I couldn't sleep and went out for a run around the town. I drew curious glances from some and disapproval from others, but I enjoyed the ozone-fresh air. I stopped by the harbour wall, listened to the sea, and looked out into the darkness. I found my thoughts turning to Cyprus, the place I was beginning to think of as home.

Another night passed and the authorisation to travel in Israel finally arrived at midday. The local police inspector delivered it and seemed to think it was amusing although he didn't explain. The papers were signed by an Israeli government official and gave me diplomatic status. I was impressed although it said I was assigned to the British Embassy in Tel Aviv.

That surprised me. As far as I was aware, relations between Israel and Britain hadn't thawed enough to justify a British Ambassador. However, I wasn't to complain. I had my authority and could start tracking down Duffy.

TWELVE

The man from Tel Aviv received the call he was dreading.

The man from Acre said, "The two men who escaped. One was a British military policeman. The other was Abu Hajjar."

The man from Tel Aviv noticed that the imbecile sounded more confident than last time he'd called. "Who's he?"

"The leader of the Orbit Men."

"The gang from years ago?"

"Yes."

"Is that relevant to the plumbing?"

"Yes," the Acre man said sharply. Not just more confident but arrogant too.

"Explain."

"He's never tried to escape before—even when he could have just walked out. I've read about him. There's something not quite right. And with the plumbing operation just a few days away. I thought someone might know something. Perhaps you need to…"

"Don't worry about me."

There was silence and the man in Tel Aviv was about to replace the receiver when the other man spoke again.

"The British soldier. The other escapee. Something isn't right."

"Why?"

The man from Acre explained the military policeman had handed himself in. He repeated that Hajjar had never tried to escape before and they both went through the tunnels.

He ended with: "It looks like the British soldier knew about them. Do you know whether it is part of the plan?"

"That he's involved?"

"Do you know?" the Acre man asked again.

The Tel Aviv man didn't know but he didn't like to admit the extent of his knowledge. He didn't want the Acre imbecile knowing that he was another part of the chain.

"He's not involved."

"That's what I thought," the Acre man said. "So, this is important. You'll pass on the information?"

"Don't worry about what I'll do. Just make sure you're ready for the shipment. Make sure nothing goes wrong at your end."

The man in Acre said, "I'll do my job."

Yes, he would. Whether his motivation was money or something else, he would do what he'd been told. No matter what.

Tel Aviv-man tapped the cradle to end the call and asked the operator to place another. A minute later he was speaking to the heavyset man in Jerusalem, relaying the message.

The man in Jerusalem was not someone who troubled the man in the organization above him. He dealt with problems and as soon as the Tel Aviv man had finished his communication, he'd picked up the telephone and called the man he knew as Tzaiad. The name meant *hunter*, and he knew he could rely on the killer to track Hajjar and remove the risk. Before Hajjar died, he'd tell Tzaiad everything he knew. Whether or not, Hajjar and the Brit were a threat to the operation, they would be eliminated quickly.

THIRTEEN

I checked out of the hotel and took a taxi to Haifa. Passing through the checkpoints was simple. Not once did anyone question me and I realized how smart Duffy had been to swap the truck for a taxi.

He'd been virtually invisible in a land where innocent people liked to travel, especially north-south and between Tel Aviv and Jerusalem. The war had stifled that urge to move and visit, but since the Armistice, it appeared that everyone was on the roads. A pent-up demand, I supposed.

In Haifa, I asked the driver to drop me at the taxi head office. Barclo Passenger Cars had a broad front and was half café, half taxi office.

The manager wanted to treat me like a hero, as though it had been my intervention that had returned his car. I was offered a glass of spirit but accepted cold water.

He explained that the taxi had been hired from Haifa to a place called Lamaqor. The passenger had been a young woman who forced the driver out of the car at gunpoint before driving off and leaving him stranded.

"It's never, ever happened before," he said. "And may it never, ever happen again." He followed this with open hands and a beseeching look to the ceiling.

"Your driver was all right?"

The manager sighed. "Praise God!"

"What did the young woman look like?"

"I told the police," he said before providing me with a reasonable description of Eva Weiss, although she'd booked the cab under another false name.

"She was alone?" I double-checked.

He confirmed that she had been, and that made me think about logistics: the moving of and leaving support transport.

I walked to the port and needed to show both my credentials and travel permit before they would release the Land Rover I'd been sent.

It was stored within a pen, and the security man, who thoroughly reviewed my papers, asked why the Land Rover had no British Army markings.

"Because I don't want a target on my back."

He laughed like I was joking, but I wasn't. To many Jews, the British were still hated as oppressors. The final years of the British Mandate had been tough with a colonial army who'd undoubtedly overreacted at times. However, the ever-present fear of terrorism can have that effect. In the perfect world, we'd have policed the situation and worked on an equitable solution. Instead, we fought fire with fire until we were forced to leave.

I had plenty of time to reflect on this as I drove out of Haifa and then south to Tel Aviv. It was slow, and I needed to queue and show my papers at each checkpoint.

By the time I drove into Tel Aviv, the sun was going down fast.

After the cheap place in Acre, I'd hoped to get a room at the relatively comfortable Scopus Hotel on the front, but it was full. So I found the St Andrews in the south, dropped my bags and took a stroll through the town where I'd stayed last time I was here.

My first stop was at the District Police HQ on the Jaffa-Tel Aviv Road. Dave Rosen wasn't there, so I left a message that I could be found at the St Andrews. Then I went up to Allenby Street and headed diagonally in toward the centre. This took me past Nahmani Street where the SIB office had been. I didn't bother visiting; it was vacant now.

I kept going and bought a meal on the go. Eventually I reached the seafront and Hayarkon Street. As I walked north, I remembered the places that had been here until just over six months ago. Things change fast in Tel Aviv. It was expanding at an astonishing rate and any sign of the British rule and military had already been subsumed by the demand for prime real estate.

I visualized the places as I walked. The military car park was now a public car park, but with signs of development underway. Then came what had been the Services Club and the RAF command post. A hundred yards later I was at the Scopus Hotel which had been the Scopus Club, followed by the Ritz Officer's club where I'd played too many hands of poker to remember. Then came the Military Police HQ and finally Gordon Street.

As I turned up Gordon Street, I realized that this is where I'd been subconsciously aiming for. I'd stayed in a lodging house run by a young widow called Erika Arnold.

As I approached the house, I thought of knocking, but forced myself onwards. She was originally from Southern Germany but looked as though she had Persian blood, with her fine features, dark eyes and long eyelashes.

Erika and I had played gin rummy and talked most evenings. And we'd made a connection which briefly became physical before I had to leave for Cyprus. I told myself it had been casual, but as I turned away from Gordon Street and Erika, I admitted that she'd meant more than a fling.

I'd promised to return, and we'd written to one another for months until she told me it had to end. She'd met another man, and the relationship was serious. We couldn't exchange letters anymore. Perhaps that was it, I told myself as I walked back to the St Andrews Hotel. The heart wants what the heart cannot have.

* * *

Dave Rosen joined me for breakfast.

"Didn't expect to find you slumming it," he said pumping my hand. That drew a scowl from the owner watching over the breakfast tables and Rosen raised an apologetic hand.

"No insult intended, madam." He grinned back at me. "Next time, let me fix you up in a hotel, Fred."

The nickname made little sense except for the fact we'd been seen as a double act—Fred and Ginger. Rosen had sandy hair and a bushy beard that we liked to call ginger although it wasn't really. He had intelligent, smiling blue eyes and was always game for a laugh.

I nodded. *And you need to stop me from wandering the streets at night, mooning over a lost love*, I could have replied but took a bite of toast instead.

We talked a little about the background to the case and I knew he was drawing things out. He had news for me but wanted me to wait.

"So, you're assigned to the British Embassy," he said, winking. "Diplomatic immunity."

"I don't think it extends to immunity, Dave."

"Good," he said. "Because you need to behave yourself. It isn't the Wild West even though it feels like it is sometimes." He grinned again. "Although I tend to say it is like the Silver Screen. Tel Aviv is the Hollywood of the east. You should consider staying, Ash. It'd be like old times. Now the war is over"—he waggled his eyebrows—"we could hit the Blue Kettle Club again. Just you and me. Like old times. What do you say?"

"Sounds good, Dave. Now stop teasing me and tell me what you've found out."

He drank a cup of coffee, continuing to make me wait.

"There's nobody AWOL."

I nodded.

"Not officially anyway, Ash."

That made sense. I suspected that even if there had been, there was no one the Israeli Defence Force would tell me about. But his words suggested there was good news to come.

"All right," I said, my voice faking disappointment.

"Woah there, old pal!"

"What?"

"I have two women officers missing, presumed killed in action."

He gave me two names. The second one made me grin.

"Wislitsky," he said. "Eva Wislitsky."

"Bingo!" I said. "Sounds Polish. Where's she from?"

"Russian parents," he said. "Born in Gam Shemuel."

I tried to picture it. "That's on the train line to Haifa, isn't it?"

"Almost midway Tel Aviv and Haifa."

"Double bingo!" I said, feeling giddy with excitement.

The owner scowled again, this time because I'd made too much noise.

"What?"

So I told him. Gam Shemuel was near Hadera which was close to the coastguard station. Eva had known the place. It hadn't just been midway between Haifa and Tel Aviv, it had been near her home.

Which told me something else.

This had all been Eva's plan.

FOURTEEN

Finding the Wislitsky residence wasn't too difficult. I drove through Hadera and found the train station at Gam Shemuel. It wasn't a passenger stop, really. There were grain silos and sheds and rail carts. It was some kind of agricultural cooperative organization running it. I thought they'd know the Wislitskys, but I asked four people and they all shook their heads.

The people I saw were hard-looking folk, middle-aged to elderly and none of them friendly—even before I spoke with my all-too-English accent.

The farms were scattered so, rather than travel around enquiring, I went back into the town of Hadera.

I'd passed a community hall and seen people outside, chewing the cud, maybe solving the political problems faced by the new state. Or maybe they just talked about the weather and the latest harvest.

For the first time, I was welcomed with nods and pleasantries. When I asked for the Wislitsky residence I was ushered inside the hut by a matronly woman who proceeded to show me a map of the area. All the properties and boundaries were marked with names.

"Wislitsky," she said with a jab of her finger.

It wasn't a farm, but alongside the small, square property was a strip of land the size of two standard swimming pools. Half was planted, half was tilled.

A battered truck was parked alongside the house. There were identical properties all along the road, most with similar trucks, and I was less than a mile from the train stop.

I parked outside and went up steps onto wooden boards that ran along the front like a veranda. There were two rocking chairs outside and a large school bell by the door.

I knocked and waited.

Eventually a man with suspicion all over his face cracked the door. I guessed he was in his sixties, but he stood straight and large; a square frame built for labour, not the schoolteacher, I'd presumed from the bell.

"Yes?" His voice was heavy with Russian.

"I'm looking for Eva," I said.

His gaze took me in slowly.

"You should have rung the bell," he said, indicating the large brass object.

Before I could question him, he stooped, picked it up and rang it; four booming clangs. Then he set it down and looked at me.

"There. Now it's rung, you can come in."

I stepped inside and he retreated to lean against a table.

"So, who are you?" he said, seeming more relaxed and perhaps less insane than a moment ago.

Behind him, I saw photographs lined up on a mantelpiece. A family history probably dating back over a hundred years.

I saw a family of four. This man, a wife and two pretty girls of similar age. They were maybe a year or so between them. The girls grew up and the older one became Eva.

"Mr Wislitsky," I said. "I'm looking for your daughter. She's missing. I'm hoping—"

"What? You're hoping that I'll tell you where she is?"

I waited a beat. "I met her recently. She's ex-Palmach and now a lieutenant in the IDF. They think she's been killed in action, but she hasn't, and I think she's in trouble."

"You haven't told me who you are," he said.

I told him and his eyes narrowed either with doubt or hatred, I couldn't tell.

I said, "She's with a dangerous man who's escaped from Acre Prison and—"

He smiled.

I heard footsteps on the boards outside and turned. The door opened and a man in overalls and a pitchfork stepped into the room. I saw more people behind him.

"Thanks for coming, Zach," Wislitsky said.

"You rang the bell," the other man said. He stepped sideways and two more men came in, each with hoes. Zach went right, the men with hoes went to the left. Their faces were full of menace.

I turned back to Wislitsky. "You knew I'd come."

"She said someone would."

"Time to leave, mister," Zach said and lowered the pitchfork, prongs aimed at my midriff.

There was a wooden chair within reach. I went through the steps in my head: right hand grabs the chair and swings it at Zach, knocking away the pitchfork. First man on the left would lower his hoe, I'd step forward and grab it, ramming the pole into him. I'd jab the last man in the face with my left. Then, hopefully with the hoe in my hand, I'd hit Pitchfork-man before he reacted.

They were big and old and slow. I hoped.

But then the dynamic changed because the three men moved outwards and around so that they were too far apart. A second later, all four men were on one side of me with the door on the other.

I took a step toward it. There was a cluster of people outside and more were arriving.

I opened the door and the ones outside stepped back so that I could move onto the veranda. Then they parted so that a channel appeared to the Land Rover.

I walked down the path, unfriendly faces glaring at me as I passed. At least two of the later arrivals had been at the station yard. They'd known where Wislitsky lived. I didn't know whether they didn't like any strangers or whether it was because of Eva.

Maybe it was a little of both, but I was sure they didn't want me to find the girl.

FIFTEEN

The taxi was no longer outside the coastguard building, but the rest of it looked the same. The rope was still on the floor. The map was still on the bench and there were the piles of cigarettes although any tobacco smell had gone.

I was here to do what I always did. When stuck, go back to the start. I'd looked at a map before and guessed we'd find Duffy near Hadera. Duffy hadn't been following a subconscious pattern. It had been thoroughly planned. They had met at the coastguard station because Eva knew the location. It was remote and unoccupied.

I realized I'd been lucky. However, you make your own luck, and often it can seem like a lucky guess, but something intuitive triggered it.

Where have they gone from here?

I picked up the map and my subconscious must have noted again the lack of dust on it compared to the rest of the bench.

They needed Eva's Jeep so they weren't restricted to the main roads. She was in uniform, which had helped us get through checkpoints. However, she'd now have two men with her, one of whom was an Arab. Would she still find it so easy?

Her father had mentioned she'd expected someone to come looking for her. She wouldn't have anticipated my continued involvement. I was supposed to be back in Cyprus having given up. Which meant she expected the police or army to come after her. Which meant she expected difficulty getting past checkpoints. I also thought it unlikely that they would go north again. Duffy's original move had been a decoy. He'd made it look like he wanted to get to Lebanon or Syria, I guessed. Which meant he didn't.

Not north. Not checkpoints.

Multiple routes ran east from Hadera into the hills. The front line wasn't far. On the downside, it was occupied territory and therefore dangerous despite the truce. On the upside, the border wasn't a barrier. There would be enemy soldiers and checkpoints, but the fugitives had a vehicle that could go off-road.

They'd gone east, I was sure of it. I ran my finger toward the mountains beyond Hadera, but the map didn't cover more than five miles from the coast.

That was when I noticed the imprints. There were lines on the map. I held it up to the window to see them better. Nothing was drawn on the map itself, but something had been put on top. That's why there was less dust. Someone had leaned on the bench over the map. If it had been a while ago, surely the dust would have been more even. So I figured this had been Duffy and Hajjar planning, maybe deciding where to go.

Without spare paper, I folded the map and decided to spend time studying it in my hotel room.

Finding the indents on the map felt like progress. I should have picked it up yesterday, and I blamed the delay on the bang to my head. I hadn't been thinking clearly.

The lines on the map made me think of the prison. In Hajjar's cell, I'd noted a tally and other scratches. Was there a message in those marks that I should have picked up on?

I looked out of the window at the sea. Yesterday, I'd been lucky. I'd followed my gut and found them at the coastguard station. I could play that luck again and drive into the hills. I could hope for divine inspiration about where the fugitives had gone.

Yesterday, it had been mostly a choice of north or south. The map in my hands showed an area of thirty square miles. Probably more. No obvious destination.

My gut said it was pointless going that way, so I folded the map and headed back to my jeep.

I drove to the prison in Acre.

It was the right decision because the warden had something for me.

"I don't know if it helps you," he said before I revisited Hajjar's cell, "but word is that Hajjar had a secret."

"A secret?"

The warden shrugged with his hands. "That's all, I'm afraid. He knew something that he wouldn't share." He chuckled. "I suppose it wouldn't have been a secret if he'd told anyone."

I didn't find it so amusing but thanked him for his help.

"One other thing," he said when I was about to leave. "Something struck me now that I remember it. Remember the prison-break almost two years ago?"

Of course, I did. It had been major news and a major embarrassment. On Sunday 4th May, twenty British soldiers and three Arabs arrived at the prison in five army vehicles. However, they'd been Irgun fighters in disguise and expected to get away with forty-one Jews held prisoner.

Timed to coincide with explosions on the roads and in the market outside, a massive hole was blown in the prison wall. Twenty-seven Irgun and Lehi fighters escaped. The irony for the Jews was that 214 Arab prisoners also got away.

"Almost a third of the men escaped that day," the warden said. "All the Jews earmarked for the prison-break remained in their cells, ready for the escape. But the Arabs took advantage, and it became a free for all."

"Right?" I said, wondering where he was going with this old information.

"Abu Hajjar," he said with a knowing nod, "also remained in his cell. He knew the attack was coming, I'm sure. But unlike the others, he didn't take advantage."

"He could have escaped?"

"Correct," the warden said. "Who in their right mind doesn't escape when given the chance?"

SIXTEEN

I returned to Tel Aviv and discovered that Dave Rosen had moved my hotel. I arrived at St Andrews and was told I was now staying at the Rothschild, courtesy of the Tel Aviv police. Which probably meant it was provided free of charge to them. It's how the world worked. A free cup of tea, a free meal, free tickets and a free hotel room. Presumably because the hotel proprietors expected something in return. Or maybe this *was* the return gesture.

Whatever, it wasn't my concern, and the room was twice the size of my previous one, with fresh-smelling sheets and flowers in a vase.

A writing desk held paper, pens and a pencil.

Using the desk lamp to identify the marks on the map, I traced them with the pencil. Then I copied it onto a separate piece of paper.

I'd hoped Duffy had used the map to indicate where he was going. However, the resulting diagram looked like regular structures with lots of straight lines. There was also an oval. So, they weren't roads or directions.

The lines didn't all join where I'd expect and I figured this was because the imprints had been secondary, beneath whatever they'd been drawing on. The paper on top had moved and so the lines didn't meet.

So I joined it up with guesswork. After a few attempts, I settled on a series of rectangles that could have been the plan of a complex property or buildings in a town.

There was something else. I missed it the first few times because it wasn't part of a diagram. It was a dot. If someone had used a pencil, they'd either rested it hard or deliberately pressed.

I decided where it fit in my diagram that I imagined as an oval room with small rooms off it, maybe cupboards. The dot was in the top left. About 10 on a clockface. A dot marks the spot? An X would have been more convincing.

I might have something. I might have nothing.

Content that I could do no more with the map, I turned my attention to the scratches I'd seen in Hajjar's cell in Acre. Despite trying different angles and interpretations, I ended up thinking that the lines still looked like a tally of the days and random doodles.

I kept thinking about his alleged secret and why he didn't escape when he had the opportunity two years ago. What was different this time?

In the morning, I had breakfast with Dave Rosen. Before he left, I asked if the police had any more information on Hajjar or the Orbit Men. I'd reviewed newspaper cuttings while I was staying in Acre but I hoped for more.

He promised to do what he could.

Late afternoon, I received a call from the hotel reception letting me know that a box had arrived for me. Following my request, a bellboy brought it to my room.

The box contained files marked *Confidential* and *Police property* in obligatory red. There was also a note from Rosen telling me to join him and the lads for a soiree at the Queen of Sheba Club. I would be picked up at 8 pm.

Inside the box were sixteen files dating back ten years. The first one I read was the incident involving Hajjar's arrest at Arad almost four years ago. The police report said that an informer had warned them of the illegal excavation and robbery.

The shoot-out was mentioned, and I found it interesting that Hajjar didn't appear to be armed. He'd been found after the eight other gang members had been killed. The fact that no police had been injured suggested that it was more one-sided than implied by the newspaper report.

I had picked up the map and located Arad. It was fifteen or so miles from the Israeli-Transjordan Armistice Line. I wasn't certain but I thought it was in a wide swathe of land that was outside the Jewish territory granted under the UN General Assembly partition agreement. It was a remote and relatively barren region.

I circled each of the other reported incidents and then studied what I'd marked. With the exception of the theft from the Dome of the Rock in Jerusalem, all of the other activity was in the south and remote. There was no straightforward cluster, no circle I could draw and identify the centre of, but I had a sense of where these men operated.

I thought about Rosen's comment yesterday about this not being the Wild West, but I couldn't help thinking it was to these men. Admittedly, they didn't target the banks in towns, but they used guns and they took what they wanted. There were serious crimes reported: rapes, abductions, armed robbery, grievous bodily harm, and Abu Hajjar was the only gang member taken in alive. Which made me wonder. Why hadn't he been shot? I added this to my previous question about why, given the opportunity, he hadn't escaped before.

There were only two other news articles after Hajjar's arrest. The first concerned his conviction and imprisonment. According to the report, the activities of the Orbit Men were over.

And, indeed, that seemed correct.

The second, a year later, reminded the reader of the gang and Hajjar's role. It went on to suggest that the name Orbit Men had been coined by the authorities. It listed other crimes that had been attributed to gangs called the Maccabees and Ghosts. I took a note to find out more about these other groups.

SEVENTEEN

The man from Tel Aviv had been monitoring reports. After his call to Cigar-man about the escape through the tunnels, he'd expected to read that Hajjar had been apprehended or found dead. So far, he'd heard nothing.

Perhaps the big guy in Jerusalem wasn't worried.

Which made no sense.

The tunnels were important. The cargo would be stored there. They could have been compromised.

The Minister of Education and Culture had closed the citadel and tunnels. It wasn't public knowledge or in their interest, but the Tel Aviv man was resourceful. He'd found out.

He rang the number in Jerusalem and heard the smokers' deep voice answer.

"Do we need a contingency?" Tel Aviv-man asked.

"For what?"

"The plumbing—after what's going on."

"You don't need to concern yourself, but there is a change in the plan. Let the man in Haifa know his trucks will be at a depot." He provided an address in Lod and the man from Tel Aviv understood.

The plan had been to leave the trucks in Sarafand where they'd stored the cargo. On reflection, that wasn't smart. If anyone was investigating, then finding where the trucks had been would connect the dots to the next phase.

"Can you arrange that?" the smoker asked, and from his tone, Tel Aviv-man suspected he'd annoyed the big guy.

"Consider it sorted."

"Good." The call was ended.

The man in Tel Aviv immediately relayed the message to the transport boss in Haifa. He despised having to deal with the disgusting man and again thought about how he'd kill him.

Afterwards, he went back to work but found his mind was elsewhere. He didn't know the history of the criminal gang he worked for. They didn't use a name. They were under the radar.

Since Hajjar's escape, the man from Tel Aviv had also been piecing things together. It was his nature. He couldn't help himself. The mystery surrounding the timing of Hajjar's escape had piqued his interest and the more he dug, the more he understood. Hajjar had been a patsy. He hadn't been the leader of the gang known as the Orbit Men and yet he'd accepted his fate and refused to escape when presented with the opportunity. Which meant the gang had something over him.

And the Tel Aviv man also concluded that the organization was that same gang. Or maybe not exactly the same but it was likely that his organization was led by the same man. He'd never asked Cigar-man about their history. It hadn't seemed relevant. All he needed to know was that he was making a lot of money for being prepared and would soon take a share of a fortune.

He had a flash of inspiration. The organization had stopped, or at least paused. Maybe the operation would have started earlier if the British hadn't left, and the War of Independence begun. And now there was an end in sight, they would begin again. Only now it was something else, bigger, more sophisticated.

He'd learned that the officer tracking down the escaped British soldier was SIB Captain Carter. He had been in the tunnels under the prison. He had investigated Abu Hajjar's background.

Carter had a reputation. He'd been involved in exposing organized crime in Cyprus and more recently, he'd been part of the team that had tracked down the nefarious Killing Crew.

Against the odds, he had solved what many considered to be a myth. Could he do the same again?

Was he a threat?

Tel Aviv man was going to tell Cigar-man but after his response about the tunnels, he decided to keep it to himself.

That evening, after too many drinks, the man from Tel Aviv found his head spinning with questions. Was Hajjar still at large? Was the British deserter still with him? Did he know what they were planning?

What if the deserter knew about the operation and Carter found him? Carter would know what was going on. Or maybe he'd simply work it out. Even stopping part of their operation would be a disaster.

The man from Tel Aviv considered himself a man of action. Carter wasn't hiding and he was local. He could be dealt with. There was no need to speak to the man in Jerusalem. No need to worry him.

It was probably his semi-inebriated state that made him draw another conclusion.

Captain Carter had to be dealt with.

EIGHTEEN

When we met at the Queen of Sheba Club that evening, I gave Dave Rosen an update. I'd needed to buy a suit because my casual jacket and trousers wouldn't have sufficed, and my British Army uniform might have been seen as provocative.

"I know, I know, it's not exactly Savile Row," I said when he eyed me with disapproval.

"Next time, let me choose the suit."

"You've been generous enough with the hotel."

He shook his head and then leaned in to whisper: "You know I get more than double what I was paid in the PPF,"—which was the Palestine Police Force—"and we're celebrating a promotion. Inspector Rosen if you please!"

I patted him on the back. "Great news! And well-deserved, I'm sure."

"And we should drink to that!" He ordered champagne before asking, "You aren't still teetotal, are you, Fred?"

"Afraid so."

He laughed. "Well, in that case, old chap, I'm drinking for both of us."

And he did. He drank, we ate, he drank, we hit the dancefloor, he drank, and we played poker. The room rapidly filled with smoke and music, loud voices and laughter.

It was raucous but civilised. There must have been almost fifty guests, including some pretty girls who I danced with between dinner and poker.

We took a break and danced with pretty girls again, then we chatted.

"Shame about today," he said. "Should I send some men and put the wind up Mr Wislitsky and his neighbours? I don't like that they threatened you, Ash."

I think it was the drink talking, so I told him it was fine.

"But a wasted trip."

I shook my head. "It completed part of the picture, and you never know, information can be useful later on. Eva stole the taxi and took it into the mountains near the Syrian border. But she needed an accomplice. I wondered if it had been Duffy but now I think it was her father. He'd have gone with her and been the ride back. She didn't walk to Acre from there, that's for sure."

We resumed the poker game, but within a few hands, Rosen was too drunk to continue at our table, so he joined a drinking game. It appeared to involve taking turns to pose a problem, a conundrum or riddle. The first person with the correct answer didn't have to down their drink in one.

I found myself listening and trying to solve the problems. Most of them were easy, but there was one that no one got. It involved a piece of string. How do you tie a knot in it if you hold both ends, one in each hand and can't let go?

I didn't hear the answer, and Rosen couldn't remember when I asked him later.

He probably knew that I went back to my hotel with an American girl. She was one of the least drunk and seemed to like the fact I was sober. She didn't smoke and her soft mouth tasted of vanilla and cherries. I remember that, and the way she sighed when I touched her.

In the morning, she got up and looked amazing with nothing on but my shirt. I was starting to wonder how we'd part ways when she started getting dressed.

I watched appreciatively.

"Did you kill any of us during the troubles?" she asked, and I knew that by 'us' she meant Jews.

"No," I said truthfully. "I'm Military Police so my job was investigating soldiers."

"Shoot any of those?" she said, cocking an eyebrow at me.

"No," I laughed. "Not until after we'd left."

"I like you." She came over and kissed me hard on the mouth. "Maybe too much."

"Oh?"

She held out her hand. "I suppose we should exchange names. Nicola Short."

"Last night you said it was Nicca."

"That's my party name." She chuckled. "Did you give me a party name or are you really called Ash?"

"I am."

"Short for Ashley?"

"Ash, never Ashley." Only my father called me that. I didn't like him and guess I'd have rebelled against any name he preferred.

"Any other names?" she asked.

"Carter."

"Ash Carter." I liked the way she said my name. She said it with a smile on her lips. "Are you married, Ash?"

I shook my head.

"Would it be a problem if I was?"

"Too late for that," I said smiling, but then stopped. "You're being serious. You're married?"

She raised her eyebrows and looked awkward. "We have an arrangement."

"We? You and your husband?"

"Yes."

"He must be crazy."

"I'll take that as a compliment."

It was. She was good-looking, fun and smart. If she'd been mine, I would be fighting other men off instead of coming to an arrangement. I guessed that meant he played the field.

She continued: "And he works for the state department—the US Embassy here, so I guess he probably is a little crazy. Has to be."

"Was he at the Queen of Sheba last night?"

"No." She closed the gap between us, and I pulled her in. After we kissed long and hard again, she said, "I'm at the Sheba most Saturday and Sunday nights, Ash. Please say we can do this again."

She stepped back and studied my face as though searching for the truth.

"Well, I know your name and where you'll be, so definitely maybe, Nicola Short."

"As good as a girl can expect," she said with a light laugh, then blew me a kiss from the door and was gone.

NINETEEN

I exercised every day. I'd done so since I'd started boxing eight years ago. While I'd been in Acre, apart from my night-time run, I'd officially been confined to the hotel until my papers came through. Now I felt a pent-up energy again. Maybe it was because of Nicola. I was conflicted. A gorgeous married young woman who was also available.

I decided to pound the streets and clear my head of the girl and get my brain back on the case.

The sun was already on its ascent in a clear dome of blue. Fresh salty air blew off the Mediterranean and I filled my burning lungs. First, I went north and passed the US Embassy. It was huge and impressive. Especially when I compared it to the British Embassy a few hundred yards later.

On my way back, I decided to go inside the British one and say hello. After all, my papers said I was officially assigned to the embassy.

I met an administrative assistant called Foley. He was a little, anxious man who seemed to think I was there to catch him doing something wrong.

"So, you're just visiting," he said after I explained for a second time.

"I don't really expect to have anything to do with your ambassador," I said. "It's just a cover story for my activities."

He tapped his nose, as though I'd told him a great secret. Then he said, "Sir Gregory isn't going to be an ambassador."

I wasn't sure what he was telling me.

"He'll be charge-de-faire rather than ambassador," Foley said. "After everything. You know, it's amazing the Israelis have let us in at all. Not like the Yanks. My God, you'd think they were running the country. So bloody arrogant." He stopped himself in case he was speaking out of turn, I suppose. "Have you had any dealings with them, Captain?"

"Only a pleasurable one," I said, thinking of Nicola and then immediately regretting it. I'd wanted to forget about her and here I was actively thinking about the next time I'd enjoy her company.

He looked at me expectantly, maybe hoping I'd provide details. I didn't.

I bade him good luck with all the boxes I could see in the adjoining room. When we'd left in 1948, the British administration took lorry-loads of records back to the UK. Those that couldn't be transported were destroyed. I figured Foley was receiving most of what had been taken and was charged with cataloguing and filing all the backdated records. Probably having to work out what they had and didn't have.

At least, I thought, Sir Gregory wouldn't have a challenging job. There weren't many Brits left in Israel, so there wouldn't be queues of people with passport or other problems needing the embassy's support. I figured Sir Gregory's biggest task would be attending formal functions. He'd have to press the flesh, and smile and try to rebuild relations with a country we'd effectively been at war with.

As I passed the US Embassy, I again thought of its stature. It was more than four times the size of the British square-box of a building.

Was Nicola's husband in there now? Was he wondering who she'd spent last night with? Did he care?

Nicola had said they had an arrangement, but I only had her word for that.

I ran harder down the coast and did my thing of picturing the old buildings that had been here during the Mandate: The Ritz Officer's Club, EFI Canteen, Scopus Club, RAF command post, Services Club, Military laundry, Military car park, Polish command post, Polish and Greek soldiers' car park. It was all changing so fast.

There was a swathe of land before Jaffa Hill. It had been Out-of-Bounds to most military personnel, being an historic den of iniquity with gangs and drugs and prostitution. The last time I'd been here, I'd seen demolition work. Now I saw brand new tenement blocks. The city was expanding on the outskirts, but there was also regeneration. And there needed to be, because of the massive influx of refugees who still came in their hundreds of thousands a year.

I continued, following the coast.

The port of Jaffa was full of activity and smelling of oranges—another difference from six months ago. Life was returning to normal.

Rounding the hill, I started looping back and hit the Jaffa-Tel Aviv Road and then slowed. I saw police outside St Andrews Hotel where I'd stayed. There were two cars, a cordon, and a crowd of onlookers.

"Trouble?" I asked a bystander.

"Someone staying at the hotel," he replied with eyes as round as saucers. "They've been murdered."

TWENTY

I tried to find out more information, but the police at the scene weren't sharing. It was only when Dave Rosen came to see me at my hotel, mid-morning that I got the story.

He looked gray and said his drinking days were over. His suit looked crumpled although it wasn't the fine one he'd worn last night. And he had a tan leather satchel over one shoulder.

"I'm going teetotal from now on. Like you, Ash," he said. "I can't do it anymore."

"Based on the amount you consumed last night, Dave? I knew you could drink, but I've never seen you have that much before."

"I lost count."

"Alcohol can do that."

He nodded sagely. "Did you hear about St Andrews?"

"The murder?"

He nodded again, then shook his head. "Let's go for a stroll. I need the fresh air."

We went outside and down to the coast and watched gulls chase a fishing boat. I waited for him to feel better and speak.

Eventually he said, "Unbelievable. The murder."

"Happens all the time, I'm afraid," I said, thinking murders weren't that unbelievable. But then I noticed he was looking at me strangely.

He said, "The man was in your room, Ash."

"The killer or the victim?"

"Well, both."

"But it wasn't my room." Then I got it. I'd paid for two nights, so officially it was still my room. Rosen explained that it was common practice for staff to let a room cheaply to someone who stayed in an unoccupied room. Of course, it was off-the-books, so they'd pocket the cash.

"You think that I was the target?"

"I think it's likely. We haven't got an ID for the victim yet, but no one except the night porter knew he was there."

"Tell me what happened," I said.

"He was found in the bed. Head smashed in. Wait for the official report, but if the weapon wasn't a hammer then I'm a monkey's uncle."

One of us might have cracked a wise-ass joke about a monkey having a wrench rather than a hammer, but we didn't. This was too serious. If I hadn't been in the Rothschild Hotel it could have been me with a caved in head.

Rosen continued: "I don't think he even woke up. No sign of defensive injuries, so small mercies I suppose."

I said nothing for a few minutes. I was thinking about the questions I'd ask if this were my investigation. I'd want to know if anyone else saw the man go to my room. What was the conversation between him and the night porter? What state was he in? Did he seem anxious? As I thought this, I realized I was clinging to the hope that I wasn't the intended victim.

Rosen broke into my thoughts. "Some people still really hate the British," he said. "Probably an ex-Stern

Gang member. Someone with a grudge against the British Army."

"Ex-military?"

"Or still military."

"Why not use a gun. Wouldn't that be the weapon of choice for a man used to killing?"

"Noise?"

Maybe, I thought, but it could have been muffled. There had been no struggle. It was quick and easy. Although the violence of the attack troubled me.

"Why not smother or strangle? The man was asleep."

Rosen inclined his head, thinking. "OK. Then he came prepared. He didn't know the man would be asleep."

I said, "I don't think we're talking about a professional hit. Not a trained killer."

"Probably not. Do you have any ideas? What about Wislitsky?"

"He might fit, but he could have killed me when I found him."

"Unless he's had time to think about it."

"Duffy would be more likely."

"You think?"

I pointed to a café on the front. He nodded and we started walking again. If we kept on going we'd come to the US Embassy. I was wondering about Nicola Short, or more specifically her husband.

An attack with a hammer could be a crime of passion. Not Nicola because she was with me, but where was her husband? Did he know? Did he care more than Nicola let on?

We took a table at the café. I ordered tea and Rosen got a large mug of sweetened black coffee.

I said, "I've upset someone."

"You?" He forced a smile. "Who could possibly be your enemy, Fred?"

I could think of quite a few people, especially the criminals in Cyprus. Maybe a few commandos too, I suspected.

I said, "It won't be Duffy. He'd be a fool to come after the man hunting him. I'm nowhere near catching the man, so raising his head above the parapet would be like a fox popping up in front of a Bassett Hound. There's no need."

"Someone else? Someone you met in Acre?"

"The prison warden. The sergeant who helped Duffy escape. And the local police officer you had help me."

"It'll be him! By golly, you can't trust the police." Rosen laughed at his own joke. Then he pushed his thumbs under his eyes, and I figured the laughter had triggered pain there.

We sat and talked about security. We ate lunch and talked security some more. He was worried about me, and I finally agreed to change room and use an assumed name. However, I wouldn't go as far as having a policeman sit outside my door.

I changed the subject and asked about a gang called the Ghosts.

"Not heard of them."

"What about the Maccabees?"

Rosen shook his head with a frown. "It's an historic name associated with Jewish warriors fighting the oppressors."

"Could they be another incarnation of the Orbit Men?"

"Not that I know of," Rosen said. "Doesn't mean it wasn't them, but I'd say the name suggests heroes rather than villains."

In my experience, bad guys justified their acts. They rarely thought of themselves as bad. They did what they did for a reason. Admittedly they may have been deluding themselves, but the Igrun and Stern Gang didn't see themselves as criminals. To the British they were out and out terrorists.

This wasn't a conversation I wanted to get into. Rosen was my friend but he was also a Jew.

I had the name of the journalist who'd written the article so I resolved to speak to him about any Maccabee connection.

He had another mug of coffee and we talked about other things. His promotion would be official on Monday but I could call him *sir* already if I liked. Then we talked about the Queen of Sheba Club and he wanted to know if I'd met anyone I was interested in. He remembered me dancing with a blonde in a green dress but had been too drunk to pay enough attention.

I fobbed him off with a response about lots of pretty girls and switched the attention to his romantic liaisons. I wasn't ready to talk about Nicola and her husband. If Mr Short was a problem, I'd find out, but for now, I thought the timing and circumstances were all wrong. If he'd been concerned about Nicola sleeping with another man, he'd have followed us back to at the Rothschild. He wouldn't have known I had a reservation at St Andrews Hotel.

So who did?

We talked some more about the evening at the club and he said the team went there most weekends and that I should join them again.

"I thought you weren't drinking anymore?"

"If you don't drink then I can abstain as well. You being there will help. Just keep me away from the drinking games."

Which reminded me: the piece of string puzzle. How do you hold each end and tie a knot without letting go? Rosen couldn't remember. He couldn't even recall the question.

It reminded him of another riddle: "What holds water but is full of holes?"

"A sponge," I said.

"Ah, you know it." Rosen looked crestfallen. "It sounds like more though, doesn't it?"

"It does, but misdirection is usually the nature of such puzzles."

TWENTY-ONE

We paid for our lunch and headed back to my hotel.
Then he asked the question that had been troubling me. "Why did Abu Hajjar escape?"
"And why did Duffy help him?"
Rosen told me what I already knew about Hajjar, that he'd been arrested in the shootout. He was the only survivor and the police had been excited to catch the leader of the Orbit Men.
"He confessed," Rosen said, "but not straight away. The police had him bang to rights, I suppose, and as a result his conviction was quick. No need for witnesses."
"What are you thinking, Dave?"
We'd reached the hotel steps and he said, "That I'm going to change your room now so I know you're alright."
I waited as he checked me in under a different name then returned and gave me a key.
We rode the lift and inside, I said, "You were saying about Hajjar?"
"That it was too easy. I don't know. But what I do know is this." He pulled a thin file from the satchel he'd been carrying. "It wasn't in Hajjar's main file because this was from years ago. When he was still too young to shave, probably."

Outside my room, I took the file and read the single page inside. It was the arrest report for young Abu Hajjar. He'd committed a theft in the town of Nablus. There was a home address too.

"Where is this place?" I asked, referring to young Hajjar's address.

"Junid? It's just outside Nablus."

"What about his other reports? There must be a whole batch that didn't make it into the Acre prison document?"

"None. None that I've been able to find anyway. He's been pretty clever to evade detection until they got him at Arad."

I said nothing.

He said, "Which could mean he's had protection. Which is likely, I suppose. A powerful man can make sure he pays off the right people."

"Who?"

"Local police. And then he gets caught when it's a national operation. Can't pay off everyone, now, can you?" He chuckled.

"And the national police force was involved because of a tip-off. Any idea who that was?"

"No. That's the nature of anonymous tip-offs. People do it so they aren't caught out. My best guess is that it was someone on his payroll. Maybe even a local policeman who'd had enough of protecting the criminal."

"True." I unlocked my door and stepped in. He stayed outside and for a second I thought he'd stay there. "No sentry duty, Dave," I said. "Remember?"

He laughed. "Don't worry, I've got important work to do."

"*Inspector* Rosen."

He snapped his heals together and saluted.

I grinned. "Game of poker tonight?"

"Not for me. I'm still delicate from last night. And too much paperwork to trawl through. I've wasted enough time today already, babysitting you."

"Thanks."

"You're welcome."

I watched him turn and head toward the lift and I closed the door.

I read through the documents again and decided to head over to the Palestine Post's sub-office in Tel Aviv. I'd thought of calling ahead but the article had been four years ago and a lot had changed. Would the journalist still be there? Possibly not and if he wasn't then I may have more luck in person persuading someone else to speak to me. I also bought a box of sweet pastries along the way.

The food gift was for the receptionist. I knew she'd be hot and hassled. She didn't need someone interrupting her day with questions and an attempt to locate a journalist.

And it worked.

"Oh he's still here," she said, taking the box and eying the contents with glee. "Changed his name, like a lot of them. I'll ring up and see if I can't persuade Yoav to come and speak with you."

Yoav had a narrow face with hard eyes, below curly black hair turning to silver at the temples. He carried a cigarette and had the tar-stained fingers of a chain-smoker.

I asked him about the article and he laughed. "What? You expect me to remember something like that? It will have been a filler. I write a thousand columns a year. I'm not going—"

"The Maccabees Gang."

I'd stopped him mid flow and he looked taken aback. I saw recognition in his narrowing eyes.

"Maccabees... yes I vaguely remember." He shrugged and lit another cigarette took two long drags that made his eyes shrink even tighter. "What can I tell you? I'd heard the name."

I wasn't convinced by his story. "In relation to the Orbit Men?"

He sighed. "Look sometimes… my editor thought it beefed up the narrative. You've got to remember this was a time of resistance—Maccabees were heroes. He thought we could do spin offs—columns inches, you know? But it didn't happen."

"And the other one—the Ghosts?"

"That was genuine although, again, my editor had a hand in it. The name I heard was Tzillay which really means shadows, but the editor thought Ghosts sounded better."

I asked a few more questions, tried different approaches but his answers were as thin as the smoke he exhaled.

He fidgeted and said he had a deadline, needed to go.

I thanked him for the information.

He'd told me nothing. Then again maybe he had said a lot. As I walked back to the hotel, the sun a hammer at my back, I wondered why he would link the Orbit Men to the Maccabees Gang and Tzillay. Was the latter even real?

I'd always suspected reporters of creating stories. The news about Hajjar wasn't very interesting, so the editor had told the journalist to beef it up. There had been other crimes. Maybe some of them had been by Zionists. To the Jews, Maccabees were heroes. That made me wonder if the Irgun or Stern Gang had been more than terrorists.

Then there was Tzillay—Ghosts or Shadows? In the end I came away from the reporter with the impression of a generic name for unknown criminals.

Now I wondered whether there was another possibility: maybe the Orbit Men was made up too. The frustrating thought made me clench my teeth.

I could just about hear the call of the mu'azzin coming from Jaffe Hill. It was distant and weak. Some Muslims were still here. They hadn't all fled or been killed, but the faintness of the summons seemed to reflect their status in this new land.

Then I realized a contradiction. Muslim. Arab. Hajjar was the leader of the Orbit Men. He wasn't a Jew. The Maccabees were Jews. There would be no point in associating the gang with something he might see as the enemy today.

I reviewed all the information I had again. I ate in the hotel and I watched the clock's hand tick round. There was a library where I picked up a hardback; fiction about a US platoon stationed on an island in the South Pacific. It was OK. I read half of the first part and found it convincing enough. The boredom, the waiting, nervous jokes and the fear that they were sitting ducks. A foxhole is only any good if the enemy don't know you're there. I sat in the corner of the dark, wood-panelled bar with a tall lemonade and a bowl of salted olives. I read my book and people-watched. An eclectic clientele came, gathered and went. I variously judged them as wealthy travellers and businessmen. There were a few who may have been local politicians and maybe a few journalists.

I watched the clock hands tick further and wondered whether Nicola Short was partying at the Queen of Sheba. I knew myself too well. I knew I was keeping myself busy so that I didn't go to the club. Two nights on the trot with Nicola and I'd seem keen. Too keen for a married woman.

That was one argument. A more convincing one might have been that there was a killer out there. I needed to keep a low profile. I also didn't want to involve anyone else and risk their lives as well.

By eleven, I was pleased with my resolve. I'd managed to stay away from the club. If she'd even been there tonight. She might come to the hotel afterwards, looking for me. Of course she wouldn't find my new room because the guest register didn't have my name.

When I finally went to my room, I went to a higher floor first and then came down the stairs to mine. I checked that no one saw where I went and locked the door behind me.

I moved one of the room's armchairs to the corner of the wall by the door. Anyone coming into the room would go forwards first, toward the bed. I would be on the left in the dark.

I'd also have my gun.

With the lights off, I relaxed into the seat with the gun in my hand resting on my left thigh.

I thought through my challenge. How would I find Duffy?

I was stuck and kicking my heels and one thing you learn as an investigator is to follow leads—any lead, because you don't know what's relevant and what's not.

I'd been back to Acre and Hajjar's cell. I'd examined the coastguard station, and I'd been to Gam Shemuel and found Eva Wislitsky's home.

I had some lines on a map. I had marks on a cell wall. I knew Duffy was smart. I knew he was working with Eva. I knew they had a plan.

Did Hajjar fit in that plan? What was his story? I had a thousand questions about him. Something seemed off. Maybe about the Orbit Men themselves.

Which took me to the smoking journalist and from there I was in a foxhole.

I didn't know where the enemy was. I didn't know if I was a sitting duck. The Japanese were coming. I could feel the tension. They were sneaking up on our positions and I no longer had a weapon.

I woke with a start, my heart thumping so hard, I thought my chest would burst. Sunlight cast fingers through the heavy drapes.

Morning.

Time to act. Not sit in a foxhole.

When I'd been revisiting my actions of the past week, I knew from experience that none of it had been wasted. Although I hadn't known where to go next.

Abu Hajjar. A lot of unanswered questions about him. He came from Junid near Nablus. So, that's where I would go.

The only downside of that decision was the location. It was in the mountains. Which meant I'd be leaving Israel and entering the occupied territory.

TWENTY-TWO

I telephoned the British embassy from the hotel lobby and spoke to Foley. I was travelling into Arab territory, and I needed an interpreter and translator. At first, the administrative assistant thought I was joking. Then he explained there was just the small administrative team at the embassy and that no translators had been employed yet.

I was about to end the call when he said, "Try the Americans, Captain. I know they have an Arab interpreter."

My call was transferred twice. The first person was just an operator unsure how to handle my request. The second person tried to fob me off with a line about being too busy. When I insisted on being transferred to his manager, I got a more reasonable man.

"When do you need this interpreter, Captain?" he said after I explained my position and exaggerated my role with the British Embassy.

"Immediately."

"It's his day off," the man said, then: "One moment, I'll check see if he's willing and available."

Five minutes later, the man came back on the line. "OK," he said. "Malik will be ready in fifteen minutes. If that suits you, I'll send him on over."

"No need," I said, "I'll pick him up on the way."

"Just for a day, mind. We need him here on Monday."

"Thank you…" I hesitated as I realized I hadn't caught his name. "Mr—"

"Short," he said, finishing my prompt. "Clayton Short, and always good to help a cousin in need."

As I replaced the handset, I muttered something. I'm not sure what. I'd just spoken to the man whose wife I'd slept with on Friday night. That was all I could think.

Clayton Short was over six feet tall and had a charming manner. I'd wondered if he'd be much older than Nicola, overweight and probably a bore. On the contrary, he was in his late twenties and lithe. He had film-star looks with perfect teeth, slicked hair, and a pencil moustache. Short had confidence enough for two men, which was just as well, since Malik held his head low and said nothing except to respond to my greeting.

I invited the Arab to climb into the Land Rover and saw Short eyeball my transport with suspicion.

"Easier for the mountains," I explained.

"No official identification. I'd have diplomatic plates at least."

"But then you're American and I'm… Well, I'm sure you know the Brits aren't so popular."

"You eventually left, though."

"And look at the mess."

He nodded sagely. "It'll smooth out soon, mark my words." Then he gave me a warm handshake and repeated the phase about helping a cousin.

I drove out of the town with Malik keeping his gaze downward.

"Is everything all right?" I asked after we passed through the first checkpoint. He'd shown his credentials to the IDF guard and received challenging questions. It was the first time in Israel that I'd been given less attention than my passenger.

"It is difficult for you and me," he said once we were on the other side.

"With the Israelis?" I thought he was referring to checkpoints.

"With each other."

"Because I'm a Brit?"

"British and a soldier. Your people and mine, we were friends for many years. I fought beside your countrymen in the Second World War. And then you abandoned us. I don't like how you treat your enemies and I like even less how you treat your old friends."

It was a fair criticism, and I told him so. I also said I kept out of politics and just did my job.

"Like me," he said with a glance across at me. "What is this job?"

I told him about Duffy going AWOL and being on the run with Abu Hajjar. I added that they were aided by an IDF soldier.

Malik didn't show much emotion, but a brief smile flickered on his craggy face.

The frontline was only a few miles east, but I decided to go north first and find a more remote crossing. My logic was that there would be more soldiers guarding routes close to the big conurbations. There would be whole units, probably tanks and big guns, just in case of trouble.

Malik said, "I know where to go."

Five miles out of Tel Aviv, he directed me toward the mountains. We were soon met by a roll of barbed wire. Malik jumped out and moved it aside as I drove through. A mile up the track and we came to more barbed wire. Only this wasn't Israeli. There was a handful of men. Arabs in Transjordanian uniforms. They checked our papers as thoroughly as the Israelis had outside Tel Aviv, only this time it was me who received the scrutiny. Malik did a lot of talking and gesticulating and, within ten minutes, they rolled the wire back and we continued east.

I decided to tell Malik about myself. Nothing about my role beyond finding Duffy. I tried to break the ice between us by talking about my childhood.

"What is Oldham like?" he asked. "I hear it rains a lot in the north of England. It must be green and beautiful, no?"

I laughed. "Not really. And rain in Britain isn't the blessing it is here. Don't get me started about long, cold, damp winter evenings."

"Why?" he said. "I thought you English liked to talk about the weather."

For a second, I thought he was serious, but then he chuckled gruffly. It was the throaty sound made by a heavy smoker.

We started to climb into the hills and passed hamlets that looked, and probably were, a thousand years old. It was so far removed from the modernity of Tel Aviv. Here, people tended goats and drove donkeys more often than trucks.

"Where do you come from, Malik?" I asked.

"A small town in the south," he said without giving detail.

He looked to be in his forties, although I suspected beneath that hard, worn skin he was probably five or ten years younger. "Do you have a family?"

"A wife and children. They live in the south. I work around Tel Aviv."

I waited for more. When nothing was forthcoming, I asked their names.

He said, "It's better that I don't say."

"Oh?

"Because family can be used against you."

It seemed a profound statement, but before I could question him, he carried on speaking, changing the subject.

"Have you been to Junid or Nablus before?"

I hadn't. I told him I knew Tel Aviv and Haifa best. I'd been to Jerusalem and driven to Transjordan—on the far side of the Jordan River.

Malik said, "Well, you're in Transjordan now." Of course, we were. We'd crossed the ceasefire line and, this land that would have been an independent Arab state under both the British and UN plans, was now occupied by the neighbouring country.

"How do you feel about that, Malik?"

"My opinion doesn't matter," he responded. There was no bitterness, just acceptance, which I'd found was typically the Palestinian Arab way.

Heat bounced off the rocks, but as the road climbed, the air cooled by a few degrees. It might not have had the sea breeze, but I could see why tribes had chosen the mountains over the coast. Although I did wonder about water.

"Wells," Malik explained, "and you must know that was how Saladin came to defeat the Crusaders?"

"No."

"He poisoned the wells so that when they swept up to Jerusalem, they were weak with dehydration." He chuckled in his throaty way. "But the funny thing is that most of the wells weren't contaminated. Saladin's men just left dead birds near them, and so the Crusaders were too afraid to drink."

I remembered Eva telling me that the Arab villagers had poisoned the wells and wondered if the modern day inhabitants had played the same trick.

We approached the mountain peaks. At first, I thought we were heading for the one on the right, but the road swept around, and we cut through between them. One second there was rock and coarse landscape and the next we were in the heart of a cosmopolitan town.

"Welcome to the *New City*."

I could see Byzantine structures and Roman-influenced buildings among the more traditional Arab, brick walls and a giant tower which I guessed to be a minaret. Overall, I figured it looked ancient rather than new. There were old people and women on the streets, but I saw no men under the age of sixty. Off fighting for their country, I presumed. The same as all the other remote towns.

"Why are we here," I asked, "rather than Junid, where Hajjar comes from?"

"Easier to ask where we'll find the Hajjar family," he said and directed me down a narrow street into the heart of the town.

We found the municipal police station, and I wondered what kind of reception I would get as a Brit looking for an Arab.

Malik went in first with me a step behind. Someone in authority was shouting and there was a lot of excited chatter. Malik stopped a policeman who barged past. I heard him say the name Hajjar and then all hell broke loose.

Malik was grabbed. Two more policemen rushed toward us and pinned me down before I realized what was happening.

"British!" I shouted in a commanding voice. "I'm a captain in the army." It was a wild attempt at regaining control and, amazingly, it worked. The men holding me let go and stepped back, uncertainty written all over their faces.

But the sense of victory lasted a mere three seconds. A sergeant charged toward us with a gun, screaming in Arabic.

Malik raised his hands, and I copied him.

I said, "I'm a British Army captain!" I moved my hand toward my inside pocket, which elicited another tirade and the jab of the sergeant's gun.

My hands returned aloft.

"Does anyone speak English?" I yelled over the shoulder of the sergeant, who looked close to shooting first and asking questions later.

"I do," a voice said and then I saw another sergeant step toward us. He waved the other men back before asking to see my credentials. Then he asked who Malik was, and I explained he was my interpreter.

"Why are you in Nablus, Captain?"

"Looking for Abu Hajjar. Looking for his family."

The sergeant's cold eyes were like daggers about to fly at me.

"You're claiming that you don't know?"

"Don't know what?"

"The whole family has just been found dead. Throats cut. Slaughtered."

TWENTY-THREE

I hoped the sergeant would be reasonable, but his next move was to bark at the other men.

"They're going to hold us," Malik whispered. "Don't react." We were immediately frisked. My Israeli travel permit was taken along with my money clip and military credentials. Then they did what no one had ever done in Israel. They patted me down so thoroughly that they found my ankle holster.

My Beretta caused more commotion. We were pushed and hurried along a corridor to a police cell. The humidity inside the police station was higher than outside and the warm air was stale and bitter.

There were no other prisoners, and I was grateful Malik and I had been put in the same cell. We sat on the wooden bench, and I was impressed at how relaxed Malik was. He stretched out his legs and closed his eyes.

I breathed slowly and tried to ignore the predicament and uncomfortable situation. Which was hard because of the continual noise and apparent level of anxiety.

After an hour, I called for water and eventually we were brought a jug and cup to share. The water was tepid and tasted of dust, but we each took a mouthful.

"They think we had something to do with the deaths," Malik said after swallowing. "Showing up now seemed too big a coincidence."

"It is," I said, "I'd be suspicious."

"It appears to be ongoing. I gather they are waiting for a police captain. He's at the scene of the murders."

We took another drink, and it didn't taste as bad the second time.

I said, "Why did you call it the new town? Was that sarcasm?" It was an ancient place with a mishmash of architecture, but then there were plenty of Biblical towns from Nazareth to Jerusalem which were similar.

"The name Nablus is an Arabic corruption of the Roman name," he said. "The Romans built it and named it Flavia Neapolis after the emperor."

"Neapolis," I said nodding, "meaning new town."

We listened to the sounds beyond our prison corridor for a while before he said, "Tell me more about why we are here."

So, I explained that Duffy had handed himself in and been incarcerated with Abu Hajjar in Acre. It had been planned.

I said, "I mentioned they were helped by an IDF soldier. It was a woman officer. She posed as someone hunting Hajjar and teamed up with me. Her intention was to ensure that I didn't find them. But I got lucky."

He raised his eyebrows.

"She knocked me out, and they got away."

"That doesn't sound so lucky."

"Lucky to track them down. Unfortunate that I didn't suspect her involvement."

"Why escape?" he asked.

"Hajjar? He had a secret, apparently."

"Tell me more about Abu Hajjar. What have you learned?"

So I told him about the gang and Hajjar's arrest four years ago.

Malik placed his fist against his lips and tapped them for a minute. I guessed he was thinking.

When he spoke, he said, "Hajjar was the ringleader, no?"

"Of a gang of criminals."

"He never tried to escape before? Even when he had the opportunity?"

"No."

"And you were told he had a secret."

"Yes?" I said, wondering what his point was.

"Antiquities," he said still being cryptic. "He was caught stealing antiquities. Weren't the gang known more for their thefts than murders? They weren't like the Jewish Lehi or Irgun or Abd al-Qadir al-Husseini and his Army of the Holy War. Not even your Killing Crew, for that matter. Abu Hajjar and his gang were, or are, different. They weren't fighting for something. They weren't against the Arabs or the Jews. They weren't against anything. Not *against*, they were *for*."

This was the most Malik had said in one go and I was pleased he was opening-up to me.

"So what did they stand for?" I asked.

"Themselves."

"There are other criminals out for themselves," I said, that's nothing new. I'd had a run in with some in Tel Aviv last time I'd been there. A Slovakian gang preying on the immigrant Jews. I'd heard of a similar Polish gang as well. Religion didn't play a part. The Mafia were a case in point. Catholic by name but criminal by deed.

Malik said, "I have a theory, if you'd like to hear it."

"I would."

"The secret is where the treasure is hidden. The men were looting when the police arrived. Eight were in a shootout. Hajjar wasn't. I think he was hiding the treasure and I think your man Duffy and the IDF woman knew that. They broke Hajjar out of prison to find whatever he hid."

I thought about that. It was a good theory and better than any of mine. It also meant that we were in the wrong place. We shouldn't have been looking for Hajjar's family near Nablus, we should have gone to Arad where he'd been arrested.

TWENTY-FOUR

It was another hour before anyone came down the corridor to our cell. Two policemen led me out, leaving Malik behind. I complained that I needed him for interpretation, but my words fell on deaf ears.

The reason was clear: my interview was with an English speaker.

"Captain Ash Carter," a police captain said in Queen's English. He had a shock of auburn hair, a dark tan and contrasting bright blue eyes.

We shook hands for a long time, warm and friendly. "You have me at a disadvantage," I said to the captain although he looked familiar.

He grinned. "You don't remember me, but then again, we were only introduced once. I'm Captain Bob Cattan. Previously with the Palestine Police Force, Arab section, based in Tel Aviv."

His name and accent sounded very British, but he looked Arabic, and I had to admit I couldn't recall our meeting.

"So, you know Inspector Dave Rosen?" I asked.

"Changed his surname. Used to be Rose." Cattan shrugged and shook his head. "Most of us joined the Arabs. The majority of the soldiers left to join us too."

"Deserters," I said.

He smiled. "One man's deserter is another man's hero." He held up my Israeli travel permit. "Tell me about this."

"It's necessary for me. I'm actually looking for a deserter"—I held up a hand—"and before you say he's a hero, this one hasn't gone AWOL to help the Arab cause as far as I can tell."

"Why?"

"He hasn't tried to join up and is involved with someone from the IDF."

"And why you are here in Nablus?"

I went through the story of the prison-break and idea that Hajjar's hometown might provide some insight. Following leads, hoping that I trace Duffy.

"So, you've not been up to Junid in the past day?"

"No, I came straight here. We didn't have an address."

"And the Arab with you?"

"My interpreter. He's assigned to the US embassy, and they kindly lent him to me."

Cattan nodded. "Did you hear about the murders?"

"Your sergeant mentioned Hajjar's family—"

"His mother, his wife, her sister and six children. They were slaughtered. Most with their throats slit. No witnesses and no suspects. I'd appreciate any insight you may have."

"None at the moment," I said.

"Please tell me what you know about the prison-break, Captain."

So I talked him through everything, starting with the route out of the prison and up to the coastguard station near Netanya. I told him about the switch of vehicles from Bedford truck to a stolen Ford taxi to Eva Wislitsky's Jeep.

"A jeep? A British Land Rover or American Jeep?"

"American with IDF markings," I said, knowing an Israeli military vehicle wouldn't get far in Arab territory. Truce or no truce.

He thought for a moment. "Easy to remove identification," he said. "They could paint it. They could burn it off."

"Why so interested?"

"Because there were no witnesses to the murders, but people in the village further along reported seeing a gray Land Rover yesterday. Which was unusual. I'm also willing to believe they saw a Jeep rather than your Land Rover."

That was interesting. Had Duffy and the others been here?

"Would you tell me where the villa is?" I asked. "I'd like to see it."

Cattan swept an arm to indicate that I was free to go. "Not only that," he said, "I'll take you there."

Fifteen minutes later, I was back in my jeep with Malik beside me and my personal items returned. Ironically, Cattan also had a Land Rover although it was black and therefore not confused with the one seen by witnesses.

I followed him out of the town, and we climbed higher on a twisting track. There were some poor dwellings and then a Romanesque villa. It looked out of place, but then I guessed the Roman period had resulted in places like this all over, just like in England, although most of those were ruins.

"It was rebuilt," Cattan said as we pulled up and got out by the low surrounding wall. The villa was north facing, with high ground behind. "The Hajjars had plenty of money. Rumour has it that the rebuild was funded by ill-gotten gains."

That made sense. Abu Hajjar was a crook after all.

We went through gates and a garden with dwarf trees and pots and urns. There was a mosaic on the patio before grand doors and Corinthian pillars.

Cattan showed me where four bodies had been found. The blood had dried without any attempt to clean it up. Flies feasted on the mess.

I noted the lines of spray which confirmed the execution by slit throats. There were bags and boxes piled up near the door. We walked through to another room—a kitchen. Here there were two blood splatters in one place and another further away.

I said, "I think the first room showed they were taken by surprise. They may have even known their killer." I paused and I guessed we were all picturing the scene. The killer had been welcomed into the home. He'd killed everyone in the first room. The kitchen implied a different scenario. I said, "At least one person was trying to get away in this room."

Cattan grunted agreement. "The two here were a mother and young child. The one by the door was the old woman."

"Where were the last two?"

"Both children, both on the hill."

"Running? Trying to escape?"

"And were shot in the back," Cattan said. "The killer intended to do it quietly. He slit throats but there were two escaping, so he had to shoot them."

I nodded.

"Any thoughts, Captain Carter?"

"Only one." What Malik had said in the cell about the reason for the prison-break was playing in the back of my mind. However, I said, "The bags and boxes in the first room make me think they were getting ready to leave."

"Maybe in a hurry," Cattan said, leading onto the patio outside. "Maybe they'd heard Abu Hajjar had escaped from prison."

"When was this villa rebuilt?"

"About four years ago," Cattan said. "From what I've learned, that's around the time Hajjar was put away,"

I said, "How old were the youngest children?"

"Three or four."

Malik grunted, and I shot him a glance.

"Yes?" I prompted.

He shook his head, remaining mute.

"My theory," Cattan said. "Hajjar, the husband, heard that his wife was enjoying his money and probably with another man. Had a child by him. That's why Hajjar escaped. He came here and wiped out the family."

TWENTY-FIVE

I sensed Malik didn't agree with Captain Cattan's assessment. There was no information on the timing of the gray vehicle that had been reported by witnesses. I'd been left at the coastguard station a week ago. If Hajjar had come straight here, then the timing was wrong. The bodies had been found today although the slaughter had occurred yesterday evening.

Would Hajjar have waited so long? Did they delay because the IDF Jeep needed repainting? That was possible, although I thought it unlikely. That wouldn't have taken long, and Hajjar needed to warn his family. No. Hajjar didn't do this.

As we drove away from Junid, the hills echoed with the evening call to prayer.

I was lost in my thoughts when Malik said, "Do you know the story about getting across the desert?"

"I doubt it."

"Rashid wanted to cross the Sahara and was told the only person to have made it the whole way was Abdul the Camel seller. So Rashid goes to see Abdul and asks the price of a camel. Abdul says he hasn't got any available but, for a price, he will tell Rashid the secret. Rashid agrees, so Abdul fetches a camel and lets it drink from a trough. When it has finished, Abdul goes behind and, with a block of wood in each hand, bashes the camel's balls. The effect is to make the camel suck up additional water.

"Abdul then hands the blocks to Rashid, takes his money and wishes him well.

"Rashid sets out, walking across the desert and is desperately dehydrated by the time he reaches the first watering hole. There's another man with a camel at the watering hole, and Rashid speaks to him, asking for assistance, before taking a long drink. When he is fit to bursting, he spreads his legs. As instructed, the other man comes up behind him and crashes the two blocks of wood together."

Malik chuckled to himself.

I waited a moment before asking why he'd told me the joke.

"Because it is about a misunderstanding."

"Rashid thinks it's about the blocks when it's really about the camel?"

"Exactly." He chuckled again. "A painful lesson!"

The light was fading fast as we drove toward the coast. The sky was streaked with pinks and purples once the sun had slipped beyond the sea.

I said, "This is your way of telling me that there's a misunderstanding. You don't think Abu Hajjar killed his family."

"I don't know. But what I do know is that family can be used against you," he said.

"That's what you said when I asked about your family."

"Yes."

"What does it mean in this case?"

"I don't know," he said again.

It bothered me that Hajjar had been reluctant to escape before. During the Irgun operation, when hundreds fled through a hole in the wall, he stayed. He'd sat in his cell waiting. Why was that? Why breakout now? What had changed?

Unless he didn't want to break out. Unless it was Duffy's and Eva Wislitsky's plan and Hajjar didn't have a choice.

I said, "How do you tie a knot in a piece of string if you hold either end and don't let go?"

"I don't know."

"Neither do I and it's been bothering me. Not because of the puzzle but because there was rope on the floor in the coastguard station."

Malik glanced over at me, but I couldn't tell if he realized the significance, so I said it anyway.

"Hajjar may have been their prisoner."

He grunted. "And maybe they killed the family. Was Duffy capable of that?"

"Or the Wislitsky woman," I said. "I don't know. Both are military trained, so it is possible."

We drove in silence for the last two miles to the frontier. He had a piece of string and was playing with it—trying to tie a knot without letting go, I guessed.

As we approached, I saw the same Transjordanian unit guarding the final stretch. The rear of the Land Rover was checked—presumably in case we were smuggling something or somebody into Israel—before we were waved through.

Malik had given up with the string when he said, "You mentioned markings on Hajjar's cell wall."

I'd told him I'd visited the prison again and sketched the lines on four sheets of paper. I'd also commented that there were too few to be a tally of his days there.

"What do they mean?" he asked.

"Probably nothing. Probably just the scratches of a man killing time if not marking it."

"Mind if I look at your sketches?"

It was fully dark by the time I reached my hotel. At reception I was told by the manager that my room had been changed again. Only he knew that I was registered under another assumed name. A letter from my friend

Dave Rosen explained that he was taking no precautions after the St Andrews Hotel murder.

From my new room, I collected my drawings of the lines in Hajjar's cell. Malik waited in reception.

"It's curious," he said, holding one of the sheets in the light and looking at it from different angles. "They don't look random."

"That's why I copied them," I said.

"I enjoyed working with you today, Captain Carter."

"And I with you, Malik," I said and meant it. He was quiet and hadn't been the necessity I'd imagined, but I'd enjoyed his quiet company. When he opened his mouth, it was to say something intelligent. He might not have answers, but he asked good questions.

I continued: "I'm going to Arad tomorrow to look at where Abu Hajjar was arrested. I'm hoping you can join me."

"Unfortunately, I work for the Americans," he said. "Perhaps in the future… perhaps it won't always be that way and we can work together."

"I hope so."

"Could I borrow this?" he asked, still holding my sketch.

"Do you have an idea?"

He shrugged. "I like a joke but I like a puzzle even more." He said nothing more about it, although I sensed he had an idea he wasn't sharing.

Since I wasn't sure when I'd see him again and didn't want to risk losing the papers, I said I'd produce a copy. After obtaining a pencil and paper, I traced the marks and lines, and the results were almost identical. However, I was copying an inexact replica and pointed it out.

"I understand."

"Thank you again for your help today," I said, paying him for the day's work.

He grinned and bowed his head. Then he waved the paper and, before striding from the hotel said, "I'll be back as soon as I have something for you."

TWENTY-SIX

Rosen's note at the hotel had asked me to be cautious and not run through the town. So in the morning, I had to confine my exercise to the hotel room and felt sorry for the occupant below. He must have thought the ceiling was coming down, such was the pounding I gave the floor.

Malik was in reception when I came downstairs.

"You have an answer already?" I said, amazed.

He shook his head sadly. "Not yet. I've sent it to Professor Khaled Khalidi, a language expert."

"Then why—?"

"I'm here because the American embassy allowed me another day off. And because you pay me more than they do." He grinned.

I was very grateful for Malik's company, not least because I'd never been to Arad. He had a map and guided me south through Jaffa. I knew this first stretch across what the British Army used to call Sector 9, through Ramala. Then we trundled on into Sector 12, Hebron. Now I was beyond my knowledge of the country. I knew that Gaza was over to the west and that some of the most intense fighting of the Arab-Israeli war had been down there.

We exchanged the odd word but said little above the rattle of the wheels and hum of the engine. I noticed he was playing with the string, trying to solve the knot puzzle.

"Yes!" he exclaimed and showed me a knot.

I was amazed. "How did you do that?"

"With long enough string, you have to create a loop and get the other loop through it."

"Show me."

He pulled the ends of the string and the knot came undone. Then he proceeded to try the looping technique again. He failed.

It was another twenty minutes of trying before he managed it again.

"That can't be the solution," I said, and he reluctantly agreed.

I drove on, through desolate, arid land punctuated by the occasional date palm grove. Goat herders watched us pass, and the villagers called with desperate voices for us to stop and buy.

With the sun beating relentlessly on my head, I took a break. I put up the roof and stretched before continuing. Malik wore a shemagh headscarf and told me to wear one next time. He was undoubtedly right.

A sign said the town of Beersheba was ahead at one point but our road curved away and round the Judean Mountain range. Up high, I could see forests and imagined a cool breeze.

Down on the road there was just heat and dust.

We passed no vehicles for almost an hour and the road got worse and worse. Stones regularly spun and clattered from the tyres. I started to wonder if we'd gone the wrong way, but Malik assured me this was the best route.

Gradually, we started climbing into the low hills. The yellow sedimentary rocks yielded to pockets of green, and the air cooled.

We'd been travelling for four hours before Malik announced we were close. And then I saw ancient stone walls on the edge of the desert.

"Is this it?" I challenged.

He studied the map. "Definitely. I think these are ancient ruins."

I stretched again and looked around before getting back into the jeep. Firing up the engine, I said, "Let's find the nearest town."

We followed a track south, looking for a village. It was a harsh landscape of rock and patches of struggling vegetation. There were sad-looking trees spotted about and I was convinced we'd reach the Judean desert without finding a soul. But then, in a shaded dip, we came upon a nest of tents and camels.

"Bedouin," said Malik.

I counted ten men. They watched us with suspicious eyes as we approached. Most of them sat under the largest tent, clustered in twos and threes. They sat with crossed arms and legs and appeared to be contemplative rather than talking.

Malik told me to stop well away from the main tent, and we got out.

"Follow me, two steps behind," he said, and I felt awkward walking toward the Bedouin Arabs. I was an alien in an alien world.

Malik raised a hand as he approached the nearest two old men. Then he told me to wait.

I stood in the baking sun as he took another four paces and then squatted. He was still ten yards away from the tent.

I copied his crouch.

He spoke in short, staccato bursts, pausing in between.

The men said nothing, their eyes moving from Malik to me and back.

Suddenly, the nearest two laughed, and like ripples in a well, the laughter went through the group. One of them beckoned and Malik stood, bowed and joined the nearest two. He waved to me, and I moved close, grateful for the tent's shade.

Malik spoke again, his voice more relaxed and the men responded. He was offered a drink and a moment later, a man from the back also brought me a cup of tea.

I nodded my gratitude, accepted the cup, and sipped the very sweet concoction. Then they gave us dates and meat wrapped in vine leaves.

Malik spoke more, and the men responded. Then the one who had waved us over stood and spoke to the others. Despite the language barrier, I could interpret the responses. They were all negative.

We finished our drinks and food, and Malik thanked them before we retreated to the Land Rover.

I said, "They didn't know anything, did they?"

Malik said the ancient walls we'd seen was what we'd been looking for: Tel Arad. "They've lived in and around the area for many years—well before the shootout with the police. But none of them had heard of it. Nor had they heard of Hajjar's arrest."

"That's odd."

"But you know, these men travel around. They may not have been in the area at the time. And they keep themselves to themselves, not least because these Bedouins are Christian. They won't mingle and talk with the Muslim Arabs."

As I drove away, I took a swig of water to remove the aftertaste of the sweet tea we'd been given. Then I asked what had happened. Why had they laughed?

"I said we were travelling in the heat of the day, which I knew they'd think was crazy. Then I used the phrase *mad dogs and Englishmen.*" He chuckled. "The English are well known for their crazy attitude to the sun."

I looked at him sharply and with mock seriousness asked, "Are you saying I'm crazy?"

He grinned. "It's not my place to judge."

"But I'm paying you for your help, so what do we do now?"

"Keep driving west and don't take the right turn. Let's ask in Beersheba."

Beersheba was the largest town in the Negev region and the scene of a recent major battle. Malik explained that the original United Nations plan had placed Beersheba in the Jewish state. When the British left, the Egyptian army took it over. However, it was populated by an Arab majority and the UN plan was revised so that Beersheba would remain Arab.

Although the Jews officially accepted the UN plan, Israel attacked with a massive strike force in October 1948 and took the town.

"Due to its strategic location and neighbouring Jewish settlements," Malik said.

He breathed loudly, like a man bearing a great weight, as we drove through the outskirts. I glanced at him and saw clenched teeth. We passed razed buildings and walls peppered with bullet holes.

The first person we saw was an elderly lady dressed in black and sitting forlornly by a broken door. She didn't even raise her head as we passed.

Another hundred yards and we saw more people, all Arabs, all elderly. They tracked us with nervous stares.

"I didn't realize it was this bad," Malik said as we rolled past. Thirty thousand Arabs fled from around here. This used to be so full of life and now look at it."

As we neared the centre of town, we were stopped by IDF soldiers. They checked our credentials and waved us through. The buildings looked in better condition. There was rebuilding activity too and people milled about. Life was returning to normal although I guessed these were Jews, maybe moving into vacant properties. It was happening up and down the country, so that made sense. The influx of Jews had created housing pressures in the major towns like Tel Aviv and Haifa and they were taking advantage of the Arab exodus.

The town square had a row of buses and we saw people disembark with luggage. There was an old, Ottoman-style train station that was being used as a temporary residence for the arrivals. There was also a civil police building that had once been used as army barracks. Both buildings were smattered with bullet holes and larger damage.

I parked outside the police building, behind an IDF Jeep.

We showed our credentials again, and I was introduced to a pixie-faced officer called Captain Kramer. He was enjoying a comfortable chair in a police chief's office. There was a ceiling fan that cooled the air.

"We're acting as de facto police until a civil unit is established here," he explained with a shrug of the hands. "Although there's no trouble now that we've the Armistice and they've agreed Beersheba is ours."

I told him about the incident in Arad four years ago. And Abu Hajjar's arrest. The IDF officer knew nothing of it, although he said I was welcome to go through the archives.

"All the old police reports are in the Records Office in the back," he said. "We haven't touched it yet, but I expect the civil police will want it intact"—again he gave a shrug with his hands—"so, as I say, you can look, but leave it as you find it."

We left Captain Kramer to enjoy the peace of the office and found the records room. It smelled of old paper and the dust that covered everything.

There were cabinets and boxes; lots of them. The good news was that everything had neat labels with dates.

I pulled out a box dated January to April 1945. Together, we took half each and riffled through the papers.

"Here," Malik said after a couple of minutes. He handed me two sheets of paper, one pink with an attached yellow sheet behind. Both were carbon copies, and I figured that the original front sheet had been sent to the Central Records Office in Jerusalem.

It was the report following the arrest of Abu Hajjar. Mostly typed in English, there were also short sections handwritten in Arabic. There were multiple corrections, places where it was illegible due to over-typing. It was brief and to the point, repeating what I already knew: Men had been found stealing antiquities. There was a shootout resulting in eight deaths and one captured prisoner.

I separated the two papers and handed the yellow one to Malik.

"What does that say?" I asked, pointing to an over-typed word and the Arabic above.

"Arad."

I held the pink sheet at angles to the light, trying to see what the typed word had been. "It could have been misspelt, but the *d* looks like it was originally a *t*," I said.

"The name of the man who completed the form is Arabic. English won't have been his first language. I suspect it was a simple error."

"Maybe," I said.

I took the yellow sheet and replaced it in the box. I folded the pink sheet and hesitated. I exchanged looks with Malik, who cocked an eye at me and then smiled. I slipped the paper into my jacket pocket.

Back in the Land Rover, he said, "Why did you take the report?"

"I have a friend in the Tel Aviv police. I'd like him to take a look."

"Will he approve of your theft?"

I chuckled. "Probably not."

I drove out of town and listened to nothing but the stones under the wheels and their rattle on metal.

Suddenly, Malik said, "Stop!"

The jeep rumbled to a halt, and I swivelled to look at him. "You're not feeling guilty about me taking the paper?"

He laughed. "Remember your sketch from the Acre prison cell?"

"Of course."

"The man I sent it to lives in Deir el Balah."

I shook my head, not knowing the place.

"It's west of here. Twenty miles, or a little more."

I waited for him to say more.

After a pause, he said, "We should go there. It's in the territory controlled by the Egyptian army."

"Marvellous," I said, dubious.

"Let's hope so," he replied.

TWENTY-SEVEN

I drove west through the desolate land with the sun hot on my neck. Within five miles the desert faded into cream-coloured rock and patches of vegetation. There were small areas of cultivated land and scattered houses.

Clusters of trees appeared and then groves of date palms and citrus trees. Birds sang and for thirty minutes, the world seemed a beautiful place.

Until we came to the army, tanks, heavy guns, hundreds of trucks and a battalion of foot soldiers. We were stopped and questioned three times before we reached the new border.

I could hear the rumble of heavy machinery a mile away. When we were closer, I saw bulldozers piling up the earth, creating a barrier that blocked the view of the territory beyond. They were still digging and moving rocks, filling the air with pounding and crunching and belched fumes.

Soldiers were also laying barbed wire, and I saw units moving blocks of concrete—tank traps, I guessed, or the start of a more permanent border.

Wire, barriers, and a vast number of men with guns blocked the road.

After showing my papers, I told an IDF captain that I was searching for a fugitive. He spent thirty minutes considering my request while his men virtually stripped the Land Rover, searching for hidden weapons. Typically, they failed to find my ankle gun, although it would have done little good had I wanted to cause trouble.

Finally, the barriers were rolled back, and we could enter the no man's land. The fifty yards, trundling toward a thousand twitchy Egyptian soldiers with guns trained on us, lasted a lifetime.

Malik called out a greeting and we were told to wait twenty yards short of the next border. There was no berm here, just rolls of barbed wire strung between wooden X-frames. Beyond a boom barrier, I could see a command post. A lookout tower had been erected beside it. At one time, it would have provided a view over the Israeli ridge. It was no longer tall enough.

We were told to stop.

After another protracted wait, Malik was called forward. He took my credentials, excluding the Israeli travel permit, and walked to the command post.

While he was gone, I thought about the ruins at Arad and finding the Bedouin. They were an unusual tribe, with their silence and contemplation of the desert. I remembered them laughing at me before they opened up to Malik. I suppose to them, the British were the odd ones.

I thought about the ruined town of Beersheba, the flight of the Arabs and the influx of Jews and the occupation of the old police station by the IDF unit. Presumably, they were now protecting the population rather than providing any real policing function.

The pink report of the incident involving Hajjar was still in my pocket. Were the edits to the report relevant? Were the marks on Hajjar's cell walls relevant?

Then I thought: Was the rope on the floor of the coastguard station relevant? I picked up Malik's string and played with it until he returned.

I thought about the Bedouin and in a flash of inspiration, the solution to the knotted string puzzle came to me.

When Malik returned after ten minutes, I said, "I've worked out the solution to the puzzle."

"What is it?"

"You like to solve puzzles," I said as I started rolling the Land Rover toward the Egyptian soldiers. I'm sure you'd rather work it out for yourself. Think about the Bedouin."

The boom barrier was raised, I trundled forward. The barrier came down and the guns came up.

I stopped.

"We need to get out," Malik said.

I was searched again. The soldiers were more tense and nervous than on the Israeli side and I breathed slowly to stay relaxed.

After checking us and again failing to find my weapon, they searched the Land Rover. When they were finally content, we were free to get back in and drive off.

"No amount of wisdom can help one escape one's fate," Malik said sagely.

"What does that mean?"

"If we are to die today, we will die. If our fate is to live then—"

"We live," I finished for him. "I wish we'd had this conversation before I agreed to detour here, Malik."

"It'll be worth it, my friend," he said, and I noted it was the first time he'd called me that. However, I suspected it might just have been an expression as opposed to a true declaration of friendship.

Deir el Balah was an old Arab town, crammed and dusty. There was a refugee camp on the outskirts and Malik told me these were much smaller than the ones in Gaza and Rafah. However, I guessed there were many thousands of people living in tents and sheltering from the sun beneath blankets on poles.

The sound of people talking was as loud as the buzz of flies. A foul stench of human excrement and rotting rubbish made us breathe through our scarves.

I squeezed the jeep down narrow streets until Malik said we'd need to walk the rest of the way. He took me into a crumbling gray-stone building and through passages. We passed families crammed in small rooms. Voices hushed as we passed, although two young children ran out to stare at me before being pulled hurriedly away by a woman.

Finally, we reached an arch with a colourful blanket as a door.

Malik called through it and we were welcomed in.

The air was filled with the strong smell of Turkish cigarettes, although some fresh air came through a window.

Professor Khaled Khalidi sat at a writing desk with a bank of books lined neatly in the shelves behind. His swept back, gray hair was tinged with yellow. I guessed it was discolouration from the cigarettes he smoked.

The man stood and embraced Malik like a long-lost son. Then he looked at me and bowed his head. After I had returned the gesture, he invited us to sit on cushions at our feet.

The professor called, and a woman came out of nowhere, serving us with cups of hot water and a platter with nuts and fruit.

"I didn't expect you," the professor said in unaccented English.

"We were travelling nearby," Malik said.

The professor looked dubious.

Malik added: "We came through Beersheba." Then he said something in Arabic which prompted the professor to shake his head.

"So," Professor Khalidi said to me, "You have something interesting. Malik tells me that it came from a prison cell."

I confirmed this.

Khalidi nodded. "Did Malik tell you about me?"

"Just that you're a language expert."

"I speak fifteen languages and can read over twenty, although not all to the same level. My speciality is ancient languages. I'm one of the best, although modesty forbids me to tell you that." He smiled but looked sad as he then raised his hands. "Look at me now. Look at what I have become."

We sat in reflective silence. Finally, he said, "Enough self-pity. Let's turn to why you are here. Malik correctly surmised that your mysterious markings could be writing."

He placed my sketches on the floor between us.

"I understand this criminal may have had a secret. You see this?" He pointed, and I leaned in. "You've heard of cuneiform, I suppose?"

I had although wouldn't have recognized it.

He said, "Cuneiform constructs letters and sounds from lines with arrows. As you can see, there are no arrows on these lines, however if I do this"—he drew lines, copying the section he'd pointed to, then he added arrow heads—"Now you have the letter P. What we appear to have here is the writing system based on a mixed language of Canaanite-Akkadian and used widely three thousand years ago in diplomatic communications." He looked up at me and grinned. "Well done for spotting it, Malik."

"I didn't but thought it couldn't be random."

The professor shook his head. "In my world that is the same thing."

I said, "But you added an arrow to make a P."

"I suspect the arrows have been deliberately excluded."

"To make interpretation even more difficult."

"Yes," said Khalidi. His eyes searched mine. "You are tracking someone. An Arab?"

Malik said, "I explained in my letter that you are looking for an escaped criminal."

"I'm looking for the prisoner who escaped with the author of these lines. The man I want is British."

Khalidi said nothing. I wondered whether he needed me to provide more justification for why he should help me find an Arab who had escaped from an Israeli prison.

Malik said, "Sir, will you tell us what you see? There is more than a P."

Khalidi nodded and pointed. "Yes, there is more. The interesting thing is that the translation appears to be English. It's P-I-L-Ah which, since the language is phonetic, I would guess means *Pillar*. Then I can't make sense of the next piece. Is your copy accurate?"

"As accurate as I could make it," I said.

"Of course," he said kindly, as though I was a simple child who couldn't be expected to make an accurate copy of what I'd seen. "There are words I cannot make sense of. It appears to be N-I-E-M-N

I said, "So the stars are Ns?"

"Correct."

"*I* is the five lines, then *E*, then *M* is the eight lines."

"And finally, an *N* again." He looked at me with eyes that seemed as old as the ancient language he was interpreting. "I've yet to make sense of it. So far, I haven't been able to convert it into anything, even assuming it's not English and considering you may have drawn it incorrectly."

"What about this?" I asked pointing to another row of lines that had first drawn my attention.

"Ah," Khalidi said, "Well done. They are letters although I haven't made sense of them yet."

"And the other marks?" I asked.

He sighed. "They are probably distractions so that anyone might assume they are the random scribbles of a bored man. But"—he smiled, showing me a row of crooked and yellowed teeth—"This and this may be something."

"Still Akkadian?"

"Yes. He's written the same thing a few times." The professor underlined a section of marks. I believe this could be Arabic. The word would be *balq*."

"Black," Malik translated.

Kaladi said, "So you could be looking for a black pillar. But here we see another word before it: *dawsa.*"

I saw Malik frown.

The professor continued: "*Dawsa* is Arabic and should be read backwards. The two words together mean *black I am finding.*"

Malik finally said what appeared to be troubling him. "That makes no sense, Professor."

"I know."

"Unless," Malik said after a moment's thought. "Could it be read from left to right?"

"Yes, it could. Well done!" Khalidi clapped his hands with pleasure. "Now it makes sense. I believe it means *black heart.*"

TWENTY-EIGHT

Our return through the Egyptian and then Israeli defensive lines was almost as painful as the way into the occupied territory. By the time we were on the main road north, the sun was kissing the Mediterranean.

We talked about what we'd learned, and I felt both elated and disappointed at the same time. I'd been right about a hidden meaning. I had a series of words, some of which made sense and some of which didn't. I was also under no illusion that the interpretations could be incorrect.

However, I had a sense that I was looking for a pillar with distinctive markings and something to do with a black heart. Or maybe the Arabic referred to looking for or beneath a black pillar. Since *black* hadn't just appeared with *heart* it could be both. The writing clearly meant something, but maybe it was just nonsense to anyone other than the man who'd written it.

The new frontier with Egypt stretched along the coast and the bulk of the Israeli Army appeared to be here. There were certainly more than at the border with Lebanon and we'd seen even fewer on the roads that led into Transjordan occupied territory. I guessed the military commanders saw the Gaza Strip and Jerusalem as the potential future flashpoints, despite the new Armistice.

When the Egyptian army invaded, they'd taken towns along the coast almost all the way to Jaffa. I suppose they intended to protect the most populated Arab towns. That's why they'd encircled Beersheba originally. But in taking the coastal plain, the invaders had overrun Jewish towns like Nizanim.

On the day the British left, the Egyptian army made it ten miles short of Jaffa before the IDF stopped them. Within eight months, they'd been pushed back to the edge of Gaza.

Despite nightfall, we could see the huge barriers being constructed at the end of the Strip. Arc lights lit up sections like daylight. Bulldozers and cranes were grinding and creaking with heavy loads.

If I could generalize and sum up the difference between the Arabs and Jews, I would say the Arabs accepted their environment and lived in it. On the other hand, the Jews were terra-formers. They developed, they transformed, they irrigated, and they grew crops.

Both were ways of life, and I couldn't judge which was right.

How long had Jews been transforming the plains? I didn't know, but we went from the harsh landscape and existence of the Arabs in the Gaza Strip, to driving past lush, cultivated land and kibbutzim, the contrast couldn't have been more extreme.

However, an hour later we were approaching Jaffa, and the natural green belt of old Arab citrus farms filled the air with the scent of oranges.

We would be back soon, and Malik said, "Tell me the solution. How do you tie a knot in a string without letting go of both ends?"

I glanced across at him in the dark. "Did you think about the Bedouin?"

"It's not a play on words, is it?"

"No," I said. "It's lateral thinking. They were sitting with crossed arms and legs, contemplating life, I suppose."

"Or contemplating nothing."

"We'll never know," I said, "but the solution is to cross your arms before you pick up the string."

He tried it and held up the resulting knot.

It had been another long day of travelling and tension and Tel Aviv's familiar streets and smells felt like I'd come home. I parked outside the hotel and paid Malik for his second day with me.

"I can't help tomorrow because of commitments to the US Consulate, but if I can ever help in the future, please do not hesitate to ask for me."

"I will. I enjoyed our time together."

"Me too, despite you teasing me with the answer to the knot."

"No teasing next time. I promise."

"Next time?" he asked.

"When I work out the meaning of the prison wall marks."

We pumped hands and he gripped my shoulder.

"I have something for you," he said. "Just words, I'm afraid but they are: be tough as a wolf lest wolves eat you. It's an old Arab saying and one I tell my new friend."

There was a message from my old friend at reception. Dave Rosen was inviting me to join him in a game of poker. On a Monday night? It seemed excessive but welcome after the one I'd had with no company but a glass of water and a war novel.

And, since I consider myself a bit of a card player, I couldn't refuse. So, after dinner I found myself with Rosen and four others in a lounge playing poker.

The game and camaraderie reminded me of my time here during the Mandate. The rest of my old unit was now in the Canal Zone, the final strip of Egypt under

British control. Would it last or would the Egyptian army decide to take that as well?

Rosen had a beer, which didn't surprise me. I knew his resolve to stay off the booze wouldn't last more than a few days.

The man who had asked the knotted string question on Saturday night was at the table. Sergeant Ben Meir was one of Rosen's favourites. Destined to go far, he'd told me.

The sergeant asked if I'd finally solved the problem and raised his glass to me when I explained the solution. I also explained it had been the Bedouin's crossed legs that had been the revelation.

The party was keen to hear about my travels but muttered disapproval when I mentioned the Bedouin. I don't know why. My experience of the tribe had been good. They'd talked to my interpreter and given us sustenance. I guess it was their different attitudes and way of life that resulted in the dislike. There had been problems in the region for thousands of years, driven mostly by religion but fundamentally by mankind's inability to accept another man's differences. It gave me little hope for the future of this land.

When I mentioned Beersheba, the men cheered. I hadn't known about Operation Moshe which appeared to have been a morale-boosting victory on the day before the agreed ceasefire in October 1948.

"They thought we'd attack Gaza," Ben Meir said, laughing. "The Egyptians couldn't imagine we'd attack Beersheba. After all, they had a whole battalion defending the town."

Another man said, "We attacked at four in the morning when most of them were still asleep in their beds. By nine o'clock it was all over."

Ben Meir said, "Most of them ran away with their tails between their legs."

There was much thumping of the table.

Rosen held up a hand. "Let's not overstate this, lads." He paused for effect. "At one point, we had sixty Palmach soldiers in the centre compared to 500 of them. It wasn't a fair fight!"

That drew raucous laughter and was followed by a round of drinks.

I sipped a Coke and let them enjoy their moment.

Later, Rosen asked to see the pink slip of a report I'd stolen from the Beersheba police station.

"I should have you arrested for this," he said with mock seriousness. "But since it's the pink copy and not the white or yellow, I'll let you off with a warning."

He read the brief report and then pointed to the reporting officer's details. "It was signed by the Beersheba police, but the report wasn't by the police."

From my time in British Palestine, I knew the police had divisions. There were Jewish and Arab police units and I'd assumed the report was by an Arab one.

"No?"

"Army," he said. "The arrest was made by a unit of Arab British soldiers."

"What about the location?"

He looked closely at where I was pointing. Arad had been written above deleted typing.

I said, "Not only didn't it look likely that the ancient place could have been the site of the shootout, but why was there a British Army unit there?"

"I don't know. It's surprising they'd be in the Negev desert, but it's before my time." He handed the report to one of his men, the one who'd told the knotted string puzzle.

He did the same thing I'd done, holding the paper up to the light, but he also reversed it and looked at the back.

"It's not Arad," he said. "That last letter is an *h*. I think... *A* something *d h*. Wait, yes! It isn't Arad it's Abdah. I'd bet my beer on it."

TWENTY-NINE

Dave Rosen told me that Abdah was the Arab name for Avdat. It was also in a remote part of the Negev. I was in two minds about travelling there. Would it be another pointless long trip?

Rosen and colleagues confirmed that Avdat also had ancient ruins, but unlike Arad, these were Roman and included pillars. I asked if anyone knew of a black pillar, but no one did.

Returning to the hotel, I was handed a letter by the manager at reception. It was in my real name as opposed to the one I was registered under.

"I'm the only one who knows," he confirmed.

I smiled although I wasn't happy that anyone at the hotel knew which room I'd been booked into.

Inside the envelope was a brief note from Nicola Short. She hoped that the letter would find me and that I didn't regret our evening together.

She'd missed me on Sunday evening and hoped to see me again this coming Saturday.

Presumably, Nicola had come to the Rothschild and discovered that I was no longer registered. Maybe she'd tried other hotels in the area and the note was a final chance of making contact again.

The paper smelled of vanilla and I thought of her soft mouth and passionate kiss.

In my room, I took the chair in the corner and slept better than the night sitting in a foxhole. I must have been thinking of Avdat because I'd gone to bed unsure whether I would travel there today. In the morning, I'd decided to spend time looking at what I knew rather than dashing off on another wild goose chase. However, a telegram arrived as I was eating breakfast. So much for my decisiveness!

However, I was increasingly concerned that my identity was becoming more widely known and getting away from Tel Aviv while a killer was at large seemed a smart move.

The telegram was from Professor Khalidi. He had either managed to send it himself or had passed it to someone who could. I had no idea how communications worked between the occupied territories and Israel.

The message was simple. He'd found what he thought was the word *Afdst* or *Afdat*. He said *afdat* was Arabic for silver. Confirmation, he suggested that I was looking for a silver pillar not a black one.

But he was wrong.

Not silver. Afdat was surely the place Avdat. It couldn't be a coincidence.

Before leaving, I called the police HQ and asked for Sub Inspector Rosen. Since Malik couldn't join me today, I wanted to let someone know where I was going.

Rosen didn't like the idea and tried to dissuade me. I'd be crossing the desert mountains. Besides the risk of breaking down in the wilderness, he thought rogue soldiers or bandits could attack me.

I thanked him for his concern but insisted on going. I packed additional supplies of food and water, just in case, and bought an Arab headscarf to protect me from the worst of the sun. As I climbed into the Land Rover, a policeman held up his hand to stop me.

"Something wrong, officer?" I asked, eyeing his holstered pistol and wondering about his intentions. Was he genuine?

"You don't recognize me in uniform?" he said.

Then I realized. It was DI Rosen's blue-eyed boy. "Sergeant Ira Ben Meir!"

We exchanged pleasantries before he swung in and sat beside me. "I'm coming with you, orders of Inspector Rosen."

I thought to eject him but then decided against it. Not only would I have company on the journey, but an Israeli policeman could get me anywhere—well, almost anywhere, providing I didn't cross a border.

After filling the tank with Derv, I drove out of Tel Aviv and went south again, through the orange groves and then plains.

Ben Meir didn't say a word once we were in the countryside, but he wasn't like Malik on our first day together. Ben Meir didn't stare into the distance. He stretched out, turned his head, and closed his eyes. This didn't appear to be the same man I'd met at the police drinking session when he'd been one of the most vocal. I suspected it was more about me than him. If I'd been a drinker, perhaps we'd have bonded and filled the monotonous journey with conversation.

We'd passed the turnoff I'd taken the day before on the way to Arad—the one that swept east around the mountains.

Ben Meir sat upright, grabbed the door, and leaned over the side. More than a minute of vomiting followed as I slowed to a halt.

He wiped his mouth, took a swig of water and spat it out. Then he drank some and flopped back in the seat.

"I don't feel so great," he said weakly.

"Drink?" I asked, knowing he'd quaffed a huge amount last night.

"Maybe. Maybe breakfast."

He was pale and looked clammy.

"Are you all right to proceed?" I asked.

He cleared his throat and took another swig of water. "I'm fine now," he said.

But he wasn't fine. Within ten minutes, he was vomiting again. He looked pale and too unwell for another hour's drive. We were outside Beersheba, and I headed to the centre, looking for a hospital. There was a building with a Star of David painted in red on the front. Too small to be a hospital, I figured it was a clinic.

I suspected my passenger either had food poisoning or the jolting journey after a skinful of beer and a big breakfast had left his stomach unsettled. Hopefully a clinic was all he needed.

I dropped Sergeant Ben Meir outside and told him to get checked. I'd be back and collect him in a few hours.

He didn't argue.

A main road arced east and then south toward a town called Nitzana and the border. This part of the journey was easy, but once I'd turned east through the hills, the road became a track.

The Land Rover pounded up over stones and spilled dust in its wake. I had the Arab scarf wrapped around my head and became uncomfortable with the heat.

Mad dogs and Englishmen, I thought. The Bedouin were right to mock me.

The sun beat down and reflected and shimmered off the rocks. When I started seeing mirages, I forced myself to take a break, stretching and quaffing a whole canister of water.

I checked the map and confirmed I was going the right way. Just approximately six miles further.

Driving again, the track twisted and turned through the hills, taking the route of least resistance, one that had been formed thousands of years ago. And one rarely used by vehicles, I decided.

There was no greenery, not even twisted dry brush. There were just cream-coloured rocks. The only variation was where shadows created brown and purple definition.

It was the definition of barren.

A vulture circled in the clear sky.

There was something dead on the ground, no doubt. If the Land Rover slipped off the track and rolled, I could be its next feast. Despite his poor company, at that moment, I wished Ben Meir was still my passenger.

Gripping the wheel harder, I pressed on. There was a hilltop peak close on my right. The ones to my left were further off, but I guessed that was the ridge that eventually became the Judean Mountains. Which meant Arad was way over to the left, maybe thirty miles distant. And Avdat was within five miles.

I passed the turn before I realized my mistake. A side track led through the rocks, and I abandoned the Land Rover in favour of walking.

The sun beat down like a weight on my neck. Now that I was no longer driving, I could feel the full force of the heat.

There was a steep path which levelled out into a plateau. The views extend for miles in every direction, with seemingly endless rocks and desert and big open skies overhead.

Ahead of me, light danced off minor ruined buildings. They may have been from a recent period, but a large structure ahead could have been Roman. The surrounding walls suggested the size of a football pitch. I climbed steps and saw stumpy pillars surrounded by more walls. A villa, I thought. From my limited knowledge of roman architecture, I figured these pillars were for underground heating rather than ceiling support.

At this time of year and day, it was hard to imagine the need to use anything but solar heat.

Walking through the rooms, I scanned for an unusual pillar. Of course, the whole *pillar* interpretation could have been totally mistaken.

I came to two engraved sandstone slabs. They were positioned like a doorway with a passage between. Beyond them, the walls curved into a semicircle.

I sensed this section was like a nave. Maybe I'd been wrong. Maybe it wasn't a villa, but rather a massive religious site.

The slabs had emblems of sorts, worn by sand but still distinctive. They each had a circle of leaves with a broad cross in the centre. My first impression was of a Crusader cross, but maybe it was specific to the people who'd lived and prayed here.

Walking beyond the curved walls, there was a courtyard, and I entered another ruined building. This one had six taller pillars.

And the one which caught my attention had a star scratched into it. Not a Star of David, but three lines intersecting.

I'd seen this star before. In Hajjar's cell.

Professor Khalidi had been mistaken. This wasn't an Akkadian letter. It was a marker.

THIRTY

Professor Khalidi had translated the Akkadian to be an unknown word: N-I-E-M-N. I looked at my sketch of the symbols. So the star wasn't an *N*. Which could mean that the phonetically the word was Niem or Iemn.

I wished Malik had been available. Were either of the words Arabic?

Khalidi had said the five lines represented the letter *I*. What if they literally meant five? What if the eight lines of the *M* meant eight?

Which left *E* and *N*.

N was another star. *E* was four horizontal lines with two at the end. Khalidi had put two arrows when he'd reproduced the second vertical line. Could it be an ancient equivalent of drawing a bar to make five? The two lines might mean six, but then why draw five lines for five?

I looked around, pondering the options before a thought struck me. Was Hajjar leaving a note for himself in case he lost his mind? Or was he providing instructions for someone else?

Was I looking for another star?

I spent twenty minutes searching before I took a rest in the limited shade I could find.

I spotted the vulture again, or maybe it was a different one. After another circle, it descended out of view.

Probably deciding to check whatever is down there, I thought.

I drank water and looked at the walls. Touching their rough stone made me think of ancient times. How many other people had touched this spot a thousand, two thousand years ago?

Far off, I heard a rumble. A land slip perhaps. Or maybe tank fire from thirty miles away. I figured the sounds of war would carry this far into the desert mountains.

But after the distant noise, I heard nothing. Had I imagined it? Was this the equivalent of a mirage? Out in the wilderness for too long and you'd imagine anything.

Which made me wonder why anyone would have lived out here thousands of years ago. With the exception of the mountain peaks to the west, and the dips and troughs, the views were spectacular.

The building was aligned north-south. Maybe to watch the road—people approaching from the south and east.

The letters. What if *E* meant east? What if the second star wasn't scratched into a pillar? What if *N* meant north?

Instructions. If Hajjar wanted to remember where he'd hidden something, maybe he'd write: Star-5-E-10-N. Start at the pillar with the star. Go 5 east and ten north.

I clambered over the wall and strode to the pillar with the star. I turned east. Five paces took me to another wall. Hajjar hadn't said what the five related to. Paces seemed logical and they had taken me to a wall. Ten paces north took me along the wall.

I looked around and at the bricks.

There was an army folding spade in the Land Rover and I fetched it.

Five minutes later, I was digging in the spot at the base of the wall.

I found nothing.

More than that, I realized there was no sign of previous digging.

Could it be under the wall? Again, I felt the stones. Heavy and secure, nothing had moved them in a very long time.

The other side, perhaps? I clambered over the wall and started digging. Just as I was going to stop, I heard the crunch of stones. And then a command.

"Drop the spade!"

I stayed in my crouch and turned to see who'd spoken.

He had short black hair and a trim beard. His face was tanned and unusually smooth apart from a furrowed brow. He was dressed like me, with a lightweight jacket over a shirt. Like me, he had a scarf around his neck, but he wore shorts whereas my trousers were long.

My shirt had been white when I'd left Tel Aviv. My trousers were khaki. Like his hair and beard, his clothes were all dark brown.

But the biggest difference I registered was the gun in his hand.

"I said, drop the spade!" he barked.

I dropped it. I raised one knee. It hid my other leg from the man. Unseen, I drew the Beretta from my ankle holster.

I stood.

Gun facing gun.

"Who are you?" I asked.

He said, "Put the gun down."

I shook my head. "I'm British military police."

"Put the gun down!"

I raised my empty right hand in a pacifying gesture. "Let's put them down together."

Our eyes locked, and I saw him quickly assess before nodding.

He held his gun away from his body and I mirrored the move. As he squatted, I squatted. As he placed his gun on the ground, I did the same.

We let go and stood slowly with our hands out, away from our bodies, non-threatening.

"Who are—?" I started to say, but before I'd finished, he'd moved. I'd never seen anyone step and kick so quickly.

Before I realized what was happening, he'd placed a boot in my stomach.

I went back, bounced off the wall, and recovered in time to block a well-aimed punch. He slapped me on the ear with his other hand, fast and stinging. A disorientating blow.

I ducked and spun, but he was there again with a strike by the other hand and then a kick.

Moving away, I managed to lessen their impacts, but he was too fast. I'm a trained boxer. I can handle myself in the ring. I can also handle myself in a street fight. Most people telegraph their moves. They are slow and obvious. Boxers are trained to predict, to block and counter. But I'd never come across a fighter like this before. I couldn't tell whether he would kick or punch or slap. His contacts weren't powerful, but that was what made him so fast. I'd block one and then he'd make contact before my counter.

Finally, I caught him with a left jab, then an uppercut that made him stagger. He tried a leg-sweep, which I avoided, but then I realized he'd planned the move. Suddenly, he was up and facing me with the spade in his hand.

I dived for his gun, but didn't make it. A boot smashed into my hand. I rolled, but he jumped across me, stamping on my side before I could get up. Then I saw the spade swing.

I ducked just in time, but he'd planned that too. His other fist caught me on my right temple. I blinked and saw the spade rushing in from the left. After that, my world went black.

THIRTY-ONE

I was thirteen years old, and my father was yelling at me. I'd dirtied my school clothes playing on the recreation ground before going home.

I knew he'd be mad at me, but I'd done it anyway. He'd give me a lashing with his belt and yet I had a sore head. Had he hit me already?

And why was he calling me Captain?

"Captain Carter?"

I tasted dust. My face stung but a greater pain was in my head. Then I remembered the spade.

I opened my eyes and the world started coming into focus. I was in the ruins in the Negev mountains. The heat, the dust. And a figure standing over me.

My first instinct was to roll—get away from my attacker.

"Captain."

There was a hand on my shoulder. I heard concern in his voice. Not my attacker.

I pushed up groggily from the ground.

"Are you all right?" The voice was less harsh now. I saw the man who was speaking, and another helped me sit and gave me water.

The man talking was the pixie-faced officer from Beersheba police station: Captain Kramer.

I looked around for the man I'd fought. He wasn't there, just Kramer and a junior IDF soldier.

"Are you all right?" asked Kramer again.

I moved my head from side to side, testing the pain in my temple.

"There was another man—" I started to say. The place spun and I blacked out again.

When I opened my eyes, I was in my Land Rover.

"Can you slow down?"

The bumping was making my head hurt.

Kramer handed me a flask of water and I gulped it.

"We're already going pretty slowly," he said.

I looked outside and saw we were trundling, probably going less than twenty miles an hour.

Ahead, I saw the dust of another vehicle.

"Is that him?" I asked.

"That's my sergeant," said Kramer. "Driving my jeep." He glanced at me. "Rest."

"Who was the other man?"

I realized my words were coming out slowly, broken by my breathing.

"I said rest, Captain. We'll talk when we get back to Beersheba."

I closed my eyes and sensed waves of consciousness. I forgot the pain in my head and was surprised when we stopped. The journey back had seemed faster than I expected.

"Stay there," instructed Kramer as I tried to open the jeep's door. We were outside the medical centre.

The other IDF soldier from the ruins plus a medic darted out with a stretcher. I waved them back but needed support to step out. I felt woozy.

With a hand under my arm, the medic said, "Stop resisting and let me check you over."

He was right. I'd taken a blow to the head and couldn't walk in a straight line if my life depended on it.

Once inside, I refused a bed but took a chair. A nurse gave me painkillers, salt tablets and water to wash them down with. Then she dabbed at my hair on the right and her wipe came away with blood.

The medic crowded in and poked until I said, "Ouch!"

He raised an index finger and asked me to follow its path. Then he blinded me with a light, checking my eyes' reaction.

"You'll live," he said, eyeballing me. "Just an abrasion although it looks like you'll have a tender lump for a few days." Then he asked me to stay where I was for an hour and that he'd check on me again.

When I frowned, the nurse explained that he was concerned about concussion.

I waited impatiently and a visit by Kramer relieved the tedium.

I said, "What happened?"

"You first."

So I told him about searching the ruins at Avdat because Duffy might have been there. I didn't explain further, but said that I thought I'd been alone. When I mentioned the man in dark brown, I realized I'd left my gun at the site. After I checked my ankle holster, Kramer held out my Berretta.

"Thought this was yours," he said. "The other man didn't take it."

"So you saw him?"

Kramer nodded. "Shabak."

That surprised me. "You know the man?"

"No. That's not his name. I mean, he's from the Shabak also known as Shin Bet—the security services."

I'd never heard of it.

The captain continued: "He thought you were a terrorist; said he'd been tracking someone and thought it was you."

I'd told him I was British military police, but he hadn't given me time to prove it. Which either meant that he didn't believe me, or he knew exactly who I was.

I said, "What happened to him?"

"He just left."

"He had a vehicle at the site?"

"Yes. I recognized your Land Rover. He had an unmarked gray Jeep."

I thought for a moment. "Did he take anything?"

"What like? He had a gun if that's—"

"Anything unusual. A sack, perhaps?" I was thinking he might have found what I was looking for.

Kramer shook his head. "There was just a spade. I assume that's what he'd hit you with. Had he been digging?"

"That was me. I thought I had a code…"

Kramer smiled. "Secret treasure?"

"Something like that. So this Shabak man just left?"

The medic returned as Kramer confirmed that my attacker hadn't taken anything. The Shabak man had been tracking me because he thought I was a terrorist. But then he'd just left. I was baffled. My working assumption was that he'd also been looking for Hajjar's presumed stash.

The medic did the thing with his finger and the bright light again and eventually said I was clear to go.

Outside, I was surprised to find the light fading fast.

"How is Sergeant Ben Meir?" I asked Kramer because I'd seen no sign of him.

"Fine. He's suffering an acute case of embarrassment. The doctor said it was a combination of alcohol poisoning and greasy food." Kramer looked awkward.

"What is it?"

"I took the liberty of inviting him to stay in our temporary barracks. He still didn't look good and it's late and you—"

I raised a hand. It was getting dark and I didn't fancy a long drive home. However, I'd noticed all the arrivals. People were camped out by the station. Housing was being built quickly, but not as fast as people were arriving.

Kramer grinned at me. "There's a room in the police station. And I don't mean a cell. It's got a cot and privacy. I suggest—"

"That sounds perfect," I said.

It wasn't until I looked in a mirror that I discovered my face was as grubby as my hands. Scrabbling on the dusty ground hadn't done much for my complexion. At least I only had a sore head and small cut. It could have been much worse if I'd been struck with the edge of the spade.

When I came back into the office, Kramer nodded his approval at the improvement in my appearance, then invited me to join him for a meal.

He took me to a café and ordered chicken soup and bread.

I learned his first name was Yonathan and he'd received a call from Inspector Rosen from Tel Aviv. Rosen had been checking up on me and told Kramer where I'd gone.

"My friend," I explained.

"Your *very* good friend! He was concerned about you after you left his sergeant at our clinic."

We talked about the war and his hopes for the future. He was a young man—at least three years younger than me—and had never known a normal life. "Perhaps now our struggles are over," he said, referring to the Armistice. "Now I can stop being a soldier and be a father."

Later, I asked him to tell me more about the Shabak man.

"What do you want to know?"

"Did he have identification?"

"You're asking whether he was genuine? Well, I didn't just take his word for it. When I arrived, he was about to shoot you in the head."

I stared at Kramer in disbelief.

The captain shrugged. "These chaps don't ask questions."

"Then I'm very lucky you arrived. Thank you, Yonathan."

"You're welcome."

"But I still don't understand. Why was he going to shoot me?"

"He said he thought you were a security issue. Said he'd been following you. I explained who you were and that you had permission. I said I'd seen your documentation, and a police inspector could vouch for you."

"And he just left?" He'd told me this earlier, but I still didn't understand.

"Yes. I thought he could have arrested you anyway, but… were you doing anything illegal up there?"

"Not unless it's illegal to dig around ruins these days."

He glanced at me to check if I wasn't joking, I suppose. "The spade—?"

I explained that I was following a code left by a prisoner. It had led me to Avdat and then the wall. I'd used the spade, expected something buried.

"And you're sure the Shabak man didn't take anything?"

Kramer shook his head. "You can keep asking me but the answer doesn't change. All I saw was his gun."

"Then, either the buried thing was never there, or I was too late."

He looked thoughtful, and I asked why.

"I was just thinking back," Kramer said. "The Shabak man did something odd. Before he left, he walked over to the wall on the other side and ran his hand along it."

THIRTY-TWO

A ship docked at Acre harbour, slipping alongside the old wall. At half-past three, on a moonless night, the sky was only marginally lighter that the black velvet sea.

Apart from the rats, the organization's man responsible for the tunnels was the only living thing on the short quay. His name was Moishe, and he was holding a lantern. It couldn't be seen until its covering was lifted. Three flashes and one came in return. Then a man shrouded in black appeared on the steps and hurried to his side.

"This way," the Acre man said and the two walked the short distance to the shop behind which the entrance to the twin tunnels was concealed. He led the way down the right-hand tunnel but not all the way to the dead end. Halfway, before the dip that would act as a trap in medieval times. He'd built a false wall with a locked door. Beyond was where the organization would stash their goods.

Moishe didn't know what they were smuggling, nor did he want to. His wife had died six years ago after protracted illness. Their daughter and her husband had been murdered in the December 1947 Arab attacks in Haifa. Now, Azael, their only child, was all the old man had. The boy had been born sickly. At four, he'd been transferred to Alyn Hospital in Jerusalem. The best, the most advanced and the most expensive. The organization arranged it and paid for everything. One day Azael would be well enough to come home. The old man knew God wouldn't let him down.

Tomorrow night, the goods would be gone, and he'd cover up what he'd done. Then he'd go and visit his grandson. He hadn't seen him for a month. The boy had looked worse but Doctor Keller had assured him that Azael would bounce back. Americans! They were always so upbeat. But the doctor's confidence had been infectious, and Moishe had left with a smile on his face and hope in his heart.

After handing the man in black the key, Moishe walked out of the tunnel. But he didn't reach the street. In fact, he'd only taken three paces before a fire burned in his throat.

A garrotte ended Acre-man's life quickly and without mess. "Sorry, old man," the man in black said. The plans had changed after Moishe's sickly grandson had died. It was just a matter of time before the old man discovered the truth. They should never have relied on someone to prepare and guard the tunnels. That was the man in black's view. But it wasn't his call. He did what he was told. However, he accepted that the new arrangement was better. They'd hide the entrance to the tunnels.

He dragged the old man's body beyond the false wall and dumped him. They'd dump him in the desert tomorrow night. Within a couple of days there would be nothing left but bones.

The man in black walked out and through the rundown shop. Within a month, it would be gone, along with its neighbours. The whole row would be replaced by a wall and a discreet door. No one would get in or out without a key. No one could pass from the citadel to the street. There would be no more prison escapees using the tunnels. No chance of prying eyes.

It took them half an hour to transfer all the goods from the boat to the tunnel.

The old man had provided food and drink for them and the man in black jokingly thanked the corpse for his consideration. Four of them had arrived on the boat, armed and tired after a two-day trip. They had to wait for tomorrow night. They couldn't go out, but they didn't have to be silent. The tunnel was deep, the walls were thick, and been soundproofed by the old man.

They should have slept but despite or maybe because of the darkness, they stayed awake and listened to the ghosts and pretended they weren't afraid.

THIRTY-THREE

"Shabak?" Ben Meir said. We were in my Land Rover and driving back to the ruins at Avdat. I'd spent a restless night thinking about Hajjar's code and my fight with the Shabak man.

I told the police sergeant that I'd never fought anyone like the man in dark brown before. Boxers can be unsettled by unorthodox fighters and the Shabak man's techniques were unlike anything I'd experienced before.

"It sounds like krav maga," Ben Meir said. Which he explained translated as *contact combat*. He went on to tell me that it was based on the best of western and oriental martial arts and was taught to all Israeli soldiers. However, from my description of the fight, Ben Meir thought I'd probably been up against a master.

"You were lucky to survive," he said. "Those men literally take no prisoners."

"If it hadn't been for Captain Kramer…" I then realized something. "Actually, I should be thanking you."

"Why me?"

"Because you called DI Rosen who then asked Kramer for assistance. Without your call—"

"The least I could do, Captain." He chuckled. "After all I'd let you down by being ill. And a self-inflicted one at that."

We followed the same route I'd taken the day before. The sun wasn't as relentless as yesterday, yet. It was still early. The purple shadows on the rocks were longer and the other way around, making the landscape look different from yesterday. However, there was one thing the same: a vulture was circling.

I took a gulp of water, remembering to stay hydrated today. I could have easily become the great bird's supper yesterday although a bullet to the brain would have got me before the thirst.

Ben Meir was a different man today. After we'd spoken about my attacker, he didn't stop. He talked about some cases they were working on. They were run of the mill, except for one. A mystery young woman had been found dead in a Tel Aviv ditch. They knew she was an Arab but she'd been brutalized, so much so that her face wasn't recognizable.

"It's good to hear that you investigate cases no matter what," I said.

"You mean, because she's an Arab?"

"Yes."

He sighed. "We do our best but it's a problem. It's hard to work with the Arab community. They're suspicious of us. Helping a Jew, even when it's to find the murderer of an Arab? Well, it's tough to solve a crime when they close ranks and won't talk."

I knew all about that. During the British Mandate, we'd had to establish Arab and Jewish police units. Even then, people were afraid the authorities would set them up for a crime rather than punish the true culprit. Only a bipartisan solution would work and the British hadn't made a good enough job of it.

However, the UN hadn't either. When the UN committee—UNSCOP—had visited Palestine in 1947, they were tasked with find a solution by partitioning the country. The Jewish community had welcomed them. The Arabs had refused to recognize its legitimacy. It was a cultural thing. They'd refused to cooperate and it had worked against them. It was a cultural issue that created a challenge for anyone trying to find compromise.

My mind drifted. My colleague Bill Wolfe had been involved with UNSCOP, he'd made a valid point. He'd questioned what would have happened if the Christians also claimed Palestine as their own? Would the UN have come up with a three-way partition of the land?

He didn't have an answer, but it highlighted the complexity and challenge of a country that was the centre of three religions. Perhaps there could never be an equitable solution.

We reached the turn that I'd originally missed yesterday, and I directed Ben Meir left. He drove as far has he could along the track.

As we parked, I thought about my attacker. Captain Kramer had said the Shabak man had been in a gray Jeep. I wondered where he'd come from. He'd told Kramer that he'd been following me.

I looked west, along the route we'd taken into the hills. A vague cloud of dust still hung in the air, not just from the wind, but disturbed by our vehicle. Wouldn't I have noticed someone following me?

"Up here?" asked Ben Meir, walking ahead.

I followed him to the plateau and ruined buildings then pointed to the Romanesque ones.

"What are we looking for?" he asked.

I kept going, between the two engraved sandstone slabs and into the courtyard beyond.

Now I pointed to the pillar with the engraved lines that looked like a star. "This mark was on the cell of the prisoner in Acre."

Ben Meir touched the three lines.

"They don't seem as old as the other engravings."

I agreed. My sense was that someone had scratched them within recent times, possibly as the marker.

He said, "But I'm sure I could find stars like this all over. Why here?"

So, I explained about the disguised name on Hajjar's arrest report. "I think the code is about something that's here. A language expert thought they were the letters N-I-E-M-N."

"But they aren't?"

"The N in the code was a star—literally a star."

"So we're looking for another star?"

I let him go with the same theory I'd had yesterday, and we both searched for a second star. We found none.

We stopped and rested and drank water. I noticed that the vulture wasn't in the sky, which subconsciously seemed better. The sun had climbed a quarter way to its zenith. By midday, it would be unbearable here.

"No more than another ninety minutes," I said.

"Then we'd better search harder."

"Or smarter."

The spade I'd been struck with was on the ground near where I'd dug. I took Ben Meir over to it and explained my logic. From the star go five east and then eight north.

"And that leads us here," he agreed.

He dug around and I checked the wall.

We stopped again and he looked at the pillars.

"Six pillars. Could the number five relate to the others?"

Perhaps there would be a mark on another. Perhaps the Akkadian symbols related to that rather than an E, for example.

There were no other clear scratches, just random erosion.

He said, "The interpreter thought it was N-I-E-M-N but you think it's Star-I-E-M-N or 5-E-8-N?"

"Right."

Ben Meir scratched the code in the dust. "N means star?"

"Right."

"But it's not N-I-E-M-Star? Not ending at the star?" Then he answered his own question. "No, that makes no sense."

"He wouldn't have a code that led to the symbol—the most obvious."

As he'd spoken, I'd written N-I-E-M-Star. A thought was just out of reach. Then I had it.

"Semitic languages," I said, "read right to left. The professor who translated it was an Arab."

I changed the code to Star-M-E-I-N.

Ben Meir said, "Wasn't the prisoner an Arab too?"

"Yes, but I remember the professor translated the Akkadian from left to right at one point. So this could be Star-eight-east-five-north. The other way around!"

Excited, I hurried to the pillar and paced it out. I was at a wall again. It was thick, about eighteen inches, and solid.

Ben Meir began digging. I waited with my hand on the wall. When I moved to take over, my weight must have shifted because I felt a stone move. The wall wasn't all fixed in place.

Ben Meir stopped and stared as I lifted a capstone away. Then we crowded over what I'd revealed.

A space. A broad gap that could hold a suitcase-worth of booty.

But it was empty.

"What do you think?" Ben Meir said after feeling around inside and coming up with nothing.

"I think someone beat us to it."

THIRTY-FOUR

"Who beat us?" Ben Meir said as we drove back to Beersheba.

"Abu Hajjar or the Shabak man?"

"What about that narrow-faced captain?"

He was referring to Kramer. I didn't think so. I hadn't shared the code with him.

I felt in my pocket. I'd written the code on a piece of paper. I'd looked at it when I'd first arrived at the ruins. It wasn't in my pocket now.

Had Kramer taken it?

We drove back into Beersheba, but Kramer wasn't in the office. I asked his staff but they denied knowing where he was—maybe they didn't know or maybe they didn't want to tell us.

We cleaned off the grime of the morning and waited in the same café I'd eaten in last night.

At a little after 1 pm, I saw Kramer drive past. He went into the police station.

He was in his office when I walked in. Ben Meir stood at my shoulder. My immediate thought was that Kramer looked hot and flustered.

"Captain Carter! What a surprise. I didn't expect you to come back."

"We found it," I said.

Kramer smiled, confused. "Found *it*? Sorry, what are you talking about?"

"Tell me about what happened after you interrupted the Shabak man."

"What, yesterday? I… We helped you up, checked you weren't badly injured. Put you in your Land Rover. You were barely with us, kept fading in and out of consciousness."

I waited patiently; my eyes fixed on his.

"What?" he said, looking from me to Ben Meir and back. I figured he was thinking that I had no authority here, but Ben Meir was an Israeli detective.

"Did you find the code?" I asked.

"What? A code? No!"

"Did you search for the treasure?"

"I… er…"

"Captain!"

"We saw that you'd been digging." Kramer swallowed, paused and shook his head. "I just took a look."

"And you found…?" I kept watching his eyes.

"What? In the hole? Nothing. You'd already dug it. There were just two holes."

Damn! He seemed to be telling the truth.

Kramer was about to say something else when we heard running feet and then a soldier came in behind us. He saluted and asked to have a word.

Kramer spoke to the man while we waited.

When he came back into the office, he said, "We've found a body."

"A body?"

"A recent death." Kramer looked at me thoughtfully. "It was just the two of you who came up from Tel Aviv?"

"Yes."

"No one else with you?"

"No," I said curious. "Why?"

"It's a coincidence, that's all then," said Kramer. "The body was in the hills not far from where we found you. Not only do we have a ceasefire, but it's a remote spot. So totally unexpected."

I thought about the vulture I'd seen. "Pecked by birds?" I asked.

He nodded. "That's my understanding. Did you see anyone other than the Shabak man who attacked you?"

"No, just a vulture." I wondered how they'd found him if the spot was remote. I asked and the captain answered.

"I don't know any details. It was reported by the Bedouin and a team has gone to investigate."

While we waited, I spoke to Kramer alone. I started by apologizing for my accusatory tone earlier.

He said, "Don't worry about it."

I waited and he glanced away.

After a few beats I said, "What was it? When I first confronted you... you looked guilty."

He pulled a face that suggested awkwardness. Then he said, "I was up to... you know?"

"No, I can't say that I do, Captain."

"With a woman—someone I shouldn't have been with." Again he looked uncomfortable.

I fixed him with a stare. "What you get up to is between you and your god," I said. "I would just like your assurance that you didn't find anything at the ruins."

"On my honour," he said, and I believed him.

An hour later, a scout car parked outside the medical centre. We watched it arrive and saw soldiers carry a body bag inside.

Captain Kramer and I headed over and located the room that had been converted into a morgue. An army medical officer was in the process of removing the canvas bag from the body and taking a first look.

"Ouch!" a voice said, and I saw that Ben Meir had come inside as well.

The body was a man and his face was a mess. He had no eyes. The cheeks and lips were gone. I could see no tongue. There were ragged tears in his neck. Below the clavicle, I saw no damage.

"Birds," the MO said, waving a hand over the face. "But nothing on the exposed legs or arms."

"He was buried," explained Kramer, "up to his neck."

I said, "There was a vulture in the sky yesterday."

Kramer clarified that I'd been in the vicinity.

The MO nodded. "Rigor suggests he died within the last twenty-four hours. His scalp's burnt, which looks recent. My guess is he spent most of yesterday in direct sunlight."

"Buried for all that time?" asked Kramer.

"Hell of a way to die," said Ben Meir and we all nodded solemnly.

"I'll know for sure once I've properly examined him."

He unwound a piece of material wrapped around the man's right hand. I hadn't noticed it because, covered with grime, it was the same colour as the man's shirt.

It was a bandage. The man was missing his right index finger.

The MO said, "Recent injury. I'd say this was shot off. Hard to tell, but possible wider burn around the site." He stepped back and instructed an orderly to cut away the man's clothes.

"He looks like an Arab," Kramer said as though thinking out loud. "Not military."

The dead man was wearing a loose brown shirt with matching trousers. He wasn't dressed for spending a long time in the desert that was for certain.

The material looked good quality and I saw no sign of wear. This was no vagrant and yet when the orderly cut the man's shirt away, I noticed a contradiction. The clothes suggested wealth and yet his body looked ravaged, like he hadn't eaten well for a long time.

I was trying to imagine what his face looked like. Could it be?

Kramer said, "What is it? Do you know something?"

"Maybe," I said. Then as the shirt came away, I asked to see the inside of the man's right arm.

Rigor mortis made the movement difficult, but I saw it immediately: the tattoo of a bird on his forearm.

"I know him," I said. I'd previously read a description of the man. I was unable to recognize the face but the tattoo was distinctive.

They waited.

"It's the escaped prisoner from Acre," I said. "His name is Abu Hajjar."

THIRTY-FIVE

I had no idea what it meant. The IDF men who'd picked up the body of Hajjar said there was no sign of anyone else there.

So, what had happened to Eva Wislitsky? And more importantly where was Duffy?

Had they killed Hajjar? Had they killed his family in Junid?

I kept thinking about the smooth-faced, neat-bearded man from Shabak—the security agent. What was he doing at Avdat? Why had he attacked me?

Too many unanswered questions although I had my suspicions. Someone had killed Hajjar recently and the Shabak man was in the vicinity. He'd told Captain Kramer that he'd been trailing me, but what if he hadn't? What if he'd been trailing Hajjar and then come across me?

I journeyed back to Tel Aviv, frustrated. I'd found the Arab prisoner but failed to find anything to locate Duffy.

We spoke of other things at first. I asked Ben Meir where he'd served in the army. It turned out that he was far too young to have seen action in the war with Germany. Although he looked about my age, mid-twenties, he had barely reached his second decade. He'd done well to have made sergeant already and I told him so.

"I'm lucky that Inspector Rosen rates me," he said.

It wasn't luck. Dave Rosen thought Ben Meir was good and had rewarded a loyal, hard-worker.

"Anyway," my driver said. "Uncle Levi wouldn't have let me join up. He's a pacifist and wouldn't even let me join the Haganah." Ben Meir went on to tell me that Uncle Levi and his wife had taken him in when he'd been sent to Palestine as a refugee. He'd been ten years old, and his parents hadn't made it.

He spoke matter-of-factly as though the horrors of the Holocaust hadn't affected him, but I was certain the scars ran very deep.

"My uncle wasn't really happy with my career choice," Ben Meir laughed mirthlessly. "He knows I have to carry a gun, but I promised I'd never kill anyone with it. He's proud of how well I'm doing."

"I'm sure he is," I said before telling him a little of my own history. I avoided talking about killing anyone and he didn't ask.

Before we were on the outskirts of the Jaffa orange groves, our conversation had turned to my job of finding Alfred Duffy. I talked through the case so far and he asked what I was going to do now.

I'd been wondering the same thing. I should probably call SIB Command again and ask them. Did they want me to stay and act as security for the embassy or should I return to Cyprus?

I knew they'd ask whether I had any leads on Duffy's whereabouts. Israel was about the same size as Wales with even more diversity. I was looking for a needle in a haystack. Normally that didn't bother me. I had good instincts. I could find people. But as the sun set over the old town and Jaffa's hill, I sensed it was setting on my assignment here.

THIRTY-SIX

There was a message for me at the hotel. Foley at the embassy needed to see me.

It was late and the embassy had closed for the night, but the night porter said Foley had left me a note. He fished it out of a drawer and handed it over. There was nothing on it except for an address on Hayarkon Street. A place called Fischbach.

"Is Foley waiting for me there?"

The night porter pouted. "I doubt it, sir. He'll have gone home to his missus, I should think. Left two hours ago."

I thanked the man then walked along the front, looking for Fischbach. It was the name of a German town, but I suspected it had been used as the name for a café or restaurant. I didn't know it. Most of the properties along the front had had British names before we'd left. New businesses had moved in. New names had been coined. But a German name? It seemed an odd choice. Of course, Germans in general hadn't committed the Holocaust. The Nazis were to blame, and they'd been defeated. And yet, Germany was still hated. I'd heard people talk of reparations. I'd also heard people talk of never forgiving Germany for the crimes.

On the other hand, there were plenty of German Jews in Israel. Maybe the name reflected their hometown.

Nothing to do with the war. No need to forget the name Fischbach.

I found it. It was a small café. A cluster of tables crammed inside. Two tables on the street. Foley needed to see me, so I expected the embassy man. But it wasn't Foley waiting for me at an outside table.

It was Eva Wislitsky's father, the old Russian with a large square build.

The man set down his cup of coffee, slowly and deliberately then stood up.

I walked straight up, placed both hands on the small, round table and glared at him.

"You've got a nerve."

The lighting was behind him, but I could see puffy eyes. He was either incredibly tired or he'd been crying. He looked at me and said nothing.

"Was it you... Did you try and kill me the night after I found you?"

"I'm sorry?"

"You're sorry?" At first, I thought he was apologizing for trying to kill me, then I realized he was confused. He didn't understand what I was talking about.

I said, "Did you come to my hotel room after I met you?"

He shook his head. "Where? I don't know your hotel," he said in his thick Russian accent and shook his head again. "I didn't want to kill you."

"Someone tried," I said.

Wislitsky placed a hand on his heart. "It was not me."

I breathed out. "All right, so where are they? Eva and Sergeant Duffy."

"Eva... She needs your help."

"She's a criminal. She aided a prison escape." I paused. "Hell, she's probably wanted for desertion by your own side."

Wislitsky swallowed hard. "Please. Eva says please."

"I need to find Sergeant Duffy," I said. "I don't care about your daughter."

"Yes. Eva says you will find Sergeant Duffy."

I studied his face and guessed he didn't know the whole story. He was just relaying a message. Eva couldn't come here because she'd be arrested, so she'd sent her father.

"Where is she?"

"Gam Shemuel." That was where I'd found him in the family home. That was where I thought they were going to run me through with a pitchfork or two.

"You will come?" There was desperation in his voice.

"Before I agree, I want you to tell me something."

"Yes."

I watched his eyes, reading whether he was going to tell me the truth or not. "Were you involved in the escape?"

His chest rose and fell. I saw him think about his answer.

"You were a driver," I said.

"I drove."

"You went into the mountains near the Lebanese border. Eva parked the taxi there and you brought her back."

He nodded. "But I didn't have anything to do with the escape. I never saw your man Duffy."

His eyes didn't waiver. They were hard and honest.

"All right," I said. "You have your truck here?"

He pointed down the street.

I pointed the other way. "I'll fetch my Land Rover then follow you."

I just followed his truck's taillights. There were no streetlights outside Tel Aviv. An occasional vehicle dazzled me as it came the other way but apart from those, it was just me, the two red spots in front and a million stars, sprinkled on black velvet overhead.

Less than an hour later, we had turned off the main road and were travelling through Hadera. We bumped over the rail tracks, and I knew the station and yards were over to the right. But Wislitsky didn't go that way, he didn't turn toward his home. He carried on into the darkness and I followed.

Was Wislitsky a brilliant actor? When I'd asked him about trying to kill me, I'd believed him. But the murderer from St Andrews Hotel hadn't been identified. Was I mistaken? Could it have been Eva's father? Was he now leading me into a trap?

Keep going, I told myself. *This is your only lead.*

My gut said Wislitsky wasn't the killer. Despite his age, he was big and physically strong but he was also emotional. Eva really had asked for my help and her father was worried about her.

So I kept following in the darkness.

Finally, he turned down a track and we bumped over rough ground, his taillights bouncing as though they had a life of their own.

And then he stopped, the headlights illuminating a wooden hut in the trees.

Wislitsky left his lights on and got out. The metal groan and slam of his truck door were loud in the night.

I swung out of the Land Rover and walked to where he was standing. The illuminated hut door was ten paces away.

He held up a hand and I waited.

A night bird called plaintively. And then I heard footsteps and wood creak. The door opened.

Eva Wislitsky came out, one hand shielding her eyes, the other holding a shotgun. And the gun was aimed at my chest.

THIRTY-SEVEN

The three commercial trucks were parked outside the tunnels and, after changing into white overalls, the man who'd been in black, supervised the transfer of the goods into them.

Night had fallen but a few people were on the streets. They attracted a few curious glances but nothing to cause alarm. An old crone, bent double as though her shopping bag weighed more than an armchair, asked the leader what was in the crates.

He smiled, pointed to the trucks' logo, and said, "Engine parts."

Whether or not the firm handled engine parts, he had no idea but the woman nodded as though she'd believed him then sighed with happiness as he slipped her a can of meat that he'd saved from the tunnel.

Once the trucks were fully loaded, they moved out in different directions making sure they went through check points in different places and different times. It was additional security and unnecessary. They had paperwork. They were a local firm from Haifa. The checkpoint guards had seen the lorries before. And since the Armistice, everyone was calmer.

The leader had been anxious about this first stage, but all three trucks arrived in Sarafand Garrison ahead of schedule. They transferred the goods into what had been the old armoury. Nice and secure. But they couldn't relax yet. Three men drove the empty lorries back out. One drove a jeep which had been left for them with two other vehicles. The body of the old man was in the back of the jeep, covered by a tarpaulin. It was dumped off-road, halfway between the garrison and a depot in Lod, on the outskirts of the airport previously known as Lydda.

How the haulage firm would arrange for their trucks to be collected, the leader didn't know or care. Nor did he care how the organization had arranged for two army trucks and a jeep to be available for their use.

THIRTY-EIGHT

"I'm not your enemy here," I said to Eva Wislitsky.

She still didn't trust me. We were inside the hut, which was mainly for farm tool storage. It smelled of rotten wood and fertilizer. There was an old table and four spindle chairs. The table had wonky legs.

Eva had me sit furthest from the door and out of reach of the table. There were sacks behind me filled with grain or seeds or something similar, I figured. Or maybe it was fertilizer. The sacks formed a kind of barrier. I guessed that was the idea because beyond them were the tools. I could have leapt over the sacks and grabbed a hoe as a weapon if I wanted to. Also, that is, if I also didn't mind being blasted with a hundred lead pellets.

Eva had the shotgun on the table in front of her, with one hand on the stock. Her father stood to her left, covering the door in case I made a break for it, I suppose.

"I have to be careful," she said, her eyes shining orange in the candlelight. The big candle on the table cast long, flickering shadows around the hut.

She was a wanted woman; AWOL along with aiding and abetting a prison-break. This was her hiding place. I guessed that only her father knew she was here. And now me. Which could turn out to be a problem—for me.

I said, "What happened after you hit me at the coastguard station?"

She glanced at her father, but I couldn't read what passed between them.

Turning her attention back to me, she said, "I need to know what your objective is."

"My objective?"

"Are you going to report me?"

I could have lied, but in situations like this, frankness often works best. It engenders more trust. So, I said, "That depends."

"On what?"

"On what you tell me." I paused a beat to let that sink in. Of course, it depended on what she'd done and how that impinged on my job. But also on my sense of justice.

I said, "If you're going to tell me you've committed a heinous crime, for example... you've killed innocent people..." Again I paused, trying to read her eyes. I saw no regret or even consideration. "If you killed the women and children in Junid—" I was referring to the massacre we'd found in Abu Hajjar's villa.

Her mouth dropped open. "Oh God!"

"Eva!" her father reprimanded.

"They're dead?"

I nodded. She hadn't killed them. "Slaughtered, Eva. They were slaughtered. Was that Duffy? What happened after the coastguard station?"

"We came here," she said and all the bravado and aggression she'd been showing me was replaced by something akin to fear. Or maybe it was distress. Her voice had a tremulous edge to it now. "We changed and we painted my Jeep."

"You disguised it so you could go into the mountains—to Junid."

"Yes."

"Why did you go there? Why did you visit Hajjar's family?"

"Because that was the deal," she said. "He was worried someone would kill them because he'd escaped. He needed them to go into hiding."

"So he wasn't your prisoner?"

"He—"

"He needed some persuasion." I remembered the rope in the coastguard station. "You used rope to bind Hajjar."

"Alfie—"

"Alfred Duffy?" I said just to be certain.

"Yes. He knew Hajjar wouldn't leave voluntarily. So the first part was a trick, then Alfie needed to subdue him before he recovered his weapon."

She started to explain but I held up a hand. "Hold on, let's start again. Talk me through it from the beginning."

"The beginning," she said after a slow intake of breath. Then she glanced at her father again and I knew he was involved somehow, not just because of the escape vehicle, but something more disturbing.

He said, "It's about my daughter."

I looked from him to Eva and then realized; the photograph on his mantlepiece. "Your other daughter?"

"Elsa." His voice caught as he said the name.

To Eva, I said, "Elsa's your younger sister."

"Nineteen," she said and shook her head. "Naïve. Innocent to a fault."

"She didn't approve of the war," the father said.

"She didn't approve of me fighting for our cause," Eva added with a shake of her head. "She didn't approve of me being in the Palmach and now the IDF."

No longer with the IDF, I thought. She won't be allowed back after deserting. The best she could expect is a dishonourable discharge, assuming the Israeli Army operated like the British.

"All right," I said. "So what about Elsa?"

"They took her," Eva said after a swallow. "She told me she was running away with her boyfriend."

"And she didn't?"

"I was suspicious of him." She glanced at her father. "Elsa didn't introduce him to anyone, said he was shy, but I spied on them. I knew he was up to something. And I was right.

"She went off with him one night and I followed. He drove them all the way south. I thought they were eloping to Egypt," Eva said, exasperated, "they were that far south."

"Where were they going?"

"I wasn't sure until later. It was on the edge of the Negev. I got turned back by soldiers. The odd thing was that Elsa and her boyfriend didn't. They drove through and I got stopped. I wasn't in uniform and had no credentials, so they wouldn't accept that I was an IDF lieutenant." She paused for breath. She'd been talking fast and now slowed herself down. "Afterwards I started to question whether they were IDF. They weren't Egyptian Army, but some of them might have been Arabs. Anyway, I started asking around. I'd had to go home and... well, when I asked about what might be down there apart from the border with Egypt. That's when I started hearing the rumours."

"Rumours?" I prompted when she paused.

"About a gang—the Orbit Men—operating in the hills, moving between Israel and Egypt."

"And have been doing for a long time," I said. "Before Israel, when Egypt was our friend."

"I told Alfie."

"And he knew about Abu Hajjar."

"Yes."

And then she told me the piece I knew. Duffy had served at Acre Prison. He knew Hajjar had been captured in a terrible incident four years ago and, as the head of the Orbit Men, had been put away for life. They decided to break Hajjar out of prison so that he could help rescue Elsa.

I had two burning questions, but Eva was on a roll, so I let her keep talking.

She told me about Duffy going AWOL so that he could be arrested. He'd handed himself in, after bribing one of the guards he knew. He'd been put in Hajjar's cell and then waited for the right moment. While working in Acre prison, a group of them had discovered tunnels under the citadel that led to the harbour.

Duffy knew the British Military Police would be sent to recover him, so he had to work fast and create a misleading trail. Eva knew where there was an old British Army truck. She'd *acquired it*—her words—and left it for him at the tunnel exit. With her father, she'd gone into the mountains in the north and left the taxi so they could do a switch. Her father had been the other driver, collecting her after the drop off and returning her to the IDF Jeep. They thought I'd go north, following the Bedford truck and assume Duffy had gone to Lebanon.

"I didn't expect you to find it in the mountains and guess he was in a taxi." She nodded with respect. "You were good, Captain. To then follow them south and guess Hadera—and then find the coastguard station."

"I was lucky," I said, thinking that the blow to my head was anything but lucky. "Although I wasn't smart enough to realize you were involved. So after Hadera you came here, changed, painted over the IDF markings and went to where Hajjar's family lived."

"They're really dead?"

I nodded.

She took her hand from the shotgun stock and placed it over her mouth. "Those poor children."

It was time to ask my first question. "Why did you spring Hajjar? Just because he'd been the gang's leader?"

"But he wasn't!" Eva said. "Alfie knew it. Or at least worked it out. Hajjar had a secret. Everyone else thought it was about hidden treasure, but it was about being framed."

I didn't bother telling her about the treasure I suspect had been hidden at Avdat in the wall and the clues Hajjar had written in his cell to remind him where it was. I figured that's why he'd done it. I knew from the *Count of Monte Cristo* that prisoners' minds could deteriorate. Years of confinement could send a man insane.

Hajjar had used code because he was worried someone else might uncover it.

"So, he wasn't the gang leader?"

"No, he was—still is I suppose—an expert in antiquities."

Eva didn't know Hajjar was also dead, but I didn't interrupt.

She continued: "They used him so they could carry on."

"Why him?"

"Because he stole from them and that also worked in our favour. It fitted with our plan."

And that's when she told me the plan.

THIRTY-NINE

The Orbit Men had threatened Hajjar. If he were to escape, they'd kill his family—all of them, from grandparents to children. All he had to do was pretend he was the ringleader.

They'd let him live and be imprisoned so that they could carry on. But they must have changed their practices because the press reports had ended.

I said, "Did you find out about the men who arrested him? The shootout?"

"Alfie told me. Hajjar said it had been in the hills near their base, but they pretended it was further away—Arad, I think."

I nodded. "And the shootout?"

"I don't think there was one. Or if there was, it was a totally separate incident."

"The soldiers who brought Hajjar in were working for Orbit?" I'd meant it as rhetorical. The arrest report I'd found at the Beersheba police station was fiction. That's why they had changed some of the detail including the location: editing Avdat for Arad.

"I don't know. I suppose they must have been."

"All right, let's go back to Hajjar and his motivation. He couldn't escape because of the threat to his family. In fact, he didn't escape two years ago when he had the chance. So how did Duffy persuade him?"

"Hajjar needed to get his family away. He also needed to retrieve his loot. We agreed to warn the family and then take him to Beersheba." She shook her head sadly. "We all thought they'd have time to get out."

"Couldn't he have stayed with them, made sure the family was safe? Surely the loot could have waited?" I was thinking that's what I would have done. But then I had the benefit of hindsight.

"He took a lot of persuading, but we needed him."

"To help find your sister?"

"Yes, but more specifically to help Alfie find her."

Eva went on to explain that Hajjar knew where the Orbit Men's base was and the layout. She said he'd drawn a diagram and I realized that's what had been imprinted on the map in the coastguard station.

"But if Alfie had just turned up looking for Elsa, they'd have killed him immediately. So he needed a way in."

"Something of Hajjar's," I said. "Something from his stash."

"It's amazing," she said. "Incredibly special. Before stealing from the Orbit Men, he'd found one of the most important documents of Judaism. A scroll. A handwritten section of the Torah."

"The Zechariah Ben 'Anan manuscript," Eva's father explained. It meant nothing to me except for the fact that the Torah was the basis for Christianity's Old Testament.

"That was the trade," Eva said. "We help Hajjar and he gives us the *Writings* to present to the gang. Duffy would pass himself off as a criminal to gain their trust, their respect and get into their base."

"But Hajjar didn't want to be helped."

"No, but once he'd escaped, he had to go along with our plan. Before we left the coastguard station, Alfie was convinced Hajjar was committed."

"What went wrong?" I asked.

She nodded. Yes, something hadn't worked out.

"First, he tried to stay in Junid with his family. We had to convince him to show us the antiquity rather than give us directions."

"You still didn't really trust him?"

"Absolutely we didn't trust him."

"Did your *persuasion* involve a gun?"

"It was the only way. He had to see we were serious."

"So you shot his finger off?"

She shook her head violently. "No, that happened later!"

"All right," I said, "The family—when you left, the family was still alive."

"Yes!"

"You went to Avdat," I said.

"How did you…? Never mind. Yes, we went to the ruins at Avdat. It took two days because of getting across the border and a lot of army activity on the road to Beersheba.

"You found the loot in a wall," I said.

"I don't know where he hid it. We had to promise to stay at the bottom of the hill so that we couldn't see. And it all seemed fine until Alfie realized Hajjar was going to con us. He wanted to get his stuff and take my jeep."

She paused and looked up. I thought she was visualizing what had happened before speaking. But maybe she was planning a lie.

She said, "He came at us with a gun and threatened us."

"You were still armed?"

"Yes. Hajjar didn't know we both had weapons. He'd only seen mine. So, when he forced me to drop my gun, Alfie moved. He dived away and drew his. Hajjar was caught by surprise and fired—although he didn't because it went off in his hand. I suppose he'd never fired or cleaned the gun. It had been hidden with his loot."

I said, "It blew a finger off."

"Yes. And before you ask, I helped him by wrapping a cloth around it to stop the bleeding."

"Did you kill him, Eva?"

"No."

"I wouldn't blame you if you did."

"No," she said again. And I believed her but mostly because of her reaction to the death of his family and referring to him in the present tense earlier.

"All right, so what happened next?"

"I'm not proud," she said, "but we left him. Alfie said Hajjar couldn't be trusted so we left him some water, and drove away."

"He's dead," I said, "Buried alive."

"Buried...? That wasn't us."

"You drove to their camp?"

"The gang's? Not straight away. We went back to Beersheba and bought another car." She glanced away to the left and I interpreted this as discomfort.

"What aren't you telling me?" I asked. Then I guessed: "You bought it with the antiquity?"

She looked horrified. "Not the *Writings*, not that! We took the ancient document, but also a bag of Roman coins. I used some to buy the car. The original plan was that I would just wait in Beersheba and we'd use the train if necessary, but I wanted to have a backup in case the trains stopped running—and we found out they aren't anyway. And if we lost the Jeep, I needed to make sure we had something to get Elsa home."

The father pressed his face with open palms, and I suspected he was wiping wet cheeks.

Eva continued: "Instead of leaving me in Beersheba, I followed in the car."

"To where?"

"Toward Nitzana."

Of course, the town on the border with Egypt. The road to Avdat split away from the one to Nitzana.

I said, "So Duffy had the goods and the map showing the layout of the base. What happened?"

Her bosom rose and fell. I saw her jaw tense.

"I watched as he approached the guards on the road a few miles before the town. I'm pretty sure they were the same ones, looking like IDF but weren't. Alfie got out. I guessed he was telling them he had something valuable. I saw them take his gun, which we expected. Then one of them hit him with the butt of his rifle. Just like that!" she breathed deeply again. "Then they threw him into the back and one of them drove off in the Jeep."

"So he's there and still alive?"

She clenched her teeth before she spoke. "I hope so."

I nodded encouragingly. "If they'd wanted him dead, they'd have just killed him on the spot. You should take heart from the fact that they just knocked him out."

"Thank you," she said.

The father leaned forward, his hands pressing down on the table so hard that it titled. Since Eva's shock over the massacre of Hajjar's family, her hand had been off the shotgun. The father's hand was now beside the stock.

He said, "Will you help us?"

"You should go to the police," I said.

Eva shook her head.

"Not you," I said. "You'll be arrested. But your father could go. Or he could tell the army. I got to know the IDF man in charge in Beersheba. I'm sure he'll—"

"We don't know who to trust," she said. "Hajjar said that lots of people are involved. Senior people. Your friend may be involved, for all you know. He's operating close enough to Nitzana, so…"

I nodded. "I suppose you could be right."

"I am right. You can't trust anyone." She looked at me pleadingly. "Except for you that is. We know you're here for a different reason."

"To capture your boyfriend," I said pointedly. She hadn't told me about their relationship, but she didn't deny it. Why else would Duffy been so willing to help her?

"So will you help?"

"You need to understand something, Eva. After we're through, I will have to take Duffy back with me." I watched her face again trying to judge whether I could trust her.

"I understand. You can trust me," she said. Which I took as a warning. I'd be a fool to trust her after everything she'd done.

I said, "You tried to get a replacement gun after yours jammed. You hadn't expected to shoot a snake in the grass." I was referring to when I'd taken her into the scrub looking for clues when all along, she knew we'd find no evidence of Duffy.

"You know that."

"But what I don't know is whether you'd have shot me."

"I won't lie to you, Captain. It crossed my mind."

"At least you only cuckolded me at the coastguard station."

"You still haven't answered my question," she said.

I nodded toward the shotgun on the table. If I didn't help them, they could shoot me. One less thing to worry about. I could report Eva's whereabouts to the IDF. She was AWOL, after all. Just like Duffy.

The father took his hands away from the shotgun and leaned away. The table righted and Eva reached for the gun. I prepared to spring for cover. I'd grab the hoe, after all.

She was fast, but the gun didn't swing up toward me. In a well-practiced move, she broke it open and popped out the shells. Then she closed it and placed the shotgun back on the table.

There had been another question in my mind. I wondered if it would come up in the explanation, but it hadn't. I knew everything about the lines and codes from Hajjar's Acre cell except for one thing.

I said, "Have you seen a man with a thin, neat beard. He's got exceptionally smooth, shiny skin."

She shook her head. "I don't know. Doesn't sound that specific. Why?"

"He tried to kill me, and he may have killed Hajjar."

"OK," she said uncertain where I was going with this.

"He's apparently Shabak."

"I've not heard of that."

"Your new secret security service. I suppose, like our MI5 or the American CIA or maybe FBI."

She shook her head.

"You still haven't answered my question. Will you help us?"

"If I don't, I'm free to go?"

She inclined her head. "I won't be happy, but yes, you can leave."

I looked at her father and saw agreement in his sad eyes.

I said, "I've made sense of a lot of what Hajjar wrote on his cell walls, but there's one thing I don't understand."

"What's that?"

"Have you heard of something called black heart?"

"I know it." She squinted at me, her face distorting in the flickering candlelight.

"And?"

"And I'll trade. You help us and I'll tell you what it is."

"Agreed."

I thought she wouldn't tell me straight away because once she'd said it, her position would be weak.

"You don't think I'll tell you yet," she said reading my mind.

I smiled and shook my head.

"Well, you're wrong, Captain Carter. I'll tell you because—well, I want to demonstrate you can trust me, because I'll trust you to stick to your word. I don't have your word you'll help, don't I?"

"You do."

"In that case, black heart isn't a thing."

She paused, I waited.

"It's a name. Black Heart is the name of the true leader of the Orbit Men."

FORTY

"So, who is he, this Black Heart?" I asked as we walked out of the shed.

"Specifically? I have no idea," Eva said. "We'll find out when we get to their base near Nitzana."

"You know that?"

She shrugged. She was speculating. I figured she was offering a further incentive for me to work with her.

We walked toward my Land Rover.

She said, "If we leave now, we'll be there by first light."

I stopped in the headlights. "No."

She looked at me, confused. "But you said you'd help."

"Two things," I said. "Firstly, we're not rushing to Nitzana. I need to know what I'm dealing with. Duffy went in there with a half-baked plan and look what happened."

"We could still leave tonight," she said.

"That's the second thing. There's no *we* in this operation. I'm going alone."

What I didn't add was that I still didn't trust her. She hadn't told me very much. She didn't know very much. If I rescued Duffy, she wouldn't be happy that I had to take him back. If her sister Elsa was dead—which I suspected had a high probability—Eva would be distraught. Who knew how she'd behave in that situation?

She started to complain, but I raised a hand and swung into the Land Rover. "You're a wanted deserter, Lieutenant," I said. "It's an unnecessary complication."

She shook her head and I saw flames in her dark eyes. However she had no words. She couldn't vocalize her anger and frustration.

I added: "Four days. Give me that."

She wrote a number on a piece of paper. "You can leave a message for me on this."

I nodded. "If I'm not back at my hotel in Tel Aviv by Monday, then come looking for me." I gave her the number for the provost marshal in Cyprus. "And speak to Colonel Dexter. He'll want to know."

She sighed and finally found her voice again. "You're crazy."

"You're crazy," Dave Rosen said when I saw him later. We were in a restaurant on the front. Not the one where I'd met Eva's father. This was big and expensive, and one of the few still open at such a late hour.

The night was clammy, but the owners recognised the inspector, and we were given the best table. We had a view and felt the breeze coming off the sea.

There were only a few people I trusted with my life. Dexter was one and Dave Rosen was another. I needed to tell him what was going on, despite Eva Wislitsky's warning. She couldn't involve or inform the police or army, but I could.

My friend rubbed his eyes, and I noticed how dark-rimmed they looked. I'd assumed it was the light at first, but now I saw that his eyes looked sunken and shaded. He was exhausted.

"Is everything all right?" I asked.

He took a long breath. "The pressures of the job," he said with a sigh. "The increased responsibility of being a full inspector."

I remembered what his sergeant, Ben Meir had told me about a difficult case. "How's it going? The mutilated young girl murder?"

He frowned at me.

"Sergeant Ben Meir told me," I said.

He nodded. "Of course. Well, we have a name at last. A boyfriend came looking for her." Rosen took a sip and stared through the window at the inky sea. He shook his head, looked at me and then away again.

"Increased responsibility. I'm looking after five sub stations now. More cases, more staff." Rosen took another sip of beer. "And pressure from above to clean up."

"Clean up?"

"Bribery and corruption in the force." Then he surprised me by chuckling and taking a bigger drink of his beer. "Give me the old days when we had a real enemy, and we knew who they were."

Now that made me laugh. Rosen was a Jew and most of the army, at least, considered the Jews to have been the enemy. Of course the terrorists came in the guise of the Stern Gang and Irgun, but anyone could help them. Teenagers were the worst. They seemed innocent enough but could be helping the terrorists. We were seen as the oppressors acting as a barrier to the creation of the promised new state.

We were undoubtedly *their* enemy.

The food came and was exceptional. We made small talk, until we cleaned our plates.

"That was excellent," I said. "Thank you."

"So what are you going to do—about Duffy?"

I told him my plan. Reconnaissance was the first thing I'd do. Eva Wislitsky had lied to me many times before. Now she was telling me that Duffy had been taken on the road to Nitzana. She'd told me that the gang were operating out of or near the town. I didn't know whether that was true.

Mr. Wislitsky seemed genuinely upset, so his younger daughter could be missing. But Eva Wislitsky was a consummate liar. I didn't trust a word that came out of her mouth.

I needed to know the lay of the land. Was Duffy working for them? Was he a prisoner? If the latter, I needed to assess the likelihood of rescue.

"You can't do it alone," Rosen said.

"If necessary, I'll involve the IDF captain in Beersheba."

"I spoke to him. Kramer, wasn't it?"

I nodded. "He's a good man. I don't know who I can trust, but if necessary, I'll seek his help."

"At least tell him where you're going."

It was a reasonable request. Kramer didn't have to know what I was doing, just my destination. Just in case I didn't return. I agreed.

Rosen said, "I wish I could let you have Sergeant Ben Meir again. Unfortunately—"

I almost commented on the lack of contribution made by Ben Meir last time. He'd been good company on the way back but had zero involvement when I most needed him. However, I appreciate that he'd been unwell. Otherwise he'd have been with me at the ruins and then maybe the Shabak man wouldn't have almost killed me. Maybe.

"—workload," he said after the distraction of paying the bill. "I can't afford to lose anyone, let alone one of my best men over the next few days."

I hadn't expected him to although he did make me promise that I wouldn't do anything stupid. There was no rush. Rather than charge in and get myself killed, I could apply for reinforcements. Or at least, the British government could apply. The Israelis had let three of us operate last time I'd come here and given us support in the form of manpower.

I wasn't convinced because I knew how long these things could take. Bureaucracy was undoubtedly greater and slower due to the unfavoured position Britain held with the new state. The paper moving sluggishly from one outbox to an inbox and then another. Like treacle.

On the way back to my hotel, Rosen asked what time, I'd leave in the morning.

I checked my watch. It was almost midnight. I planned to leave before daybreak and get most of the journey done before the heat of the day hit me.

"In five hours?" he said. "Nowhere is open."

"I'll get provisions in Beersheba."

He nodded and shook my hand warmly, and in the morning, I found a bag in the back of my Land Rover. Rosen had packed bread, meat and fruit. Enough food for two days, I thought. He'd also provided two canisters of water.

With a brief note, I also found a bar of chocolate. "For your sweet tooth," it said. And added: "But eat it before it melts!"

I devoured the chocolate immediately and set off for the mysterious town of Nitzana.

FORTY-ONE

I drove into Beersheba again, approaching from the west, seeing nothing but Jewish settlements and settlers. People arrived at the rail station in packed buses, carrying their bags and bundles of hope, looking for their future. A future without conflict, they'd pray.

The police station looked just the same. No police, just army men acting like the police. Making people feel more secure, I supposed.

I parked outside and walked past a few men. I didn't recognise them but then again, I hadn't expected to come back. I caught a couple of glances and nodded at them in case they remembered me.

I knocked on Kramer's office door and let myself in.

There was a man behind the desk. Folded in his chair he looked rangy—tall and thin. Not Kramer. The name on the desk plate read Colonel P Schattenmann.

He looked up from a pile of paperwork, his face hot and sweaty. It was also dark for most Jews. I figured he was part-African, maybe Ethiopian, based on his physique. His surname had a German origin: Shadow man. I suspected it related to his heritage.

"Yes?" He eyed me with curiosity then leaned one way to look behind me. I guess he was checking whether I was alone, or someone had shown me in.

Then he repeated, "Yes?" He sounded somewhere between stressed and frustrated. Perhaps both at the same time.

"Captain Kramer?" I asked. "Is he here?"

"You are?"

I told him.

He blinked and focused on me. I saw a hand move from the desktop to below. For a horrible second, I thought he might draw a gun. However, when the hand reappeared a breath later, it was empty and extended toward me. Not a handshake, a request.

"Your papers?"

I handed over my documentation.

He glanced at it then met my gaze. "I don't want any trouble."

"Colonel—" I began, then heard the click of a gun being cocked behind me. I turned and saw three soldiers, all armed, all pointing their weapons at me. The man at the front was a sergeant. The other two were corporals. They had rifles. No use in this office. But the sergeant had a handgun.

I turned back to the colonel and shook my head. I figured he'd rung an alarm bell when he'd reached under the table. He'd called for security.

"What's going on?" I asked.

"I need to hold you for questioning," Schattenmann said tersely. Then he spoke to the sergeant. "Take him away."

I was escorted from the colonel's office. The soldiers seemed nervous of me, as though I would try and bolt. Maybe try to grab a weapon and they'd find out how impractical a rifle was at close quarters.

I complied with instructions and walked calmly to a desk where I was processed by another man. He took my details and I emptied my pockets. Threatening a search, he asked if I was carrying a weapon. Honesty was the best policy until this was sorted out, so I pulled up my trouser leg and let one of the soldiers remove my ankle holster and Berretta.

They searched me anyway and removed my watch and shoes. Perhaps they'd had a bad experience involving a prisoner and footwear.

Less nervous, but still uncomfortable, they escorted me to the rear of the building. It was stuffy back there. Hotter than at the front, with little or no air. The cell had thick concrete walls on three sides. Only the entrance had bars. There was a slit at the rear, high up. Maybe that was a window, but air didn't circulate.

The cell block was dimly lit and I couldn't see light through the slit. If I was held for hours or days, there was no way to judge the time by light and shadow.

I stepped inside and saw relief on the soldiers' faces.

One of the corporals locked the door.

"What's going on?" I asked the sergeant.

He shook his head. Either he didn't know or couldn't tell me.

"At least tell me where Captain Kramer is," I said.

"Been reassigned, sir."

The *sir* made me smile. I had no official status in Israel.

"And Colonel Schattenmann?"

"Come in as a replacement." He paused, and a thought appeared to cross his face. Then he said, "Sit tight. I'm sure this will be cleared up soon."

It was a few minutes before nine in the morning. There was a background buzz of a working police station and town life. They left me.

I should be on my way soon, I thought. The Colonel will clear things with his HQ and I'd be released.

I sat on a bench, leaned back, and waited.

And waited.

More than two hours later, I called out. There was a bucket for a toilet, but no drinking water.

Without a word, I was given a canteen before being left alone again.

I'd been in similar situations before. The trick was to stay calm and rest. Breathe and ignore the rising heat. Given water, drink it no matter how bad it tastes—and prison water usually tasted bad: warm and metallic at best. At worst it could make you wonder whether you'd need the metal bucket sooner than normal.

The water wasn't too warm, and it tasted clean. I gulped it down and immediately felt better. I just had to wait, and things would get resolved. It was all a misunderstanding. Schattenmann didn't know me, and Kramer wasn't here. I'd be released soon and get on with my mission. The day was already too hot. I'd learned that lesson the first time I'd been in the Negev. My reconnaissance could wait. Evening would be better.

I removed my shirt and rolled it up. Using it as a pillow, I lay on the bench, closed my eyes, and listened to the background noise.

After a few hours, a soldier came into the block. But he wasn't there to release me. Making no eye contact, he pushed a plate into my cell and walked away. There was a chunk of bread and a bowl of something creamy.

I asked him for the time but if he answered, I didn't catch it.

The food in the bowl was like gritty porridge, sweet but otherwise tasteless. The bread was dry but edible when washed down with water.

I sat back again. About an hour later, another man came in and asked for the plate.

I skimmed it under the cell bars.

"What time is it?" I asked.

After a hesitation, he told me it was about half-past three.

"Please could I see the Colonel?" I asked.

The guard looked at me blankly.

"I've been here most of the day," I said unnecessarily. I stood and approached the cell door. "Perhaps I can explain what—"

"It's out of the Colonel's hands," the guard said backing away.

I questioned what he meant but he said nothing more. He just turned and walked away.

I was alone again. At least the temperature was easing.

It was cold when I awoke. The lights didn't change, but the temperature told me it was night, maybe very early morning. Any residual heat from the concrete walls had long dissipated.

The daytime police station hubbub was gone.

Donning my shirt, I began exercising, partly for fitness but mostly warmth. After a few minutes, the shirt was off again.

I was well into my well-practiced routine, although running on the spot and jumping rather than pounding streets, when the block door opened.

I paid the man no attention as he just stood and watched from the doorway. Perhaps he was intrigued or bemused.

"Captain Carter?" He strode to the cell. "What...?"

I stopped jogging. It was the first face I'd recognized since returning to Beersheba. The IDF soldier who had been with Kramer at the Avdat ruins.

He said, "I heard a noise back here. Didn't realize it was you, sir." Then he asked what had happened, and I told him about arriving, meeting Colonel Schattenmann yesterday morning and having been in the cell since.

He was just a corporal with an authority which stretched only as far as offering me an apology and a cup of coffee.

I accepted and a few minutes later, I was handed a chicory-based drink laced with enough sugar to mask the bitterness.

Then he told me what little he knew. Captain Kramer had been reassigned without notice and replaced by Colonel Schattenmann.

"The man's a pen-pusher from Jerusalem," the corporal explained. Rumour is that Kramer was being punished for a misdemeanour. Although it's nonsense. The captain's a good man. It'll just be a misunderstanding."

"In the army?" I said with sarcasm. "A misunderstanding?"

He shrugged and smiled ruefully.

"What did you hear about me?" I asked.

"Nothing except a prisoner was being held in here. POWs are usually in the pens outside in the courtyard. I heard you were an officer and were waiting for someone to interview you." He paused and looked awkward. "You haven't…?"

"I've not done anything wrong. I came here to speak to Captain Kramer. I really am just looking for a deserter."

He nodded, relieved. "Then I'm sure it'll all be cleared up quickly when the official gets here."

"Thank you, Corporal—"

"Bastuni."

"Thank you Corporal Bastuni," I said.

He checked on me again an hour later with more chicory coffee and a bowl of figs. His shift finished in another hour but assured me he'd have a word with his replacement. I'd get better treatment, and everything would be sorted soon.

He was mistaken on both counts.

The temperature climbed from chilly to pleasant to uncomfortable. The air became thicker. I called for someone to replace my toilet bucket, but my request fell on deaf ears.

I returned to my position on the bench with my shirt rolled up as a pillow. With my eyes closed, breathing calmly, I waited.

Lunch was a thin soup with stale bread and delivered by the untalkative guard from yesterday.

Then, in the afternoon, they finally came for me.

The three guards didn't speak except for the sergeant in charge who instructed me to turn around with hands at my back.

I put on my shirt and dusted myself down. Taking my time. Then I turned with my hands behind me. They entered and the manacles were snapped around my wrists. With one ahead and flanked by the other two, I was escorted from my now stinking cell.

We left the cell block, walking along the corridor. I thought we'd go upstairs but we passed the flight of stone steps I'd been brought down yesterday. We kept going. One soldier coughed and I guessed the stale, dusty air was getting to him. I was used to it by now.

There was a light at the end by the stairs and another a long way off. It was a tunnel under the police station, maybe going its whole length. We walked. Both men behind me coughed a couple of times and then we came to a series of doors where the sergeant stopped.

One door was open. I followed the sergeant inside and saw blank concrete walls and nothing but a hard chair and a desk. And a big man standing behind the desk.

I knew then that I wasn't going to like what was coming next.

FORTY-TWO

There are two types of interrogator; I suppose you could categorize them as brains versus brawn. My initial impression may have been doing this giant a disservice. Maybe I was wrong to judge his ugly, twisted face. His heavy brow had lumps above each eye suggesting Neanderthal ancestry and it was impossible to imagine that he had much intelligence behind his malevolent eyes.

Of course, the lumps may have been caused by repeated headbutts.

I was on the chair with my hands around the back. The guards had left. The door was closed.

As I'd come into the room, I'd registered what was on the table. Things I didn't like the look of.

One of those things was now in the giant's hand. A cosh.

He took a pace and stood over me. Intimidating. I could smell his stale sweat, although I'm sure my body was equally rank.

I looked him in the eye. He'd speak first.

But he didn't speak. He didn't even wait for me to break under the intimidation. He just smashed the cosh into my face. White light and pain exploded. I tasted blood. My tongue found an upper left molar that now moved. However, the rest were still firm.

The Neanderthal stepped back. I'd thought about kicking him, but his positioning had been good. Any effort from me would be weak. It'd have no impact except for encouraging further violence from the giant.

"Don't bother with the name, rank and number," he said and despite his gruff, possibly Arab accent, I heard intelligence. Not a Neanderthal after all. Which was a good thing. Maybe he played on his appearance, maybe he wasn't a thug.

Or maybe he was. He hit me again, and I spat blood onto my shirt.

"What?" I said, realizing he may have spoken first, but he'd won the game of getting me to speak. "Just ask me what you need to know. I'm not hiding anything."

He put the cosh on the table but kept his hand close.

"Ask me a question," I said, spitting out a little more blood.

"Who is Alfred Duffy?"

I told him. Not much, just his position in the army and that he was AWOL. "I'm here to find him and take him back."

"Where is he?"

"I don't know."

"Why are you here?"

"Because I believe he's been through Beersheba."

"Going where?"

"I don't know," I said.

I saw the giant's jaw tense, and light dimmed in his eyes, like a cloud veils the moon.

He picked up something from the table and showed me as he slowly pushed his fingers through a knuckleduster. "What is Duffy's connection to Abu Hajjar?"

"Who?"

He took a pace to my left. I imagined a metal glove doing more damage than a cosh to my face.

"Why did Duffy escape with Hajjar?"

The giant didn't wait for an answer. As soon as he'd finished his question, the fist piled into my left ribs. I tensed at the last second. I did my best to ride the blow, but the chair was fixed to the floor and I couldn't move far.

"Where's Duffy?" he asked.

I shook my head and he hit me again in the same spot.

I'd been beaten before. In Cyprus, hooded in a shed, I thought I would die at the hands—and feet—of a mob. That time it had been a threat. A warning. This was different. The giant wanted information and he didn't care how much damage he caused to get it.

I closed my eyes. He asked another question but I wasn't listening. I was remembering a case during the British mandate. An SAS undercover operative had been captured and interrogated in a similar way. He'd survived and I'd heard his story third-hand. He'd said, the secret was to remain civil or say nothing. Make them realize that beating you gets no answers. Hold out until they can be reasonable. We are British! Make them appreciate they'll get more from a polite, gentlemanly conversation rather than thuggish behaviour.

I wondered whether the giant had been his interrogator. Did he know that rule?

Pain burst like a water balloon across my chest. Air, spit and probably blood rushed from my mouth. I tried to dissociate. I tried to picture myself in the boxing ring, taking blows and ignoring the pain. *Dodge and weave*, I told myself.

Quick jabs. Look for an opening and then counter.

He was shouting now, and I dimly registered more pain but couldn't place it.

Then it stopped. Abruptly.

There was another man in the room. I listened and heard Colonel Schattenmann's voice behind me.

A minute later, the door closed and I was alone.

For the first ten minutes or so, I thought it was a tactic. The giant would return and start again. Break me down in stages. Maybe psychologically the prisoner would go from despair to relief to despair and start talking.

But after about half an hour, the three guards came in. I was given a ladle of water and, after I'd gulped it down, one of them wiped my face with a wet cloth. My tongue checked my teeth. More teeth were loose and there was a gap where a lower premolar had once been. My body felt battered and bruised, like I'd been run over by a three-ton truck, but I sensed no broken bones.

The guards gave me a moment, then helped me stand. By the time we started moving, I was beginning to feel half-human.

The sergeant led, and the other two held me under the arms. We went along the corridor and then up the steps. Slowly.

The journey was arduous, and I was focused more on putting one foot before the other than on our destination. However, I registered climbing a second flight of steps and lots of doors. I heard far-off voices but saw no one else. Not until we went into another room.

I saw natural light streaming though dusty windows. It wasn't like the dungeon. But the figure waiting inside was just as intimidating as the giant had been. With his inscrutable shiny face and cold dark eyes, it was the man from the ruins. The man who had almost killed me. The Shabak man.

FORTY-THREE

The early afternoon sun beat down on the small convoy as it rumbled through the abandoned gates that marked the boundary of Sarafand Barracks. Two army trucks led by an army jeep made their way slowly along the dusty road.

Their previous convoy had passed through multiple checkpoints on the journey from Acre. They'd had their cargo checked twice. Of course, the real cargo had been hidden at the rear of each truck. Soldiers never suspected a thing. They weren't looking for what was in the back. Despite there being little reason for such a shipment. Commercial trucks would stand out. Army vehicles would not.

They reached the open road; the jeep crunching along ahead of the trucks which kicked up plumes of dust.

The driver looked at him and he nodded back, acting confident. The truth was, he would only breathe easy once they'd passed the halfway point. Two hours to Beersheba. Two more hours to the border.

Beersheba was the greatest risk. There was still a large army presence there. But the boss had promised the army would be suitably distracted. The gang need only keep their nerve and continue playing their roles.

An IDF jeep tore toward them.

"Just nod," the leader said. They'll shoot right by.

But they didn't. The jeep's headlights flashed. They were slowing.

Would the leader be challenged? Would his paperwork hold up?

He stole a glance at the gun he had under the dash. If he had no choice, he'd have to do it. Then it would be a race to the border before the murders were discovered.

The leader waved for his driver to slow. Behind them, the trucks responded with grinding brakes.

The other jeep trundled alongside. Windows came down.

"A mile up the road, it's bad," the passenger of the genuine army jeep said. "Take it easy with those trucks."

He smiled and threw a salute and then the driver gunned his engine, and they disappeared.

The convoy continued. They need only keep their nerve and continue playing their roles.

When the buildings of Beersheba finally appeared ahead, the leader tensed, gripping his pistol under his jacket. But just as promised, their passage through the city proceeded without incident. There were no army vehicles and he saw only a handful of soldiers. There were lots of civilians, although they barely glanced up from their cigarettes and newspapers.

Once clear of the town, with only empty wilderness ahead, the leader finally allowed himself to relax. Nothing else to worry about now—just miles and miles of open desert. As the convoy turned onto the final eastward road, he permitted himself a fierce grin of anticipation.

Beersheba disappeared in the dust behind them and the road started its long curve. The leader shifted in his seat, trying to ease his stiff back muscles. Almost there. Just a straight shot south now. He could practically taste success, like the mineral tang of the desert air on his tongue. All the planning and preparation had led to this moment.

Not long now, he thought. *Not long now.*

FORTY-FOUR

The man with the neat beard and shiny face was sitting behind a desk. He watched me unblinking as I was put in a chair with my hands over its straight back.

"Leave," the Shabak guy said. It was a simple word, not loud, not barked, but it carried a ton of authority, maybe menace too.

I heard the door shut behind me. Shabak-man's eyes stayed on me, and I wondered whether he ever blinked. I noticed again how smooth his tanned skin was. Even the fixed ridges on his forehead looked unmoving and polished.

On his desk were my papers. He picked them up as an illustration rather than for reading.

"What are you doing here, Captain Carter?"

I met his gaze. "Who are you?"

"The man asking the questions."

"As you can see, I've already been asked lots of questions."

"Did you answer them?"

"No."

There was an open window to my left. The air in the room was much better than fetid cell and dungeon rooms. I breathed deeply and slowly and felt a little better. Outside, in the courtyard, I heard the tramp of boots. Soldiers marching.

"Any serious damage?" he asked.

"No," I said.

The Shabak man raised one of the documents. "This says you are assigned to the British Consulate."

Despite the threat he posed, I sensed he was taking the civil approach. After a pause, I answered, "I am."

"What were you doing in Avdat?"

"Looking for someone."

"Who?"

"Sergeant Alfred Duffy. British Army deserter."

My second interrogator waited for more. I said nothing and waited him out. Was he also going to ask about Duffy's connection with Hajjar?

Eventually Shabak-man raised the second paper. "Your authority to travel to Akko." He used the Hebrew name for Acre.

"Yes."

"Authority to collect Sergeant Alfred Duffy from the prison and leave the country."

"Prior to the authority to stay, working for the consulate."

"Is Duffy relevant to your diplomatic duties?"

Of course he wasn't. We both knew that the role was a cover for my continued activities.

He said, "And you were in possession of a concealed weapon."

"I surrendered it."

He scrutinized me. "Before it was found. You'd already been detained and were about to be searched."

I could have mentioned that my ankle holster was rarely located by IDF searches but it would have served no purpose.

He put down the papers and placed his hands flat on the table, leaning toward me. "Tell me the truth, Captain. What are you doing here?"

"Looking for my deserter."

"I don't believe you." He leaned back. "Perhaps I should send you back to your cell. Perhaps another day or two will loosen your tongue."

I shrugged. "It's the truth."

"You were looking for the deserter in Avdat?"

I said, "Did you kill the other man?"

For the first time, I saw something else in his eyes, although I couldn't read it.

"What other man?"

Interesting. The Neanderthal had known, but Shabak-man didn't. They weren't working together.

I made a decision. I told him about Abu Hajjar and the escape from Acre. I told him everything except for Eva Wislitsky's involvement.

At the end, I said, "You didn't know about Hajjar."

I didn't expect a response and was surprised when he confirmed it by shaking his head. He was thinking.

After a pause, he said, "Has anyone mentioned today's date?"

"Relating to my investigation? No."

"So the timing is a coincidence?"

"You'll need to tell me more," I said.

He thought again. "Give me a name. Who can vouch for you?"

I gave him Inspector David Rosen's details.

"Anyone else?"

"If you don't mind trusting a Brit, then if you want a full reference, the provost marshal of the 221 MP in Cyprus would be a good starting point." I gave him Lieutenant Colonel Jim Dexter's details.

Without a comment, Shabak-man stood and left the room. I heard someone else come into the room before the door closed and figured he'd been replaced by a guard.

There was a clock on the wall, and I watched the minute hand move through forty-two steps before my interrogator returned. At least that's what I assumed when I heard voices outside the room and the door open. But it wasn't Shabak-man. It was a different sergeant and two guards.

The sergeant instructed me to stand and did so with difficulty. My legs had stiffened after the walk from the dungeon and then sitting again. The chair went over as I transferred my weight getting up.

Walking in the same formation as before, with a man on each arm, they walked me along the corridor. I sensed tension. Instead of taking the stairs down to the cell block, we kept going.

"Where are you taking me?" I asked.

No one replied.

Was this another way down to the dungeon and a beating by the Neanderthal?

I stopped my shuffle-walk. The guards tugged at me, but progress wouldn't be easy. The sergeant at the front turned and drew his gun.

"Where are you taking me?" I asked again.

He spoke reluctantly. "Outside."

"Outside?"

"You're not our problem anymore." His jaw clenched. "Now let's move."

I stayed put. The soldier on my left pushed me with his free hand, urging me on. It was a foolish move. I was exaggerating. My condition wasn't as bad as I must have looked. I could have walked unaided. And I could have swivelled and taken the guard's gun—despite my cuffs. Maybe. If I'd been desperate.

I looked hard at the sergeant and shook my head.

He said, "All right. The man you just talked to—"

"The intelligence agent?"

The expression on his face suggested he had no idea who the man had been. He was just doing what he'd been told.

The sergeant said, "All I know is he's taking you back."

"Back?"

A facial shrug. "To Jerusalem, I suppose."

"All right," I said. Happy that I wasn't about to be summarily executed but disappointed that I was still in custody and going in the wrong direction.

I started walking again although they didn't help me this time. We went to the end of the building and down a flight of steps on the opposite side. Each step jarred me. Pain stabbed in my left side, and I realized I wasn't just bruised.

There was a Jeep waiting at the door. The Shabak man sat behind the wheel with more expression on his face than I'd seen before. Frustrated, I surmised.

He indicated that I should be put into the passenger seat.

"Cuffs?" I said to the sergeant. "Can't sit with these behind my back."

"They stay on," Shabak-man said.

"Really?" I tried to read his eyes, but they were just cold and expressionless.

"Get in, Captain."

I stepped up and shuffled onto the seat with exaggerated awkwardness, although twisting made me wince. He didn't care.

The sergeant shut the door and turned to go.

"My things?" I asked.

He used a thumb to indicate the rear of the jeep. I could have swivelled and presumably seen my personal things in a box. I didn't. No point in checking. No point in aggravating my injury. They were there, or they were not.

We pulled away and I concentrated on protecting my ribs from the movement.

Someone was standing at the main entrance. Colonel Schattenmann watching me go. A relieved pen-pusher, I suspected. His problem was being taken away.

Everything looked like it had yesterday when I'd arrived. I scanned the outside of the police station and then streets. I don't know whether I wanted to catch sight of the Neanderthal or not, but I didn't see him.

The road worsened, and I shifted in my seat, trying to get comfortable. We hit a rock and the jolt unseated me.

"Injured?" he asked as the last of the town buildings were behind us.

"Ribs. It won't look good when I arrive battered and bruised."

"Who's going to care?" He shot me a glance and I had an awful premonition. In the police station, I'd imagined them shooting me against a wall. Now I had a flash of being shot and dumped in the desert.

Then the Shabak man surprised me.

He laughed.

FORTY-FIVE

It wasn't an evil laugh. The man just chuckled and as I wondered if my concerns were unfounded, he said, "We'll stop up ahead."

We came to a village, and he parked out of sight of the road. He got out. Now I saw the box in the rear. He reached into it, pulled out my shoes, and handed them to me.

I turned my back and showed him my cuffs.

"Don't do anything you'll regret," he said and the next moment, my hands were free. I rubbed the skin where the metal had chafed it.

"Let's get you looked at," he said. Carrying the box, he walked into the nearest building. It was a home. Two rooms at the front and probably the same at the back.

The Shabak man called out in Hebrew and an elderly man appeared from the room behind. He had a wrinkled pointy face like a rubber glove puppet with the fingers drawn together. The two men embraced and spoke quietly while the old man threw glances my way.

Then he disappeared and the Shabak guy said, "He'll get you cleaned up."

The pinched-faced old man did more than clean me up. He ran his hands over my body and made me wince as he checked my ribs. Then he bound my chest with a bandage. After confirming it was just a couple of ribs I'd cracked, he gave me oil to smear on my gums. I figured it was either clove oil or something similar because it eased my aching teeth. Despite this, I found my tongue regularly checking the gap where the premolar had been.

"You look a little better," Shabak-man said.

I thanked them both.

"Are you hungry?" Without waiting for a response, he spoke in Hebrew and the old man abruptly scurried away.

We found a rickety wooden table and I was relieved that the ribs didn't trouble me as I sat.

From the back, I heard chatter, like an argument between the man and a woman. A minute later, the old man was back. He gave us each a glass of something lukewarm. I'm not sure what it was, maybe a fruit-based tea. It was sweet and, after the second sip, reasonably palatable.

I said, "You spoke to Dexter and Rosen?"

"Just your provost marshal." He nodded. "After checking him out as well."

I wondered if that meant he'd investigated whether Dexter had left a mark, had a bad reputation in Israel. Some men, some units had been hated by the Jews. In particular, the Sixth Airborne had been labelled worse than Nazis. I considered it unreasonable, but the Jews were fighting for their Promised Land. We'd been the enemy, the oppressors. And on occasion we'd been heavy handed.

The pinched-faced man reappeared with two steaming bowls and set them before us with considerable pride. At least, that's what I read in his face. Either pride or disgust. It was hard to tell.

The food was a pottage, thick with vegetables and grains and the occasional chunk of meat. It tasted good and the intelligence agent nodded at my obvious pleasure.

After watching me devour half the bowl, he said, "I have a problem."

I looked a question at him as I chewed on a morsel of tough meat.

"You're not the man I'm looking for." He paused. "But you may be able to help."

"How?"

"I think *your* manhunt and *my* investigation are linked somehow." He took a mouthful, and I waited for more. He said, "I have pieces of intelligence. We believe arms are being shipped via Israel to the enemy. Another piece of intelligence is Saturday. Happening on Saturday."

It took a moment for my brain to catch up. "Today?"

"Possibly."

I knew arms shipments had occurred before. From mid-1947, the Jewish Agency made several purchases of arms from Czechoslovakia. However, in December of the same year, the Czechs did a similar deal with the enemy sending weapons to the Arab Liberation Army. Fortunately for the Jews, the Haganah caught wind of it and intercepted the large shipment destined for Arab fighters. Ironically, the weapons were ex-Nazi Germany's, and I had noted that no one highlighted their questionable provenance.

Had there only been one deal with the Arabs? I doubted it. However, I wasn't lying when I said, "I know nothing about any arms deals."

"What about gold? More specifically, white gold?"

I shook my head and he read my eyes.

"You might know more than you think," he said. "What haven't you told me?"

I finished my food.

"Do you want more?" he asked, indicating the bowl. "I'm paying for it, so eat as much as you'd like."

"I've had enough, but I do want something."

"What's that?"

"Let's start with your name. I've been thinking of you as Shabak-man because the captain who stopped you from executing me told me what you are."

He eyed me for a moment. "Joe. You can call me Joe if you must have a name."

It wouldn't be his real name, but that was fine. I said, "All right, Joe, what's really going on?"

"Going on?" He smiled although creases didn't move around his eyes.

"Back in Beersheba. The police station."

"Me and the IDF, you mean? I don't trust anyone. I tell them what they need to know, and they do what I say—most of the time."

I figured he was alluding to Captain Kramer interrupting my execution. Joe wasn't a man to be argued with.

"Did you arrange for Captain Kramer's reassignment?"

"No." He pulled at his beard. "And I don't like that Colonel Schattenmann was rushed in as his replacement."

"You think someone high up in the army is involved? Do you suspect treason?"

Joe's eyes gave me nothing. But he didn't deny it.

I said, "Was an Israeli involved with the intercepted Czech munitions in '47?"

He waited a beat, considering his answer. "Most likely."

I nodded. He didn't know who to trust, but I was an outsider. He hadn't called Inspector Rosen for a reference because the inspector was part of the Israeli establishment. But Joe had accepted the word of a British provost marshal. At least a degree more than he trusted his own people. The irony wasn't lost on me.

I said, "Why might I know something?"

"Abu Hajjar was a mobster," he said. "The leader of the gang. It's a huge coincidence that he escaped less than two weeks before whatever happens."

"And you didn't kill him?" I challenged. "He'd been buried up to his neck. Someone tortured him. Someone, I suspect, wanted information."

"Not me." Despite being unable to read Joe's face, I saw no reason for him to lie.

I said, "What about the other man who questioned me?"

He asked me to describe the Neanderthal and then shook his head. However, I didn't believe it. His eyes told me he recognized the description.

"Who is he?" I asked.

"I've no idea." He shook his head again. "He's not one of us."

I told him what had happened and how Schattenmann had interrupted the beating—presumably because Joe had arrived. "What was the giant doing at the Beersheba police station? Colonel Schattenmann must have known him or been told to let him interrogate me."

"I don't know."

"The giant was worried about Duffy. He seemed to think that I'd already found him. Why would that be a problem?"

"What did you tell him?"

"Nothing."

"And have you found Duffy?"

"No."

The pinched-faced old man topped up our drinks. When he'd left, Joe said, "Tell me what your plans were. How would you find your deserter?"

"Duffy was going south from Beersheba. He had a location for the Orbit men's base."

"Where?"

"In Nitzana or nearby."

"Why?"

"A personal matter. I believe he's looking for a girl."

Joe pondered.

I added: "There's something else. It seems that Hajjar might not have been the leader. It looks like he was a scapegoat."

"Hajjar in prison so that the true leader could continue…" He paused, considering it. "Which would only work if their activities changed; if it looked like the gang had disbanded. What was their previous criminal activity?"

"Petty stuff mostly, and antiquity theft according to the press. That's where Hajjar came in. He was an expert in antiquities. No reported murders and nothing about arms dealing. And no reported activity for the four years Hajjar was in prison."

"Plenty of time to refocus," he said. "Lay low and wait for the right time."

"Your War of Independence?"

"Or the armistice. Easier to move arms when the bullets stop flying."

"I have two more things," I said. "Hajjar was obsessed with something. We think it's a name: Black Heart."

The Shabak man shook his head. "Not something I've heard. The second thing?"

"Lines that look like a map. They may have been instructions for Duffy."

"Best guess?"

"A plan of the Orbit men's base."

"In or near Nitzana?"

"Yes."

Shabak nodded and stood. "Then that's where we'll go."

He picked up the cardboard box by his feet and handed it to me.

My silver money clip was the first thing I withdrew. The money wasn't there but it didn't matter. The clip had been a gift from my mother. My watch wasn't expensive and hadn't been taken. My gun was still in the holster.

As I removed it, I noted a twitch in the corner of Joe's eye. He didn't totally trust me. If I tried anything, I'm sure he would have been ready. I was under no illusions. This man could kill without compunction. With no evidence except for that I was in the wrong place at the wrong time, he'd almost executed me. If it hadn't been for Captain Kramer's intervention at the ruins, I wouldn't be here now.

"Let's go," he said. "You can put that on in the Jeep." He called out and gave the old man a bear hug when he appeared. We said goodbye and I followed Joe's rapid strides into the daylight.

FORTY-SIX

Joe skirted Beersheba and went south. He drove fast, and I used the door and windscreen frames to reduce the jarring.

"How are you feeling?" he said once we were on a smooth section of road.

"I'm better on the flat, but it hurts less than it did."

"And the tooth?"

"Bearable."

I could see the hills ahead and left. They looked different today. A thick layer of cloud deadened the light, reducing the contrast. The hills appeared flat and bland but I welcomed the protection from a cruel sun.

Joe said, "There's something I didn't mention."

I wasn't surprised. "Yes?"

"My thing may have happened already. I may be too late."

"Your intelligence pointed to today."

"It might have been last Saturday. I may be too late."

The desert road ran west for over five miles. I'd been wondering about Saturday. Last week, I'd been at the club and spent the night with Nicola Short. It was the same night someone had murdered the poor soul who'd taken my old hotel room. Was the attempt on my life connected?

When we passed where I'd gone into the hills looking for the ruins of Avdat, my thoughts turned darker.

I'd had a lucky escape. Joe had been about to execute me, and now I was riding shotgun with the killer. Perhaps the pain had affected my mind. Was I a fool? Was I being played? Joe and the Neanderthal could have been working together. The giant wanted Duffy, it seemed. And now I was potentially leading Joe to him.

My wounds had been treated. I'd been fed and watered. I'd trusted the man who'd taken me away from the monster who'd beaten me.

Had I made a schoolboy error?

"Stop," I said.

He complied and watched me as I got out. Casually bending down, I drew my gun and stood.

Joe's gun was already levelled at me.

"What're you doing?" he said.

Neither of us moved for a few beats. I saw curiosity in his eyes rather than an intention to shoot me.

I breathed in and out, turned and fired my weapon into the ground. If Joe had been conning me, it wouldn't have been loaded or wouldn't have fired.

I said, "Just checking my weapon… you never know."

As I climbed back in, he said. "Good army training. Always check your weapon."

I nodded, and he grunted. I'm sure he knew what I'd been thinking.

"Are we good?"

"Let's go," I said.

I didn't know what I was looking for, but after five miles I figured we'd gone too far, mainly because the road was barricaded. A sign warned of mines. There was also barbed wire strung out at least a hundred yards on either side.

"Not in the town then," he said. Then he must have guessed what I was wondering because he added: "It's a potential route from Egypt. The whole area has been mined to stop them coming at us from this side."

I looked down the dusty track and at the hills. The ones on the right were steep. On the left the terrain undulated randomly but with lower peaks.

He said, "Your man didn't come this far. Or he did and gave up."

"Let's back up."

Joe turned around and we drove east, slowly. I was looking at the low hills that were now on my right. There was a gap. I hadn't seen it from the other direction and the flat light made me question what I was looking at. However, when I noticed a faint track run from the road toward it, I pointed.

"Off-road here."

The route didn't run straight and, covered by dust, it wasn't easy to make out. But after two hundred yards, we reached a crest that then dropped into a gorge.

And we were no longer alone.

There were goats and caves.

It wasn't exactly an oasis, but there were patches of grass that meant a goatherder could graze his flock.

A face appeared at a cave entrance and looked at us nervously, then ducked back inside.

Joe stopped at distance and called out in Arabic. He climbed out and took a parcel from the back. Holding it in one hand like an offering and with his other in the air, Joe approached. I stayed in the Jeep.

He stopped just short of the entrance and spoke again. A boy came out, snatched the package then shrunk back.

I could hear Joe speaking, and the boy responded. I saw him point and shrug.

Joe returned. "He doesn't know anything about Orbit Men, but people used to live here. There was a well that ran dry."

"What was he pointing at?"

"There's a way up to the top. He said we might see what we're looking for from up there."

"But he doesn't know of anything?"

Joe shrugged. "Got a better plan?"

I hadn't. We found the base and followed a zigzag path up the rocks. I'd seen Ibex mountain goats climb steeper cliffs but it gave me no confidence as stones slipped beneath our feet and tumbled down.

Joe had fished a pair of binoculars from his bag and used them once we'd reached the crest.

I could see the road from Beersheba and the barricade before the minefield. What I guessed was Nitzana was just a sandy outline to the south.

Joe swept his binoculars across what looked like hills, but were mostly dunes, opposite. Then he paused, focused north, away from where the gang's base might have been—if Eva's information was correct.

"Something's coming," Joe said. He was focused on the road.

I could see the dust and watched it approach and move from right to left. It was going fast.

Joe handed me the glasses and I found the vehicle.

A gray Land Rover. It was open and I could see the driver. A big man.

The jeep came closer.

"It's him," I said. "It's the giant who beat me."

"What's he…?" Joe took back the binoculars and watched. The Land Rover passed where we'd come off the road and I realized I'd been holding my breath. Was he looking for us?

The Neanderthal kept going. Fast. No hesitation.

Then he came to the barricade. And he did something that shocked us both. The big man got out and moved the blockage aside.

FORTY-SEVEN

The Neanderthal drove through, then got out and dragged the barricade back into place.

After a few hundred yards I couldn't see clearly, but Joe said the Land Rover had gone into the town.

He passed the binoculars to me, and I could see the walls of Nitzana but no vehicle. In fact, I could see no sign of life at all. If he was still driving then no dust tail gave an indication of his location.

"Where did he go?" I asked.

"I lost him."

"Do people still live in Nitzana?"

"They shouldn't. We cleared everyone out before mining it."

I said, "The road isn't mined."

"And he knew it."

Joe started moving and I followed him along the crest. He was getting closer to the town and, I figured, trying to find a better observation point.

We kept going for half an hour, but the crest swept away and, if we wanted to get closer, we'd have had to descend. Which would have meant being unable to see over the town's walls.

Joe nodded back the way we'd come, and we clambered over the rocks to find the zigzag path.

Descending a narrow cliff route is even more perilous than a climb. Joe moved faster than me and didn't comment when I finally reached the bottom.

I'd asked on the way down but he hadn't responded. As we neared his Jeep, I asked again: "Are we going after him?"

"Yes. Unless…?"

"No, I don't have a better plan."

But as we exited the gorge, Joe stopped and backed up.

"Something else is coming." He jumped out, got the binoculars, and leaned against the rocks. "Another vehicle."

I waited.

"Trucks," Joe said after a few more seconds of watching. "No, two trucks and a lead vehicle."

"What sort of trucks?"

He waited, presumably until he could see them more clearly.

"Covered. Israeli military with an army Jeep."

Then I could see them too. They passed us, heading the same way the Neanderthal had gone over an hour earlier. They travelled slow and steady and close together. Dust billowed in their wake.

"They've reached the barricade," he said.

The dust settled.

A Jeep and two covered army trucks heading south. They'd either come from or through Beersheba. Did they know about the mined region? Would they turn back?

Of course not.

It took them a few minutes before the three trundled forward and stopped. I couldn't see clearly until Joe handed me the binoculars. Then I watched three men moving the barrier out of the way back. They were all in IDF uniforms.

The trucks moved off.

Joe looked at me. "Change of plan."

"We're not following?"
"We need back up," he said. "We need an army."

FORTY-EIGHT

The cloud cover had been constant and the light flat for so long, I'd lost sense of the time. But the sun must have been going down. The clouds took on a purple hue, and it was darker ahead than behind. We were about three miles outside Beersheba, driving faster than was comfortable on uneven, stone-strewn roads.

Another car—a small black one—was almost upon us before we saw it coming. Joe reluctantly slowed so that we could pass without either car swerving off the road.

I saw the face staring back at us as we passed.

"Stop!" I said, and Joe slewed to a halt.

Similarly, the black car skidded to a standstill behind us.

The man who got out was Ben Meir, the police sergeant from Tel Aviv.

"Who is it?" Joe asked me as the police officer approached looking hot and flustered.

I told him then jumped out and shook Ben Meir's hand.

The detective sergeant glanced from me to Joe then said, "Oh my... I can't believe... I've been looking for you, Captain. DI Rosen released me to assist..." Ben Meir was excited and out of breath, like a dog who'd been chasing around, looking for his master. "You didn't report in yesterday and... I've been driving around. I didn't pass you, so—"

"We haven't got time to chat!" Joe shouted irritably.

I pointed to the black car. "Follow us back to Beersheba. We're going for reinforcements."

Ben Meir frowned heavily. "I've just come from there. There's something up."

"What?" Joe asked.

The police sergeant shot the intelligence man a glance. "Who's your driver and what's going on, Captain?"

I briefly explained that Joe was from the intelligence services and tracking an arms shipment.

"For the Arabs?"

"That's what he thinks. And we've seen suspicious trucks going toward Nitzana."

Ben Meir frowned like none of it made any sense, and I suspected I'd think the same if I hadn't seen them go past the barricades. He didn't ask how Duffy fit into all this. If he had, I'm not sure how I would have answered. Was Duffy even involved?

Ben Meir strode closer to our Jeep.

"If you're looking for the army, you're wasting your time." Ben Meir shook his head. "I've just come through Beersheba. There's nothing but a skeleton force there."

"What?" Joe said.

"Some sort of exercise—manoeuvres in the east." Ben Meir shook his head again. "And the guard I spoke to said the telephone lines are down. If you want reinforcements—"

Joe looked at me and I figured we were both thinking this sounded suspicious. The army had moved out of the way just as the shipment passed through. It looked like Colonel Schattenmann was as involved as the Neanderthal who'd driven ahead of the convoy.

"Are you armed?" Joe asked the sergeant.

"My gun's in the car," Ben Meir said.

"You'll have to do as the reinforcements. Get your gun and get in." Joe didn't wait for agreement. He fired up the Jeep and swung it around. But he waited fifteen yards away from Ben Meir's car.

"Are you wondering why I trust him? You British have an expression: Hobson's choice," Joe said as we waited. "There were two trucks. I saw two in the jeep. Three men came from one truck and moved the barricade. I figure that's eight men in the convoy. Three of us. Better odds than two."

Ben Meir pulled his car off the road, out of the way.

"Could be more in the back of the trucks," I suggested. I was thinking of three-ton troop carriers. "There could be a whole platoon in there."

"If it's men in those trucks, then this is something else entirely. If they are genuinely the army, then it's not my problem. But if the cargo is the arms—"

"This is your problem."

"And it needs to be dealt with now. Before the trade happens."

I thought he was being optimistic. The trade might have already happened.

Ben Meir climbed into the rear of the Jeep.

His breathless relief at finding me had been replaced by enthusiasm. He leaned forward with bright eyes. I figured his day job didn't often involve working with the intelligence services.

"What makes you think they've got illegal arms?" he asked.

Joe spun the tyres and accelerated before speaking. "Intercepted messages," he said. "Trucks in the wrong place at the right time. Too big a coincidence. Add that to whatever's going on in Beersheba."

"And you found them, just like that?" Ben Meir leaned toward me. "And how are you involved?"

Joe said, "Just following hunches and leads."

"Me too," I said. "My deserter came this way and didn't come back. Another coincidence."

We drove south and the sky darkened.

"How many men do they have?" Ben Meir asked.

"Could be six but my best guess is eight," Joe said.

He sounded convincing although those trucks were going somewhere. They would be met. There could be any number of enemy combatants waiting for us. And there was the Neanderthal.

We passed the first sign warning of mines. We passed where we'd turned off and found the goatherder and what might have once been the Orbit Men's old base.

By the time we reached the barricade, the sky behind us was washed black, fading to indigo.

Joe stopped and I jumped out. The barrier was a coil of barbed wire around a wooden frame: Three Xs with a hollow metal boom bar across the middle. Ben Meir joined me, and we swung it in an easy arc, following the grooves made by the men from the trucks.

I could see Joe was thinking. We climbed back into the Jeep.

"How far from Nitzana?" he asked.

I hadn't judged it from our vantage point in the hills. I was still thinking when Ben Meir beat me to it. "About a mile and a half," he said.

I squinted ahead. In the fading light, I could see less than half that distance. The road vanished into a gray blur.

"Agreed," Joe said and then started forward. After a hundred yards, he pulled off onto rough terrain. He went left. On the right, it looked furrowed, like giant ripples in the sand left by a retreating tide. Too difficult to drive over.

"What about the mines?" Ben Meir asked.

"There are no mines," Joe said. We knew there weren't any on the road but what about the outskirts? Joe couldn't know for sure, but he sounded confident.

We bounced and rattled and kept veering left. He drove slowly and watched the ground ahead of us. In places, it dropped into gullies and Joe steered away, just in time. As soon as he could, he went left again.

None of us spoke. The clouds and the night were rushing in. Apart from the Jeep and the moving sky, everything seemed eerily still.

I figured he was avoiding a direct approach and wondered how far around the town he was going when he stopped.

"It's over there," he said, pointing. "Another half a mile. We approach on foot."

I peered into the rapidly fading light and couldn't see if he was pointing at a structure. I guessed his eyes or sense of direction were better than mine.

From the back of the Jeep, Joe unlocked a metal box. He'd taken his bag from it earlier. Now he pulled out a dark shirt and flung it at me.

"Swap this for your white one," he said.

My once-white shirt, I thought. It was grubby from my night in the cell and streaked with blood where I'd spat and dribbled during the beating. The clean shirt fit and felt cool.

When I looked back at Joe, he had a sub-machine gun in his hands. It was a US Tommy gun with a stick magazine rather than the gangster-style round ammo box. Maybe it was an Eastern European copy. He slung it on his back and drew the gun from his holster.

Ben Meir had a Webley revolver, probably an old British Palestine Police issue weapon. It was a powerful gun with the right ammunition, but a shortage meant they were commonly loaded with the lighter Smith and Wesson .38 bullets.

My Beretta was small in comparison, about half the weight but with a higher muzzle velocity for the same bullets. Which meant better effective range and better stopping power. The Italians got a lot wrong in the

Second World War, but their service pistol wasn't one of their mistakes. I'd take the Beretta over the Webley every day.

"We split up," the Shabak man said, slinging his bag over the other shoulder. He told me to go left and Ben Meir right. He said we would be less obvious, less of a target. We'd move forward slowly, a pace a second. We'd stay in line, and we shouldn't talk unless necessary. He said he'd signal with a whistle, then demonstrated with a high pitched, but quiet hiss through his teeth. One meant *stop*, two meant *go*.

I looked at Ben Meir. The sergeant still looked eager and unconcerned. He looked fearless. But bravery can be the bedfellow of ignorance. He didn't have military experience. Worse than that, he'd told me about his lack of gun experience. It was probably a good job that Joe didn't know our reinforcements were probably useless in a gunfight.

I figured Joe didn't want us to stay together because he wasn't certain about the mines. Walking apart, if one man triggered a mine, then the others would survive. Ben Meir probably hadn't worked that out either. Foolish bravado.

"Let's go," I said.

We started. I thought: half a mile, more than eight hundred paces, less than nine hundred. A pace a second would mean fifteen minutes to cover the distance.

At irregular intervals, the clouds thinned. Not enough to see the sky, but in the monochrome light, I could make out the shapes of the other two men. The shadows clung to us like living things. Joe was half a pace ahead of me, Ben Meir slightly behind.

Our leader signalled for us to crouch and pointed to the sky and his eyes. I got it. Wait until it's darker.

The thicker cloud cover returned. Joe whistled twice and I heard the faint sound of feet on stone. We continued onwards toward our hidden objective.

I stepped slowly and carefully with a sweeping motion. I checked for stones and uneven ground before transferring my weight.

Twenty-six paces. A slither to my right. It reminded me that people weren't the only danger out here. Hopefully, what I thought were silent steps were thunderous to the desert snakes.

Apart from that slither, I heard nothing.

Without a break in the cloud cover, I began to question whether my sense of direction was off. I felt utterly alone.

And then a gunshot shattered the illusion.

FORTY-NINE

As I dropped to the ground, my brain registered that I'd also heard a thud. My senses strained for any sign of the enemy. After more than a minute, I whistled through my teeth. There was no response.

"Joe?"

Still nothing.

I crawled right and found him. Joe was on his back, staring at the dark heavens. He didn't move with my contact. I could see his face was misshapen. A bullet to the head.

Ben Meir hissed.

I whispered, "He's dead."

Seconds later, Ben Meir commando-crawled to me. I'd already located the Tommy gun and Joe's pistol and bag. There was a magazine inside which I put in my pocket.

"Sniper," Ben Meir whispered.

"Where? I didn't see anything."

He pointed ahead and right. "I think I saw a flash, that way."

If a sniper had a bead on where Joe had been, we'd better move.

I began to crawl away; forward and left. It sounded like Ben Meir was a few yards behind me.

The clouds thinned, and I stopped and squatted.

I could see the ghostly outline of the town. We were still a hundred and fifty yards out. Maybe more. The road was thirty or so yards to the right. We needed to keep away from that direct approach.

Ben Meir shuffled up beside me.

Ahead and to the left, I spotted something. A low wall. I looked at Ben Meir and pointed.

"As soon as the light goes, we run for it," I whispered. He nodded.

We didn't move for five long minutes. The light remained, and I still saw nothing in the town. No movement, no odd shapes, no pinpricks of light.

If it hadn't been for the shot that killed Joe, I could have believed we were the only people here.

The cloud closed up and I was on my feet, running in a crouch. My ribs complained but I bit my gum against the pain.

Ben Meir was right behind. I heard him slip and grunt, then start running again.

I reached the wall and sheltered behind it. There were other low walls. A demolished stone building or buildings. There could have been someone waiting for us here. Another sniper. But I was sure there wouldn't be and there wasn't. They didn't expect anyone tonight. They didn't have sentries posted out here, and no one had run from the town to this remote spot.

I had Joe's Hi-Power in my left hand. With quick movements, I released the magazine and replaced it with one from my pocket. The chambered bullet ejected as I racked the slide. Good to go.

Ben Meir bundled up behind me.

"What are you doing?" he hissed, frowning at the Browning in my hand.

"Checking it," I said. "It's a good gun. Better than your Webley. Better stopping power."

I gripped the Tommy gun, stock wedged under my right arm, and held out the Browning.

He glanced, thought then took it. Sensible.

He slotted the Webley into the holster. I switched my Beretta to my favoured left hand and moved the machine gun to my right shoulder, ready to swing into action.

The clouds thinned. I got my bearings, and when the darkness rushed in again, we made a beeline for the town, keeping to the eastern side, well away from the road.

There were no shots or shouts, just the crunch of our running feet.

The buildings loomed suddenly in the dark and hit an outer wall. Ben Meir was close, but I didn't wait for him. I started moving around the perimeter, making my way to where we'd seen the trucks disappear.

Using Joe's communication system of low whistles, we moved, stopped, listened, and moved. Within a minute, we'd covered a hundred yards. Not far now. Maybe two buildings further.

Ben Meir came up close. I could see his face. He looked nervous and excited.

I nodded a question. *All OK?*

He gave me the thumbs-up.

With my Beretta, I signalled for him to continue. I'd go around.

We split up, and I moved along an alley between crumbling buildings. No one had lived here for many years. I kept thinking about the trucks. Where had they gone?

By the time I reached Ben Meir, I knew.

There was a tunnel.

It was disguised by outer walls, but the tyre tracks told us everything. The road had come in, turned right, and gone beneath the old town.

We went down.

FIFTY

We found the two trucks parked side by side. There were three other vehicles. Two Jeeps and one Land Rover. They were all gray and one of the Jeeps had the army logos over-painted. Eva Wislitsky's vehicle, I guessed.

A string of well-spaced, dim electric lights had taken us along the tunnel. It hadn't gone directly beneath the town as I'd expected. The direction suggested we were curving east, away from the town and there had been nothing for about a mile. Then came a parking area and a door.

The trucks were painted in IDF colours. Inside, I saw packing cases. I checked three and found electrical items. No sign of armaments. However, I also noted that three quarters of the trucks' load-space was empty. Which probably meant the electrical items were a decoy and the boxes with arms had been removed.

Ben Meir listened at the door, tested the handle and opened it an inch. Then he went through. I followed. Beyond was a corridor and silence.

It was akin to going from Kansas to the Land of Oz. The town dated back hundreds of years. The tunnel had been hewn out of rock, rough and possibly ancient. But the corridor had concrete walls. And there were side doors with windows. It was brighter too. I could imagine I was in a windowless office building.

Ben Meir's face was full of questions.

I waved my Beretta. *We go this way.*

At the first door, I looked through the porthole window. A desk and charts. We moved on. The next was similar plus cabinets. A commercial building with administrative offices.

There were two more rooms. All appeared in use, but empty.

At the end of the corridor was a T-junction with doors left and right. We went right. The lights were off and I got a whiff of something I'd barely registered before. Something acrid, something animal. Beyond another door, the stench assaulted me. I could also hear the creatures now. The odd low growl and chatter.

And then we came to cages. The first block had baboons. The next had big cats of some kind. Maybe lions. I could see their eyes watching us in the faint light.

There were cage-like barriers leaning against the walls.

What the hell was this? A subterranean zoo?

Narrow passages appeared on our left. I felt air as we walked past and, at the third one, I directed Ben Meir along it.

There were steps and a caged platform. A thick rope ran from the low ceiling. A pulley system to raise the platform.

The back of my mind must have been processing. The corridor, the offices, the T, the blocks with animal cages. By the time we reached the top of the steps, my senses alive to any whisper of movement, I understood. We were outside, the dark sky above and gritty sand at our feet.

The light was good enough to see curved walls. This was the oval from the map. Not just an oval, an ancient arena, an amphitheatre.

This was the diagram from the coastguard station. This was what Hajjar had drawn and left its imprint on the map.

The night hung heavy with menace.
I looked at Ben Meir and then down.
His gun was pointing at me.

FIFTY-ONE

Ben Meir said, "Don't!"

My Beretta had risen involuntarily. I let it fall to the ground. I wasn't a threat. There was no point in me expressing surprise or begging for my life. I just needed to know something.

"Before you shoot me," I said. "Tell me what's going on."

"An arms deal," he said. "I'm sorry, Ash."

His aim raised to my face.

I didn't flinch.

His finger tightened on the trigger.

And nothing happened.

I swung up the machine gun. "Drop it!"

He let go of the Hi-Power but his hand immediately fumbled for his Webley revolver.

I could have shot him, but I wanted answers, so I jabbed the machine gun into his face. The barrel smacked into his mouth, breaking teeth. He stared with shock, but not for long. I reversed the gun and swung it into the side of his head.

He staggered and went down. I kicked him in the gut. Three rapid blows—jab, smack, kick—leaving my opponent stunned and disorientated. Joe would have been impressed.

Ben Meir's hands were shaking. He coughed and spat blood.

I pulled the Webley off him and stuck it in my waistband. It was a heavy, thuggish gun but I didn't know how many of the enemy were here. Joe had guessed eight. I reckoned more, possibly a lot more.

Then I located my Beretta, picked it and pointed it Ben Meir's face. His expression was full of fear and confusion.

"How did you—?" he spluttered through his broken mouth.

I'd guessed there hadn't been a sniper on the approach. I'd heard the shot and thud. Almost simultaneous. My brain hadn't registered it immediately, but when it caught up, I knew the shot had been close. Joe would have gone down before I'd heard the shot if it had come from distance.

Then it was a matter of making sure Ben Meir didn't shoot me. While I'd been waiting for Ben Meir outside the town, I'd ejected a perfectly good bullet from the chamber and removed the magazine. Before that, I'd tampered with a magazine from Joe's bag and inserted a stone. When I racked the slide, I knew it would jam.

Ben Meir hadn't been in the army. I relied on him being unused to checking and testing. He'd seen me prepare the gun and he liked the sound of a more powerful weapon. A great gun, but also prone to jamming. Easily cleared if you know how, but when it had dead fired, his only thought had been to go for his Webley.

I didn't answer his question. Instead, I said, "Call for help and I'll shoot you. Lie to me and I'll shoot you."

He looked up at me, probably running through his options. No doubt buying time, he nodded.

"Are the arms still here?"

He took his time answering. "Yes, they'll still be here."

"Where?"

Ben Meir glanced to my left, toward the south end of the arena. I didn't think anyone knew we were here. I didn't think anyone was coming to his rescue.

"I don't know. I've never been here before. Will you let me live?"

"Answer my questions and I'll consider it," I said. I honestly hadn't decided. "How many men are there?"

"I don't know." I think he smiled, but it was hard to tell because of the busted mouth. Perhaps he was encouraging me to believe him. "I really wasn't involved in this part of the operation."

"What *was* your role?"

He glanced to the south again, more deliberately this time.

I repeated the question.

He said, "Just making sure the goods were picked up—and then that you didn't get involved."

"Is Duffy here?"

"I don't know." He spat out blood and wiped at his mouth.

"Who is Black Heart?"

"That's not a name I've heard."

The light wasn't great, the clouds were closing in again. However, I could see the confusion in his face. So far, I believed him.

I said, "Who killed Abu Hajjar?"

"Look, Ash, I'm not important. I just did what I was paid to do. I know they brought the arms here to meet with the buyers."

He was lying.

"Was it the giant?" He raised his eyebrows unconvincingly and I continued. "You know who I mean. Ugly with a prominent brow. What's he called?"

"Tzaiad." He paused, looked away. "He's the enforcer. He'll have tracked down and killed Abu Hajjar. But, Ash, Hajjar was a known criminal—"

I opened my mouth to speak and Ben Meir surprised me. I hadn't seen him prepare. Seemingly from nowhere, he flung a handful of grit at me and dived. As he hit the ground he rolled. I think he'd intended to reach the steps that led down to the animal enclosure. But he fell short, and I was over him as he tried to spring and dive again.

"Stop!" I barked.

He didn't. Like a frog, he kicked off, driving low, toward the steps.

He made it but he was dead when he hit the ground, shot in the back and then the head.

The twin shots boomed around the amphitheatre and a cacophony erupted from the animals like a shockwave.

The men inside hadn't heard the shot that killed Joe. They may not have heard me shout at and then shoot Ben Meir. But they couldn't fail to hear the animals.

The covert stage was over. I was about to find out just how many men were in this hellish place.

FIFTY-TWO

Hajjar's map had been symmetrical. It didn't show steps around the amphitheatre, but I hoped I'd find them on the opposite side.

I figured the grunts, growls and howls would attract attention. They'd go to the animal enclosures rather than the other side. Better than fifty-fifty odds, I thought.

I was wrong. I was halfway across the arena when I heard a clunk from my right. The direction Ben Meir had looked. He really had expected help to come that way.

A door opened in the wall and light spilled out with a silhouetted figure. Dropping down, I trained my gun on him as he came forward, but he didn't look my way. My eyes had adjusted to the darkness whereas he'd not see much for a few minutes. He was heading for the steps to the animal enclosures. Then he pulled up sharply and I guessed he'd spotted Ben Meir's body.

He spun around, a gun in his hand, his eyes sweeping the arena.

His aim came up and he took a pace in my direction. I figured I must have looked like a dark patch on the ground. If he kept on coming, he'd see me for sure.

But he stopped, turned and started sprinting for the lit doorway at the end. Rather than confront me, he would set off an alarm.

I switched the Beretta for the Tommy gun and let off a burst.

He went down with a scream then stayed still.

I waited. Would someone else hear that? Probably. The rapid percussion still rang in my ears.

The door remained open. No one came through.

I couldn't see any hatch on the opposite side to where Ben Meir lay, but the ground sounded hollow when I stepped on it. A second later, I had the hatch open. After a final check that no one was coming across the arena, I descended steps into darkness. At the bottom, I hesitated. Not only was there no light down here but I couldn't even see contrasts. Above had been dark, but this seemed pitch black.

The animals were still howling and I thought I could hear human voices, too. Maybe more people had gone into the amphitheatre. Maybe there were other steps. Maybe they were coming after me.

My shin banged into a wooden bench. I ran my hand along the wall and touched leather and metal. A row of four short swords, then a trident. An image flashed into my head. An arena above and a room with fighting gear. Gladiators. Then I thought about the animals. Not a zoo. Was this what Romans called *venatio*—the hunting of wild animals?

The gang had built their new base under an ancient amphitheatre. That made me think there were a lot more than eight men here. A permanent unit in need of entertainment. They dressed up as Roman fighters and slew animals.

At the end of the passage were doors to my left and right. I eased open the left-hand one. Another dark room, although there was faint light coming from the other side. My hand touched a light switch, and I threw it.

The room was for exercise—including practise for fighting, I suspected. There were weights and a couple of wooden fighting dummies. There were also wooden equivalents of what I'd felt in the passage before. I crossed the room to a door on the far side, where I'd seen the faint light.

Next to it was a table and chair. An empty mug sat on the table beside a plate with chicken bones and a chunk of unleavened bread. A bunch of keys hung from a hook on the table's side. On the floor were empty containers and a bucket half-full of water.

Through the door, a rank stench assaulted me. I already knew why. I could tell by the smell. This was a cell block. The desk outside was for a guard.

There was one dim bulb on this side of the door. Enough light to see four doors on the right and a water tap and trough on the left.

The doors were solid, not the usual barred type, like I'd seen in Beersheba. Each had a peephole in the middle and slit for food at the bottom.

The first cell was empty. But there were two men in the second and also the third. I could just about see them in the light coming under the door. Three were lying on benches. The fourth sat and looked toward me. I guess he assumed I was the guard. His face was dark and his hair long. I didn't recognize him.

But I did recognize the man in the last cell.

He was alone and standing and I could see him clearly enough.

He'd lost weight and looked ragged, but there was no doubting who this was. Pale skin, ginger hair. This was Alfred Duffy, the man I'd come to find.

I went back to the table outside, picked up the keys and tried them until Duffy's door opened.

He didn't move, just stared at me.

"Who the hell are you?" he said. His voice grated, perhaps hoarse from shouting or lack of water. Or maybe he always spoke like that.

"The man who was sent to find you," I said.

He frowned and raked a hand through his hair. "To set me free?"

"To arrest you for desertion."

"Rank?"

"Captain. Special Investigations Branch."

"Should I be impressed?" Then, before I responded, he said, "I need water."

I backed up and he moved out of the cell and turned on the tap. The trickle wasn't great but he used his hand and scooped it into his mouth. Water he missed went into the trough that ran for a few feet before it gathered. Rather than a drain, I guessed it conserved water for use elsewhere.

I fetched the empty cup and handed it to him.

After a mugful, he straightened and ran a wet hand through his hair. "What's your plan?"

"I take you back."

He nodded at me. "You're well-armed."

"I might need to fight our way out."

He shook his head. "I'm not going." There were noises from the other two cells. I guessed the inmates were trying to hear our conversation and work out what was happening.

"Don't be an idiot, Duffy."

"I can't leave. Not until… D'you know what's going on?"

I heard a distant shout and figured someone had finally found the bodies I'd shot.

"We need to go," I said and indicated with my Beretta.

"Girls," he said. "They've got girls."

Of course they had. If Eva's story was true, the gang had her sister. They probably had a few more unwilling brides. I'd seen it before. They'd keep a few girls like sex-slaves. We could release them, or I could do my job and get the Israeli authorities to do theirs.

I said, "It's more than that, it's about illegal arms trade."

He shook his head.

"They've just arrived," I explained. "I was with someone from Israeli Intelligence... We haven't got time for this. Come on. We need to go before the whole lot of them work out I'm here."

"No," he said.

"Sergeant!" I snapped. "We go now."

A heavily accented voice from one of the other cells was loud. "Not arms!"

Duffy said, "They aren't trading arms."

"White gold," the other voice called.

I stopped and stared at Duffy. Things were clicking into place. White gold.

I said, "Girls."

"Yes."

"Fair skinned and virtuous?"

"Yes."

"Two trucks arrived this evening."

"With girls." He must have seen my dilemma. "We can't leave them here."

I heard shouts from beyond the exercise room. Probably in the passage with the weapons and steps to the arena.

I made a decision, pulled Ben Meir's Webley from my waist, and held it out.

Duffy took it, checked it, frowned. "Five rounds."

I handed him the Hi-Power and he grinned. However after trying the slide, he shook his head. "It's jammed."

"It'll clear."

He released the magazine, let the slide go forward, inserted the magazine and racked the slide.

The small stone I'd loaded it with ejected, and he was ready. Just in time.

Two armed men burst into the exercise room. They stopped, stared, raised their guns, and died.

I cut them down with a blast from the Tommy gun before they could cry out. Duffy fired as well, which was a waste, and I told him to conserve his bullets.

"I trust the other men here," he said. "Free them too. We'll need everyone."

I gritted my teeth and handed Duffy the keys. I figured that more men would add to the confusion.

I kept the machine gun trained on the door opposite. I heard doors open and men spill out. Within a minute, Duffy and the four others were with me. Wild determination flamed in their eyes, and their faces were set with grave determination. I didn't need to tell them. They knew what we were up against.

They gave me their names. Farid and Yusuf took the rifles from the dead gang members. The other two held up calloused fists, ready with nothing but wiry strength.

We reached the passage. No one was waiting for us but I could still hear shouts of alarm. They were looking for the intruder. Two had found me here but the others had probably split up.

I'd wondered if the other prisoners would run. I was also thinking that Duffy and I had two weapons each. There were six of us and two men were unarmed. I needn't have concerned myself because they were all selecting short swords and tridents. Even the two with rifles stuck swords at their waists.

They started forming up around me, waiting for instructions.

"Where are the girls held?"

"We don't know. We hear the men talk but none of us has seen any."

"Who knows this place best?"

"Yusuf," Duffy said. "He's been here longest."

Yusuf dipped his head at me.

I looked toward the steps and then the other door. When I'd come through here, both doors had been shut. I'd taken the one on the left. The one on the right was now ajar. That's where the two attackers must have come from.

"What's that way?" I asked Yusuf.

"They call it the barracks. Where the men sleep."

"What's at the end of the arena. There's a door."

"The Dome." He shrugged. "That's what I've heard men call it."

"They must join up," Duffy said.

"You and you," I pointed to Duffy and another man. "With me. The rest of you through the barracks."

Yusuf grinned, showing broken yellow teeth.

I said, "Let's find those girls."

FIFTY-THREE

When we emerged into the arena, flashlights sliced through the oppressive gloom. Shadows danced and writhed. Gang members fanned out around the arena, assault rifles glinting dully in the pale beams.

"Two of them," Duffy whispered.

"Three." I was sure I'd seen a figure without a torch. I glanced at the man with us. He had a sword and grim expression. Before we came up, he'd said his name was Mo. I gave him my Beretta. "Don't shoot unless you're sure. Or you're drawing fire."

We split up. Duffy and the other man edged left toward the door. I went right.

Crack! Crack! Gunfire split the night. Duffy and Mo returned fire and the flashlights extinguished. The firing stopped and I figured the enemy were seeking a better position.

As soon as I moved, the shots began again. I heard metal hit stone but not close. I circled and sped up. The enemy were all shooting at the other guys.

I passed the north end and saw more men coming through the door at the other end. One went down straight away but the other scooted into shadows.

A light flashed close by, and a man shouted. He must have gone clockwise toward me. He let off a single shot before his call morphed into a scream as my bullets tore into him.

I ran faster now. The enemy's gunshots pinged on my side of the arena but they were too low. After shooting the man with the torch, I'd gone higher. I was running around the penultimate row of stone seats.

As I passed the hatch to the animal enclosures, a bullet whizzed past. I blasted the seats where I guessed the shooter had been and got a hit.

Across the way, Duffy was in a firefight with at least two. I found a man searching for me and took him out with a quick burst.

More shots rang out. I dropped flat behind the benches and returned fire. Two dark forms that had been shooting at Duffy, spun and collapsed. The third turned tail and fled for the lit doorway.

I thought we'd got them all, but as I crept along the benches a bullet smacked into the stone inches ahead. I saw the shooter two rows down.

I swivelled with the machine gun and fired. Only I didn't. I got a dead-man's click. Empty or jammed? No time to check.

The man below me hadn't shot again either. Probably reloading a single-shot rifle.

I dived over seats onto him. My forearm caught the man across the throat and my momentum took us down three more levels. His head smacked stone like a heavy, wet towel.

Except for the blood pounding in my ears, silence rushed in.

I finished my circuit.

"Duffy?" I hissed.

The two of us met in the shadow above the southern door.

"Think we got all but the one who fled."

"Mo?" I asked.

"Didn't make it."

Duffy handed me my Beretta.

A quick check told me there were only two bullets left. I smacked the magazine back in and gritted my teeth. Duffy had a different pistol than the one I'd given him.

"Browning was done," he said. "Picked this up. Has four shots left."

"We'll find more," I said. I don't know whether he believed me but my confidence helped. "What's beyond the door?"

"I don't know. None of us did. We were just here to fight each other."

"And the animals."

"No," he said after a hesitation. And before he explained, I already started to realize. Roman-style amphitheatre entertainment. Not *venatio*. Not men hunting wild animals."

"Oh—" I tasted bile.

"Yes," he said, breathing hard. "That's what some of the girls are for."

I shook an image from my head and gripped my gun. "Let's go."

FIFTY-FOUR

There was carpet on the floor. My brain registered the unusual sight just before bullets chewed the doorframe. If we went through, it would be suicide. For one of us at least, if there was just one shooter.

We needed a better option.

Duffy wasn't waiting. As soon as the gun fired, he was moving.

He sprinted and I saw him dive to the left.

Damn!

I followed and went right.

My ears rang with gunshots, and as I rolled, I expected pain. Not just my ribs. I expected at least one bullet would strike me before I found cover. My shoulder screamed as I hit the ground.

I needed cover but couldn't see any. I tried to scan for the shooter but my vision blurred as I rolled and I had to risk it.

I landed in a crouch and aimed where I thought the enemy would be. Opposite the entrance.

But the shooter wasn't there. He was on my left, where Duffy had gone.

My movements and aim were impulsive, but I stopped myself from firing. The scene wasn't as I'd imagined.

To my left I saw Duffy and two other men. One was Yusuf. Then I saw a dead man on the floor and figured he'd been shot by Yusuf as we'd come into the room.

"This way," Yusuf said as I stood. "The girls are this way."

Duffy threw me a look and I figured he'd seen all the blood on me for the first time. But it wasn't mine. It had come from the man whose head had smashed on the stone outside. However, I suddenly felt weak. My brain had been ignoring the pain in my muscles. I'd been beaten a few hours ago and even my teeth were aching again.

There were four of us left. We'd lost one man and so had the team going through the barracks.

We slipped down carpeted hallways, as hushed as ghosts. We could have been inside any good Tel Aviv hotel.

There was a body, bloody and crumpled. Joe, the Israeli intelligence man, had suggested eight gang members. I counted eleven enemy deaths that I knew of.

"How many did you get?" I asked Yusuf.

"Six."

"Did you kill the giant?"

Yusuf shook his head.

Of course there had been more. And there was at least one man still alive. The Neanderthal called Tzaiad.

We stepped over a fallen gang member whose blood had made a mess of the carpet. He had a holstered gun. Killed before he'd drawn it.

"They're in these rooms," Yusuf said, nodding at the doors ahead. "Eighteen of them. Three look special, like they've been cared for. The others—" He looked at me, possibly unsure how to say the rest.

"They'll be for the animals. The other entertainment," Duffy said sickly.

"Can you get them out?" I asked Duffy. "There are trucks in the tunnel."

Yusuf nodded.
"All of you," I said to Duffy.
"What are you going to do?"
"Find the Neanderthal," I said.

FIFTY-FIVE

I took the gun from the guy on the floor. A Beretta with a full magazine. I discarded my clip and reloaded using his. The action steadied me.

The carpeted room, where we'd charged in, had a door at each end and double doors near to where the shooter had been killed by Yusuf.

Five paces took me to the doors, and I nudged them open. The floor was shiny white marble. There were five tables set for dinner. A stylish restaurant near a ghost town in the desert. A lavish contrast to the harsh stone and dust of the amphitheatre just yards away.

Another five paces took me to two more double doors.

I was moving faster now, conscious that I needed to find the Neanderthal. It was a visceral thing. I was blaming him for this grotesque business, but I also wanted answers. I needed to know whether he was the leader, whether he was Black Heart.

Beyond the restaurant was a kitchen. Knives glinted on the marble counters. There was a door to the right.

The kitchen looked clean and new. It smelled clean, too. No cooked food. Probably not in use, which explained why it was empty.

But it wasn't empty.

As I crossed the room, I saw a movement to my left. Someone cowered by the ovens. Wearing white. A chef, my subconscious processed. No threat.

I checked to my right in case anyone else was hiding. A cleaver spun inches from my face. I ducked behind a unit as a skillet clattered where I'd been standing. Then a metal rod of some kind. The chef was up and throwing at me.

He dropped down and came up. He'd moved around a bench and was now armed with two throwing knives. I fired a single shot, catching him in the arm.

He howled and disappeared again.

When I circled the bench, he was crouching with a knife, ready to leap at me. But he was looking the wrong way.

"Drop it or you'll die," I said.

He swivelled, his face full of terror. "I just a cook!"

I pointed the gun. "How many men are there beyond the doors?"

"One."

"A big man?"

"Yes."

"Which door?"

He whimpered something about the officers' wing then pointed a shaky finger. "Others for guests."

"How many guests?"

"Not arrived. Tomorrow."

"Is there only one way out?" I indicated with my head. "The tunnel to the south?"

The chef waved toward the restaurant. "Guest way in. Tunnel to Egypt."

"Go." I waved the gun. "Go that way. Don't come back."

It took a moment for the man to realize what I meant. I wasn't going to shoot him. He stood nervously, took a pace away from me then ran out of the kitchen.

I listened, heard nothing but my own breathing, and went through the other door.

There was a corridor with five doors off it. Two were ajar.

A glance into the first told me it was a bedroom. Well furnished. Comfortable. Officer's quarters, I thought. The next room looked like a shower area. Then there was a closed door.

Tzaiad had gone to ground here like the animal he was. He was defending his lair.

A gun shot from behind me made me swivel.

Had the others found trouble? My mind recalculated. Tzaiad wasn't here. The chef had lied. I cursed my generosity. Maybe I should have been more persuasive. Maybe he had been faking it and I'd missed the lie.

I made a quick decision and hurried back through the kitchen and restaurant.

The door to the amphitheatre remained open. I could see figures crossing the arena. They were hurried but not concerned. Duffy and the others leading the girls away, I thought. Not the source of the shot.

The door opposite where we'd gone to find the girls caught my attention.

It had been shut but was now open. The chef had come this way. I'd sent him to the southern tunnel, through the guests' quarters.

I followed.

A corridor was like the one on the other side. Rich carpet but even more fancy decoration.

I moved swiftly through the guests' quarters. Plush carpets muffled my footsteps as I passed meeting rooms and bedrooms furnished for comfort. Rage simmered in my gut. The gang's leaders lived in opulence while tormenting innocents.

I found rooms with gold filigree mirrors and damask chairs.

Then I took a turn and saw the chef on the floor. Shot no doubt by Tzaiad, thinking he was a threat. Blood splattered the chef's white uniform, but he was still alive. Barely. A bloody foam formed at the corner of his mouth as he tried to speak.

"Where is he?" I asked.

The man's eyes flicked toward the end of the corridor, and I ran.

It was big and heavy and I recognized the door as the twin of the one at the end of the northern tunnel, where we'd come in. This was the way out.

The handle turned easily and I crouched. Human instinct can't help but expect someone at head height. If someone was waiting on the other side, I'd get a second's advantage before their brain kicked in. I'd see them first. I'd shoot first. Hopefully.

I swung open the door. No one waiting. Then I heard muffled sobs ring along the rock-hewn tunnel. My stomach twisted. Tzaiad had a hostage—a girl, I guessed.

He wasn't far, but if he reached a vehicle, he'd get away.

As I opened the tunnel door, I realized I was already too late. An engine turned over.

No longer cautious, I ran fast and approached the cavern where they parked vehicles. There was one. A jeep about twenty yards ahead.

The engine kept cranking. It hadn't fired up.

I saw the giant get out and drag the girl from the rear. He started walking up the tunnel, oblivious to me. I liked that. He was moving into the open. I could use the jeep.

He passed a light bulb and the girl's fair hair caught the light.

"Tzaiad!" I yelled as I reached the jeep.

He spun and fired wildly at me. I crouched behind the vehicle and trained my gun on him.

"Keep your distance," he shouted.

The girl struggled and I caught a glimpse of her face. Her cheeks were large and her eyes wider apart than most. I guessed her eyes would be blue because I knew exactly who she was.

Eva Wislitsky's sister, Elsa.

Tzaiad said, "I'm just going to walk out of here." He started walking backwards. His thick forearm was around the girl's neck, using her as a shield. Her feet dragged, which slowed his progress.

My throat had gone tight. After a cough, I said, "Release the girl."

I think he grinned as he shook his head. I was processing options. Could I shoot him without hitting her? Or could I shoot through her? Could I kill him without it killing her? A shot through her shoulder, perhaps?

He moved as though reading my mind. But it wasn't necessary. I wasn't confident at my ability. With a rifle, maybe but not with my pistol.

I fired into the tunnel. A deliberate miss out of frustration, perhaps. However, it made him stop.

I said, "I'll trade. Give me the girl and I'll let you go."

"Lower your gun," he said calmly, sounding reasonable. Then he fired and the bullet ricocheted off metal, too close for comfort.

"Release the girl," I repeated.

He lifted her onto her tiptoes. I caught a flash of her eyes, rolled up, not focused. Beyond terrified. Petrified. Just a mannequin the Neanderthal could hide behind.

I said, "So there are no illegal arms? It's all about girls?"

He laughed. "Entertainment. You've seen the Pleasure Dome."

I shook unbidden images from my head.

He said, "Although we're planning to sell the good ones."

"The white gold?"

"It's not too late. Join us." He didn't mean it.

"It's over, Tzaiad."

He laughed, a harsh bark. "Over? Our work has just begun." His eyes glinted with madness. "Do you know how much the rich pagans will pay to watch young girls consumed by lions and tigers? Baboons are even better. We can make quite a sport of it. Almost as much as they'll pay for the pure ones."

Revulsion roiled through me. "It's insane. Release her!"

"First, your gun. Throw it over there."

"If you'll let the girl go. And I have a question I need answering. Are you Black Heart?"

"You seem very informed."

"So are you?"

"I'll tell you what," he said, and surprised me by dropping his weapon. "Now do the same and I'll release the girl and tell you everything."

I hesitated. His bulk was easily twice my size; I'd need an edge to beat him hand-to-hand. But the girl's eyes were focused on me now, pleading. I tossed the gun aside.

Then he did something I hadn't predicted.

He walked toward me, using the girl as a shield. Because there was another gun in his meaty hand.

He fired. Rapid shots as he kept getting closer. I snatched up my gun and scrabbled backwards to the rear of the jeep. Before I made it, my left arm burned white hot. My gun spun from my hand, and he continued to close in. Now I was down, he was going to finish me.

Time slowed. I saw my gun, just out of reach. The girl was pushed aside. He raised his gun again. I focused on my Beretta. I started moving.

The girl had sunk to the ground. I stopped watching the approaching big man and just pictured myself grabbing my gun with my weaker hand. I'd keep the momentum going. I'd empty my magazine at where he'd been standing. I wouldn't even look.

Then three shots shattered my hope.

I reached my fallen gun and kept diving; I'd bring it up and shoot. The desperate, final shot from a dying man.

But I missed it. My grip failed and I slewed across the floor just as a body thudded to the ground, almost touching distance from me.

Tzaiad. Or what had been the Neanderthal. Half his head was now missing.

And behind me stood Duffy.

FIFTY-SIX

As soon as he'd discovered that Elsa wasn't with the other girls, Duffy had started looking for her. She was in shock and didn't show any recognition when he picked her up and carried her back into the underground base—what the giant had called the Pleasure Dome. A reference to the Coleridge's poem about Kubla Khan? Probably. A created paradise in the face of tyranny and war. However, this paradise was warped. I'd seen enough evil in this world, but the depths of human depravity never failed to sicken me.

Yusuf hadn't left with the others. We met him coming back through the administration block near the northern tunnel.

He wished us luck but said he had a job to do.

We didn't question him. There were enough vehicles. If he wanted to take something from this dreadful place, after what he'd been through, who was I to deny him?

Duffy selected Eva's repainted jeep and I drove it out of the tunnel. He sat in the back, comforting Elsa. He'd wrapped her in a blanket and spoke calming nonsense.

I drove steadily to where the barricade had been. It was now wide open and it wasn't until we'd passed through that I felt relief wash over me. The cool night air rushed past like a cleansing cloth. We were back in the normal world.

It was over.

We'd rescued the girls and defeated a despicable gang. I'd also recovered Duffy.

"How did you find me?" Duffy asked, snapping me out of my reverie.

"Eva. She told me where you were."

He didn't respond straight away. Then: "She took a big risk. You know—"

"That she's also a deserter?"

"She was worried about Elsa. Rightly so."

"And you," I said. "I think she felt guilty. Maybe Elsa wasn't there. Maybe she wasn't alive. And she'd sent you into a hornets' nest. She thought she'd lost you both."

Before I could finish, the sky in my rear-view mirror, flared orange. Then the percussion cracked the night's peace. I stopped and we swivelled to see the glow that came from the direction of Nitzana.

Another small flash and boom followed by a rapid cluster of more explosions.

"Yusuf?" I asked.

"They never planted the mines," Duffy said. "Yusuf said they had them stored somewhere."

I had mixed feelings. I understood his need to raze the evil place, but he was also destroying evidence. And there were the animals. Even if they'd escaped, they wouldn't last long in the desert.

Nothing I could do about it, so I faced north and drove.

I suppose the animals prompted thoughts about what Malik, the translator had said to me when we parted ways. "Be tough as a wolf lest wolves eat you."

The man must have been psychic. I felt like we'd been in a wolves' lair. We'd fought them and won.

I had questions, but they could wait. Duffy, on the other hand, needed to talk. He returned to our previous conversation.

"I still don't understand how you found me. Eva didn't know."

"She'd sent you toward Nitzana."

"But she didn't—"

"It was close enough." We had the time, so I told him about the man who'd called himself Joe. We'd seen Tzaiad and then the two fake army trucks.

"Joe thought they were transporting weapons to the enemy."

Duffy snorted. "No, just willing to entertain warped people with anything and at any price. It makes me sick to the stomach just thinking about it. Thank God Elsa seems unharmed."

Elsa was undoubtedly one of the white gold girls. She'd have been well cared for until sold to the highest bidder. She, and the other special ones, would have been whisked off to Arabia or North Africa or someplace else and never seen again by the outside world.

Duffy was probably imagining the same thing. He leaned back and held Elsa tighter. And said nothing more until we were in Beersheba.

I hadn't told him about Colonel Schattenmann and the involvement of the army. Nor had I told the other men. However, Beersheba was on the road out of the desert. We had a choice: go through it and risk Schattenmann or take a massive diversion. Minor roads that jagged across the desert toward Gaza. No choice really. Plus I needed to know that the rescued girls were being taken care of.

There was an IDF truck parked outside the medical centre and, despite the hour, the lights were on inside. There were soldiers outside controlling the gathering crowd.

I stopped a hundred yards away and no one paid us any attention.

"Does Elsa need medical attention?"

"I... er..."

His hesitation might have made me smile under other circumstances. I knew what he was thinking.

So I said, "Does she seem all right—physically?"

"Yes."

I steered away and took back streets around the town until I came out on the other side. Duffy didn't question the manoeuvre, nor did he ask why I stopped in a village a couple of miles later.

"Wait here," I said and knocked on the door.

I figured he'd be in bed, but the old man with the crumpled face of a rubber glove puppet, answered quickly.

He looked at me then past me at the jeep. His eyes stayed there for a minute, and I saw his chest heave with a juddering breath. When his eyes turned back to me, they were full of a question. He already knew the answer.

I shook my head. "He didn't make it." The old man might not have understood my words, but he understood the implication. Joe was dead.

Another deep breath, although this time it was full of resignation. Then he beckoned me inside.

I pointed to the others, and he nodded.

Once inside the front room, the old man first checked Elsa. She mumbled some words that sounded like Yiddish and the man switched his attention to me.

Another quick check told him most of the blood wasn't mine. Upon manual instruction, I raised my borrowed brown shirt and showed him the bandages. They were grubby but still in place. He offered to change them but I shook my head. However, he insisted on washing and dressing the bullet wound on my forearm. Despite it being just a flesh wound, when he applied iodine, it stung worse than when the bullet had originally seared the skin.

He finished and looked a question at Duffy, who was slumped in a chair. "I'm fine," Duffy said. "Just tired and hungry."

The old man seemed to understand. He motioned eating and Duffy nodded.

I put my hands together before a request. "Could you look after them? I won't be long." It took three attempts with hand gestures before he understood and nodded.

"You're miles from anywhere except Beersheba," I said to Duffy. "There are no vehicles in the village. If you try and run, I will find you."

Duffy nodded. "I'm not going anywhere, Captain. My job is done." His voice was loaded with acquiescence and exhaustion, and I believed him.

I went into Beersheba police station with the Beretta in my pocket. My hand was on the trigger.

As I marched toward Colonel Schattenmann's office, a figure stepped out and intercepted me.

"Captain Carter!"

I recognized him: Corporal Bastuni—the one who'd given me chicory coffee in the jail.

"Where's Schattenmann?"

"We don't know, sir." Bastuni shook his head, his eyes narrowing. "Were you involved in the thing at Nitzana?"

I gave a curt nod. "Not now. We need to get Schattenmann. He's involved."

A lieutenant interrupted us. "Captain Carter?"

I repeated the need to arrest Schattenmann.

Realization lit the lieutenant's eyes. He waved me toward the office. "That's why he took off. As soon as the trucks arrived with the girls—"

I stopped him.

"Are you in charge now?"

He double blinked. "I suppose so—if the Colonel isn't coming back."

"He's not," I said. Then I made sure he'd report to Command and tell them Schattenmann was on the run. I also said they shouldn't just treat the rescued girls but take them somewhere safe. Most would be foreign and need repatriation.

"I need a full report."

"Make the call," I said.

After he'd gone into the office, I asked Bastuni for a telephone. He gave me one by the front desk. I'd have preferred privacy for the call but went ahead and asked the operator for the number Eva Wislitsky had given me.

When she finally came on the line, I kept the news short and told her not to speak. I said that I had Elsa and Duffy and both seemed all right. I had no doubt Elsa would have mental scars that may never heal but now was not the time to say more. I told Eva where we'd rendezvous and ended the call.

The lieutenant was still on the telephone in the office. Bastuni was watching me.

I said, "I need a favour. I'll provide a full report in the morning but for now I'm leaving."

It took a few seconds for a response but he eventually nodded and I hurried away before anyone could stop me.

Had Duffy been foolish? Had he fled the house? I suspected he'd thought about escape on the journey from Nitzana. I guessed my journey with him through the back streets of Beersheba had given him hope. The longer it took to hand him in, the more a chance to escape might present itself.

But being in a village, miles from anywhere in the dark?

We'd see.

FIFTY-SEVEN

Duffy and Elsa were still at the house when I returned. The old man had also fed them and they'd both gained colour and energy.

I was offered a bowl of broth but refused and thanked the old man for everything he'd done. He gripped my good arm and nodded. A thousand words in a simple gesture.

Elsa curled up on the back seat with a blanket that the old man had given her. Duffy was in the passenger seat.

Before getting in, I'd checked and found my handcuffs were still in the door pocket.

I handed him the cuffs and told him to put one on a wrist and one on the door handle.

He did it. No hesitation. *Click. Click.*

Of course he could punch me with his free hand. It's what I would have done. But Elsa was in the back. If he hit me and I crashed, he'd risk injuring her.

It was now after three in the morning. I thought back to when I stepped out of the house into a still night. Nothing left to do but drive back to Tel Aviv.

The Jeep ground through the miles slower than I'd driven before.

With residual warmth in the rocks and the hum of insects, the world had seemed changed. I may not have the elixir of ancient quests, but evil had been defeated and I could return home.

Duffy broke into my thoughts that verged on the delirious. I should have accepted the food back in the village. However, talking helped keep my mind on the road.

He said, "You're going to take me back?"

It wasn't really a question. He knew I had a duty to perform. I was a Royal Military Police officer. He was a deserter.

"You know I have to."

"Even though it was for a good cause? Those girls needed rescuing."

"But not by you. You have an obligation to the army, your paymaster. You should have reported it. Let the police handle the gang."

I spotted the movement of his head in the dark. He disagreed but he was resigned to his fate. "Eva didn't know who to trust. She didn't know who in the police and army were involved. You saw it couldn't have happened without them either directly or indirectly helping."

I understood. I hadn't suspected Ben Meir. My friend, DI Rosen would be horrified when I gave him my full report in the morning. One of his men. We both knew corruption ran deep in most police departments, but it was usually petty stuff. Treachery and betrayal by a trusted lieutenant on the other hand would cut him more cruelly than an enemy's dagger.

My thoughts turned back to the case and things I hadn't fully pieced together.

"The man you killed—Tzaiad—he tortured the prisoner you escaped with."

"Hajjar was a good man."

"His family were massacred, I'm afraid."

I heard Duffy sigh. "Oh. Abu said the gang would go after them. That's why he'd stayed in prison—for their sakes." He paused, lost in his thoughts for a few beats. "He begged for us to leave him with them."

"But you needed him."

"I should have trusted him. He told us where some artefacts were hidden."

"In the wall at the ruins in Avdat."

"He wrote on the cell wall, told me to memorize the spot, but I didn't trust him."

"You were desperate."

"If we'd gone there and found nothing... but it was pointless anyway. We thought an artefact would prove my worth. We thought they'd let me join the gang." He laughed mirthlessly. "It was a stupid plan."

"But he drew you a map. In the coastguard station. I saw the circle and lines but didn't know what they were until I was inside and saw the amphitheatre."

"How did you persuade him to help you?"

He said nothing.

"Duffy?"

"I feel awful—especially now I know about his family." He glanced back at Elsa. "All those lives—the children. It doesn't seem a fair trade."

"That wasn't the trade," I said. "You stopped the murder of young women for sport—as well as selling others. Plus, it wouldn't have stopped there. They were building a business. Who knows how many lives you saved?"

"I suppose."

"Believe it, Duffy. You may have nightmares about that evil place, but don't you dare blame yourself for anyone's death."

"I told Hajjar his family would be safe. I told him we'd stop the gang, and they couldn't harm him."

"But there was more." That wasn't the reason Hajjar had left with him.

"The antiques. There were more. He'd stashed them years ago. The gang had paid well for his role. Pretending to be the leader meant his family could live in luxury. But he wasn't with them and—"

"And one of Eva's ruses was to suggest Hajjar's wife might be unfaithful. By escaping, Hajjar could recover his treasure and—"

The realization struck me like a blow to the head. "Did he plan to kill his wife for her infidelity?"

"Possibly, but it turned out the younger child was her sister's."

He asked again about how I'd tracked him. We talked and I found the conversation ate away the miles. When the smell in the air changed from dry dust to earthy vegetation, I knew the scent of orange groves wasn't far away.

There was another set of headlights at the broken-down farm. Approaching reminded me of another case and the good man who'd been murdered there.

Perhaps I should have picked a different place. Or maybe the reunion of the sisters would dispel the sad memories from this beautiful spot amid the orange trees.

I had my gun ready in case Eva planned to spring her boyfriend, but as I pulled up, she was already running to us, empty-handed. Giving us no time to get out, she jumped into the rear and hugged Elsa. Duffy waited and then she pulled away and hugged him over the back of his seat.

She was crying openly. They spoke happy, comforting words to one another that merged until they made no sense to my ears.

Then she looked at me. "Thank you."

"I have to take him back."

"I know," she sobbed. "I know."

"Let's get Elsa into your car," I said. "You need to get her home."

Duffy rattled his handcuff against the door and looked at me.

To Eva, I said, "I'll help you with Elsa. Then you can come back and say your goodbyes to Duffy."

I got out and we eased Elsa out onto her feet. We'd helped her into the Jeep at the old man's village. With the support of her sister, she walked taller now.

After Elsa was eased into the other car, Eva returned to Duffy and they hugged and cried.

He said, "I'll find you after I've served my time."

"I'll wait for you," she said. "Doesn't matter how long, Alfie. I'll wait."

I started the Jeep, and she stepped back, reaching over the door, still holding on.

"Take care," I said to her, but she wasn't listening.

He reached under his seat and pulled out a roll of something.

"I hid it. It was still in the Jeep," he said almost laughing. "They didn't want the manuscript. They weren't even interested. They had a new business."

He held it out toward her and she shook her head.

"No. I can't do anything with it."

Like Duffy, she was a deserter. She'd have to lie low until she was declared dead. They'd probably think she was killed in action.

"Will you take it?" Eva was speaking to me. "Give it to someone you trust, Captain. It's important."

"Is this the document you told me about?"

"It's part of the Zechariah Ben 'Anan manuscript. It's important," she said again with soft, imploring eyes. "Please."

I agreed, honoured that she trusted me. I took the scroll and put it in the door pocket, then I rolled the Jeep forward. Eva kept hold of Duffy's shirt and walked alongside for a few paces before letting go. She was trying hard to hold back the tears.

Duffy's voice cracked as he called out his love.

I drove from the old farm building and realized I'd created a second sad moment rather than dispel the old one.

"Damn!" I said and stopped.

Duffy was looking over his shoulder. Eva was standing by her car, frozen, hand in the air.

"Damn you, Duffy," I said, making a decision. "You saved my life."

He swivelled to look me in the eye.

"Take them off." I passed him the handcuff key. "Get out. Be with Eva and disappear."

EPILOGUE

The grand hall glittering under chandelier light was filled with dignitaries in their finest regalia. Tonight, we celebrated Israel's hard-won place at the table of the United Nations. But tension still simmered beneath the optimistic façade.

I straightened the jacket of my dress uniform, scanning the crowd for people I recognized. I was more comfortable with smaller groups and informal situations. Worse still, I stood out. There was plenty of colour in cummerbunds and sashes worn with black-tie, but being tall and in a scarlet SIB uniform I looked as incongruous as a sunflower in a cabbage field.

Five weeks had passed since I'd returned from Beersheba. I was still in the country. I was still in Tel Aviv, assigned to the British Embassy. It looked like I'd be here for a while, encouraged by an atmosphere of entente cordiale, whether real or disingenuous.

I missed the greenery of Cyprus and the comradery of provost officers. However, I did have my friend Inspector Rosen and the occasional glimpse of an interesting case. I also had the romantic interest of an attractive woman. Which helped, despite her marital status.

I'd written reports about what happened to the gang at Nitzana. Rosen gained some comfort by tracking down the haulage company in Haifa who Ben Meir had coerced into providing transportation. It was clear that someone associated with the tunnels at Acre must have been involved, but no one was identified. Despite protesting their innocence, both the prison warden and guard who'd helped Duffy escape were dismissed.

Colonel Schattenmann was found hanged in his garage by his gardener. I heard from Rosen that it was a clear case of suicide because of the note he'd left. In it he claimed to be the leader the gang, having orchestrated everything including supplying military vehicles and distracting the army in Beersheba.

I kicked myself for not realizing. The reporter had told me about the other gang names: Maccabees and Ghosts. Only the translation hadn't been Ghosts, it had been Shadows. I thought it was just an expression, but it wasn't.

The colonel was Schattenmann. Literally *Shadowman*. He was the leader and of black heritage. The clues had been there, and I'd been too distracted to realize. The language professor had translated *black* a number of times. Black heart had been a guess.

And he was dead. It was over.

My report on Sergeant Alfred Duffy was that I hadn't found him. I wrote that I believed he'd approached the gang and been killed. There was no trace of his body.

I never heard from him or Eva but I occasionally pictured them living the good life, working the land near Hadera and having nothing more to do with guns or criminals.

"How are your ribs?" It was the debonair Clayton Short from the US Embassy. We spoke briefly and I relaxed when he moved on, glad-handing other guests, then haunting the edges of the room, circulating with his easy charm.

His wife Nicola was notably absent. No doubt she was back in Tel Aviv, ensconced in the smoky warmth of the Queen of Sheba Club. The thought quickened my pulse.

I realized I'd been watching out for him and continued to watch. He closed in on a pretty Italian attaché wearing a stunning blue dress that showed off her assets. He was clearly flirting, and it helped suppress the guilt I felt about his wife. Perhaps that's what I'd needed to see.

"Congratulations," a Jewish man said, offering his hand. "You are the hero who recovered the *Writings*." He was a heavyset man with a bear-paw of a hand. I noticed he smelled of expensive cigars which probably explained the rumble in his voice.

I asked his name but he waved it away as inconsequential and said something about being an unimportant government administrator.

"It must have been very dangerous," he said.

"I was trying to find a deserter."

He laughed. "You make it sound like nothing, but all that fighting... The rescued girls... Animals, I hear!"

I said nothing.

"Seriously," he said in more of a hushed voice and a hand wave. "I would love to hear the details. More than in the police report."

I shook my head. "I'm afraid—"

Suddenly, the room shifted, people moved. They sensed the arrival of someone important. The bear-man melted into the crowd.

I strained to see what was happening ahead and a ripple of disappointment passed through the room. It wasn't David Ben-Gurion who'd entered and approached the stage. Israel's pugnacious prime minister no doubt had his reasons, but I too felt a pang of regret. I would have liked to take his measure in person.

In Ben-Gurion's place, the Minister of Education and Culture, Shem-Tov, took the podium. He spoke effusively of forgiveness, unity, and brotherhood between peoples. But his soothing words rang hollow to many ears in the room. With hawks like Ben-Gurion at the helm, tensions with the displaced Palestinians and neighbouring Arab states would continue to fester. The Christians aside, two faiths claimed this land and despite recognition by the UN, the path to true coexistence remained uncertain.

Shem-Tov concluded his speech on a conciliatory note, announcing the reversion of King George V Street to its former name. The Zionists had defiantly renamed it after their ancient monarch, King David. Now, in a gesture of goodwill, the British king's name would once again grace a Jerusalem thoroughfare.

More speeches followed, along with presentations of gifts and honours. Then came my turn for recognition. I strode to the podium amid warm applause from the British contingent, who knew my service in the region well. Shem-Tov presented me with a handsome certificate honouring my return of a priceless Jewish relic. I had simply been acting at the behest of Eva and since I'd never officially met her or found Duffy, I had to claim responsibility. Despite the subterfuge, it gratified me to know my small contribution might help mend relations between our two countries.

As we shook hands, my gaze snagged on a large, dark mole on Shem-Tov's wrist. I looked again. Could it be? Was it the shape of a heart?

A black heart.

I managed not to react outwardly, but inwardly my gut twisted. This cultured voice of reconciliation was the architect of so much evil. I wanted to seize him by his spotless lapels and expose his vile hypocrisy before all assembled.

However, I had nothing but circumstantial evidence. Shem-Tov's responsibilities included culture and antiquities. His office oversaw the citadel at Acre. He must have been behind the secrecy about the tunnels. And then there were Tzaiad's words. When I'd asked if Black Heart existed, he'd said I was well-informed. *Black heart* had been the correct translation after all.

Schattenmann, like Abu Hajjar before him, had taken the fall. Yes, I thought, Black Heart, the gang leader, is real and I've just held his hand in friendship.

I forced myself to smile blandly as cameras flashed around us. When I could finally withdraw from the spotlight, I headed for the door, the taste of bile sharp on my tongue. The demon remained free for now, but someday, I would see him pay.

There were few cars on the road to Tel Aviv that night. As I chased a sun that had long since sunk beyond the horizon, I was alone with my thoughts. The miles unwound beneath my tyres, showing no regard for the burdens of those journeying their length. I envied the asphalt's obliviousness, able to play its part without weighing wider consequence.

Like the road, I couldn't meaningfully change things—without evidence. I could wait. There was no rush. One day Black Heart would get his just deserts.

I rolled down the windows and let the warm night air clear my head. The miles rolled on. The velvet heavens stretched far and wide: a vast night sky full of stars, possibilities and hope.

By the time I arrived at the club, pleasant anticipation had displaced the bitter weight in my chest. Tonight was not for revenge or justice. Those could wait. For now, my only wish was to lose myself with Nicola in a haze of music, laughter and abandon.

I'd banish the darkness, if only for a few hours. Then see what tomorrow might bring.

AUTHOR'S NOTE

The story was inspired by the Crusader tunnels in Acre (Akko). Officially they were discovered in 1994, however I thought it not unreasonable to imagine that they were rediscovered at this time and known about during the British Mandate for Palestine.

All places in the story exist with the exception of the gang's base. Nitzana is an ancient town that once had 1,500 inhabitants. However by the 8th century it was a ghost town. During the War of Independence, the Egyptian army used the border crossing at Nitzana to race across the Negev to reach Beersheba. Later, the Egyptians established military positions in and around Nitzana which had by then become the Demilitarized Zone. They were finally expelled in 1955.

Military operations, information about the trade in arms and the Armistice are based on fact whereas the gang and its activities are not.

It should also be noted that, with the exception of David Ben-Gurion, all characters mentioned in the story are fictitious.

Thanks to Pete Tonkin and beta readers, Cherie Knox and Rosie Amber for edits. As always, thanks to my wife, Kerry for encouragement and support. This story took much longer than planned. My father inspired the Ash Carter stories, and after his death, I think I was writing for my mother. At the end of 2022, she died unexpected while I was working on this book and I had to stop. It took a while to recommence, with the story taking on a new significance. *The Killing Crew* was her favourite story of mine, and I'm now satisfied she would have enjoyed *The Prisoner of Acre*.

Finally, I've made reference to a case being investigated by Inspector Rosen. My inspiration for this came from a book by Jonathan Dunsky set in the same period. If you enjoy a clever mystery, I highly recommend *The Dead Sister*.

THE SINGAPORE
ASH CARTER THRILLERS

WOLFE'S GAMBIT

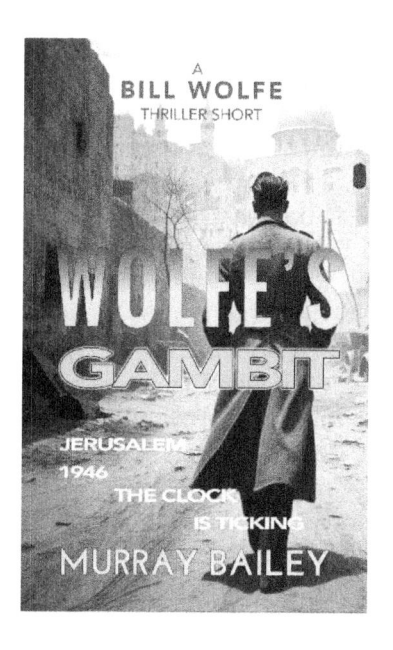

Jerusalem 1946:
Bill Wolfe is a captain in the RMP Special Investigations branch.
An insignificant case turns out to be something much, much larger.
And all the time, the clock is ticking.

"I found myself, on the one hand, racing through this story but, on the other hand, forcing myself to slow down a bit as I didn't want to miss anything!"
Grace J Smith, book reviewer

Read on for the first chapter of my short thriller.

Extract of
WOLFE'S GAMBIT

05:50

It was Saturday the twenty-second of July 1946, and one of those days upon which history would pivot, only Bill Wolfe didn't know that yet.

He woke with a start, remembering where he was and what he had to do.

The sun was barely up, but the ancient city was already bustling with activity outside the tiny room. He lay still, listening to the familiar sounds of Jerusalem coming to life—the clip-clop of donkeys pulling carts down the stone streets, the call of the mu'azzin ringing out from nearby mosques, the distant peal of church bells. Beside him slept Rosa. These were her rooms and he stayed with her when he could.

She worked late and he kept her up later. So he knew it was only fair to let her sleep now.

Slipping out of bed he splashed tepid water on his face from the basin in the corner. After dressing in lightweight trousers and shirt, he checked his Webley revolver and slid it into the holster on his hip. Already bracing himself for the oppressive heat that would bear down as the day wore on, he shrugged into his jacket. As an SIB detective he'd be in civvies. He could do without the jacket but being seen with a gun and no uniform could invite unwanted trouble.

Wolfe felt the growing tensions every day as he walked the ancient alleys and winding market souks. He could see it in the resentful stares from shopkeepers getting harassed at checkpoints, in the furtive whispers between men wearing the distinctive pillbox kaffiyehs of the Arab population.

Rosa was nervous too. She was a Coptic Christian. A small community sandwiched between the two big religions.

"They could both turn on us," she said. "Jerusalem will be the worst place to live."

She knew he'd leave one day. The British Mandate would end. He'd be shipped out. What she hadn't said was that she wanted to go with him. She wanted a ring on her finger. But more than that, she wanted the security of British citizenship. Of that he was sure.

He was less certain he was ready for matrimony.

He always said he had two things running through his blood: the military police and Yorkshire. Rosa knew what he was like. A straight talker, with little patience for beating around the bush. And yet he knew they were both avoiding talk of the future.

It's because she knows what I'll say, he thought.

He'd told her he'd protect her, but they both knew that was far from the same thing.

"Oi! Watch where you're going, will ya?"

He'd bumped into a couple of British Tommies. They had rifles and arrogance.

He straightened. At six foot he was no giant, but he was from good farming stock and had the shoulders and chest of someone who could work the fields from dawn till dusk. And he was bigger than these boys in uniform, barely out of nappies.

They eyed him suspiciously, wondering why he hadn't spoken, no doubt.

The bolder one on his right said, "You're in our way."

In a move that took them by surprise, Wolfe jammed his forearm under the left-hand man's chin. He drove the Tommy back into a wall.

The young soldier choked and spluttered. Anger swelled. The other man reacted. He was swinging his rifle from his shoulder to the fore.

Wolfe remained calm. With his left he pulled something from his pocket. Not his gun, but a wallet. As he rotated, he swatted the rifle aside as it came up, and kicked the kid in the balls.

The second man went down. The first was still pinned against the wall.

"Are you finished?" growled Wolfe.

Neither Tommy was capable of speaking. The man on the ground had his hands between his legs and sucked in louder than a train's piston. The man on the wall was gagging. Wolfe let him drop.

He kept his left hand out with the wallet, now flicked open.

The first man saw the warrant card and gagged some more. He kicked at his friend on the floor. The other man looked up and fear transformed his face.

"MP?"

"Pick up your weapon," barked Wolfe. "And get up."

The men stood side by side, no longer arrogant overlords but school kids about to be given a detention.

"Now fuck off!" snarled Wolfe. "Get out of my sight and think yourselves lucky I don't introduce you to a hot, stinking cell for the rest of the day."

The two men scarpered. Someone clapped and Wolfe eyed an elderly Jewess with a bag of shopping.

He nodded at her appreciation but recognized the sad state of affairs. On the whole, the British soldiers were despised. Of course Wolfe was one of them but the military police were hated by the soldiers. Over drinks with the team from 75 Provost Company, they would often say they were the fourth party in this mess. At least they were hated by the populace less than the common soldiers.

He walked on, looking out for trouble. Not a formal patrol, just one to keep an eye on behaviour and unrest. On any side.

He passed through Jaffa Gate's handsome stone archway and into the enclave of the Old City. Here, suspicion hung as heavy as the smells of warm confectioner's shops selling sticky Arab pastries.

Twenty minutes later, he passed a platoon of nervous infantry recruits in unfamiliar territory, tin pots too large on their heads, Enfields held tight across their chests. Wolfe felt none of their fear. He'd been based here for a year. He knew Jerusalem's shadows like old friends, her smells as familiar as a childhood home. The stink of donkey dung in the narrow alleys, throat-catching spice smoke from tiny bakeries, dust and sweat and a thousand scented oils—this place got inside a man, became part of him.

He kept moving. Eyes watched him and he flicked his gaze left and right. Searching.

The peal of bells from the Church of the Holy Sepulchre reached him. And then the mu'azzin song. The incongruity seemed a haunting reminder of the zealotry that infected this place. Three religions crammed within this fortification, resulting in a fragile coexistence. A tinderbox.

Through the winding alleys of the Jewish Quarter, he slowed his pace. Would he find what he was scouting for? Had Rosa been right about the message?

And then he saw it: a yellow ribbon on a scarred wooden door.

END OF EXTRACT.

Wolfe's Gambit is currently only available in ebook format. I intend to write three short stories / novellas featuring Bill Wolfe and publish them together as a paperback.

SINGAPORE GIRL

When a headless body is found on the causeway between Singapore and Malaya, Ash Carter is asked to investigate.

This second adventure takes him through Malaya visiting Johor Bahru, Kuala Lumpur and Penang. Is the murder a warning by the Chinese communists or a drug lord? Or is this something else entirely?

CYPRUS KISS

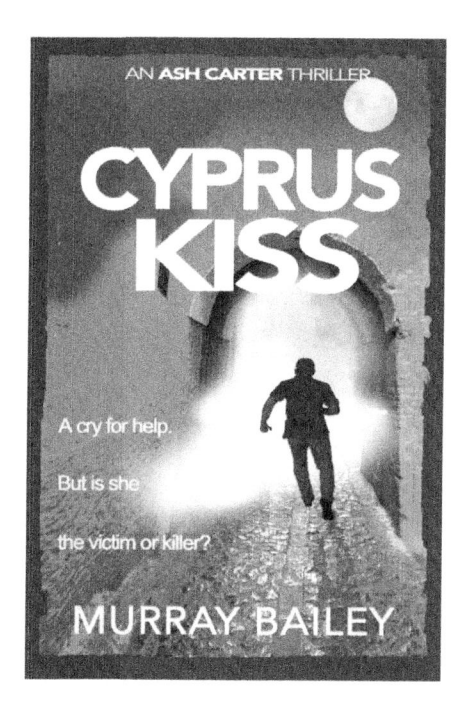

Ash Carter, is drawn into a mystery. Who is the missing woman? What's her secret? And is there a connection with the gang known as Kiss?

After another murder, Carter realizes it's personal and has limited time to find out what's going on.

"Twists and surprises abound. A five-star read."
Roger Price, author

THE KILLING CREW

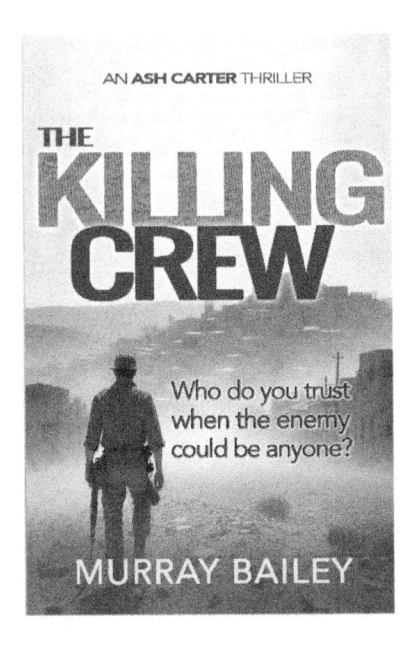

In the newly formed state that's at war with the Arab nations, hated by Jews and despised by Arabs, the two SIB officers think they face an uncomfortable task.

But when they become targets they realise this is more than just a job.

It's life or death.

"Took me totally by surprise."
Jonathan Dunsky, author

murraybaileybooks.com

IF YOU ENJOYED THIS BOOK

Feedback helps me understand what works, what doesn't and what readers want more of. It also brings a book to life.

Online reviews are also very important in encouraging others to try my books. I don't have the financial clout of a big publisher. I can't take out newspaper ads or run poster campaigns.

But what I do have is an enthusiastic and committed bunch of readers.

Honest reviews are a powerful tool. I'd be very grateful if you could spend a couple of minutes leaving a review, however short, on sites like Amazon and Goodreads.

If you would like to contact me, I'm always happy to receive direct feedback so please feel free to use the email address below.

Thank you
Murray
murray@murraybaileybooks.com

Printed in Great Britain
by Amazon